MRya

AN ACQUAINTANCE

Published by:
Daybreak Press
Minneapolis, Minnesota, USA
Rabata.org/Daybreak-Press

Library of Congress Catalog Control Number: 2017962400
ISBN: 978-0-9992990-0-5

Cover illustration by Reyhana Ismail
Book design and typesetting by scholarlytype.com

Printed in the United States of America

A Crossroads Novel

AN ACQUAINTANCE

SABA SYED

DAYBREAK PRESS

2017

Dedicated to my beloved husband, for his constant encouragement to live my dreams and his endless support, contribution, and generosity to make this book come alive.

I

I passed by the bookshelves and the desks in my school library, towards the fire exit in the back that opened into the faculty parking lot. Breathing in the crisp aroma of books, I peeked through the back window to get a glimpse of the crowd. The small parking lot was empty of any cars because it was a weekend, but people were gathering up to protest. Although only a handful of people had assembled so far, the writings on their banners made my heart sink.

One poster read

No to Shari'ah Law!

while another was emblazoned with

Terrorists Go Home!

I didn't recognize any of the protestors, which meant they were probably from out of town. Wickley, located on the far northwest edge of Pittsburgh, consisted of one major street and a handful of stoplights. Most everyone was familiar with everyone else. I was happy to see that none of the people I'd grown up with was out here. This seed of hatred had been sown by Anti-Islamization of America, which was a well-funded group of rabid Islamophobes.

I watched another lady join the crowd and unwrap the banner in her hand before holding it up and proudly waving it around. The writing on it felt like a dagger to my heart.

FUTURE ISIS BRIDES HAVE NO PLACE IN OUR CITY

My shoulder muscles tensed, and I took a deep breath to stay calm. The brisk sun of October was shining through the trees, whose gorgeous fall colors lit the parking lot. Fall was one of the prettiest times in Wickley, a time to roam around town and enjoy the fresh air—I guess they hadn't gotten the memo.

The unfamiliar faces were either strangers bussed in from other towns or newcomers from the outer edge of Wickley who had only arrived within the last few years and treated wickley like a bedroom community—commuting to Pitts for work and shopping.

I walked toward the front side of the library and sat down at one of the desks, trying to form the right words in my head. I had to keep reminding myself not to react emotionally—although, let's face it, this entire venture was emotional. I wanted to make it clear to those protesters that I condemned extremism, that violence was wrong and against my beliefs; I wanted to remind them of our unity, of how Muslims had lived in this beautiful town for years without any conflict.

Oh God, what would I say... what *could* I say? My head was spinning, and I felt an nauseating wave of frustration. I wished the people outside would put themselves in my place and understand how it feels to suddenly be declared a stranger in your own home, to be considered a threat, even though I would give up my life to protect my town. I put my head down on the table and felt tears rolling down my cheeks.

I would have gotten over my emotions shortly and sensibly, if only Gerard and his equally loathsome friend, Leo, hadn't interrupted my pensive moment. What were those two freaks doing here? Then I remembered I'd left the library keys in the keyhole. I'd picked them up from our librarian, Mrs. Harold's, house. She was a friendly older lady who often let us borrow the keys if we needed to study over the weekend.

Gerard and Leo must have seen the keys hanging in the slightly open door while they were roaming the hallways. They were sophomores, and not exactly the friendly type. I always kept my distance from them, even in the best of times, because they'd never pass up an opportunity to razzle someone up. Of course they had tried to tease me about the AIA event at school, but I'd ignored them. They must have come to enjoy the protest. I slunk down further in my chair, hoping I could make myself invisible. Unfortunately, however, my red scarf was a bright flash of color in the otherwise dark library, and they honed in on it.

"Look who's here!" Leo jeered, nudging Gerard and pointing at me.

Gerard sniggered, "Osama's sister!"

"Are you here to blow up the school?" Leo smirked

I had never feared those two clowns, but that day in their sagging jeans and dark hoodies, they seemed unusually menacing. I didn't feel my usual bravado either, but I tried to look defiant.

My tears were still obvious, though, and the two bullies grinned at each other. "What happened?" Gerard taunted.

"Are you crying because you're going to be kicked out of school the way you deserve?"

"Why don't you leave her alone?" a familiar voice said from behind them. I hadn't seen Jason entering the library. He must've been at soccer practice.

"Jason..." Gerard turned around. "Hey man!" he said in surprise.

Jason approached them slowly, his hands tucked into his jeans pockets, trying to gauge the situation. He stopped when he had made his way between me and the younger boys.

"You two should go," his voice was stern and his gray-green eyes were fixed on them.

Gerard and Leo glanced back and forth between me and Jason, their leering eyes coming to the same conclusion. Gerard made a point of looking me up and down, his smile lewd. All of a sudden, for the first time that I could ever recall, I felt dirty, as though the way he looked at me was stripping me of something more than my clothes.

"She *is* hot, right?" Gerard told Jason. "I wouldn't have thought you'd go for her... *type...* though," he added in mock surprise.

Jason's expression hardened further, his eyes burning with anger. "Get *out* of here," he said harshly, stepping in closer and looming over them. The threat in his voice was clear, and the two cowards backed off, but not without a final leer in my direction.

I sat up quickly and made a show of fixing my *hijab*, but mostly I was just trying to compose myself again. Jason had slipped into the chair across the desk, right in front of me. I tried to avoid his gaze, looking down at my lap as he studied my face.

2

Y ou should have been ready by now!" Jasmine couldn't have sounded more annoyed at me.

I rolled my eyes as I packed books into my bag from my study table. "What's your problem?" I drawled, ignoring her irritation.

She followed me through my bedroom as I walked around, gathering my stuff. "We're going to be late on the first day of school!" she insisted.

"Late?" I never understood why she always wanted to be the first person at school. "It's not even seven yet. There's still over an hour before school starts."

Jasmine crossed her arms stubbornly, trying to seem tough. She was dressed more like a teacher than a student, and her business-like skirt and blazer hadn't been picked as a special first-day-of-school outfit; they were her everyday attire. Her neatly-wrapped white scarf contrasted with her dark skin and chocolate eyes, which were aimed at me from underneath raised eyebrows. Jasmine could seem intimidating to others, but her stern looks had no effect on me. To me she was my other half, the best friend I'd known since before I learned to walk.

"I want to get there and get my class schedule and locker and settle down before school starts," she snapped, but there was no real anger in her voice.

I rolled my eyes at her again. "Jaz, you won't get your schedule or your locker until the first class starts, and that's not til 8 o'clock."

She started tapping her foot, the next step in her "annoyed Jasmine" routine. "Can't you just hurry up?" she pleaded. "I want to be there before the parking lot fills up!" When it came to school, Jasmine would *never* run out of excuses.

I laughed. "Wickley barely has enough people to fill up any parking lot!" I was only half-joking.

Turning away from Jasmine, I examined myself carefully in the full-length mirror that leaned against my wall. Eyes the color of toasted hazelnuts looked back at me before glancing at the rest of my reflection. I was wearing a flowing black maxi skirt topped with a teal blouse. Its see-through sleeves were covered with a black cardigan, and my dark brown hair was neatly tucked into a blue-grey cashmere scarf that settled softly around my shoulders. For good measure, I flashed myself a smile—the 'smart, confident Sarah Ali' smile that most people in Wickley knew well.

Satisfied with my appearance, I slipped on my flats and hoisted the strap of my school bag onto one shoulder. A twinge of guilt passed through me at leaving my room so untidy. It meant our housekeeper, Paula, would clean it before I even got home. But Jaz was already downstairs, so I clattered down behind her, knowing that if it wasn't for her, I'd probably never make it to school before fourth hour. I could hear my dad singing in the kitchen.

Professor Omar Ali, as he was known by most of Wickley, was the best dad anyone could ask for. He'd come to the U.S. from Pakistan to study at the University of Houston when he was only sixteen, which was when he'd first been introduced to the Muslim Students' Association. His outlook on life became more spiritual as he became involved with the MSA.

It was when he was pursuing his Ph.D. in Chemistry that he'd been introduced to my mom through mutual friends. Even though my dad's family wasn't too pleased, Mom and Dad were adamant—they shared common goals and religious beliefs, and eventually my grandparents gave their blessing.

My dad always looked happy from the outside, but he had been through a lot. When I was very young, my mother had been diagnosed with uterine cancer. She went through the treatment for almost six years, and just when we thought she'd finally beaten it, she had a relapse when I was ten. For the next year, all we did was pray that the worst would be over soon. In a way, it was. She died when I was eleven, and my older brother Adam had barely turned fourteen.

Now Dad and Adam were seated at the breakfast table, having already gotten started on their scrambled eggs. They both looked up as Jasmine and I walked in, and I couldn't help but feel a swell of love for them. My dad and my brother were my family, and after Mom had died, we shared a closeness not many others enjoyed.

Although he had just turned fifty and his laugh lines had become permanently etched into his face, Dad looked younger than his age. His few grey hairs were masked by the rest of his sleek black hair and dark, full beard. Dad was always full of lively conversation that meant you never got bored in his company.

Adam, on the other hand, was the quietest of us all. His thick black hair was always tousled from his habit of running his hands through it when he was thinking, and his neatly trimmed beard gave him an aura of maturity. His dark eyes were usually thoughtful, except when he was teasing me.

"You look lovely, Sarah," Dad said warmly, and gave Adam a pointed look. It was a tradition in our home for my brother to compliment me every morning—Dad was adamant about it. Not that I needed the ego-boost, but it was a sweet gesture and I always appreciated it, even if Adam tried to get out of it as much as possible. My older brother glanced at me and rolled his eyes. "You look nice," he said grudgingly, but I could hear the hidden sincerity in his voice.

I popped some frozen waffles into the toaster for myself while Jasmine poured herself a bowl of cereal, reminding me we only had 10 minutes to eat. We left for school soon after Adam left for his university in Pittsburgh, about forty-five miles away. I tried to convince Jasmine to walk the mile and a half, but she was not to be deterred from arriving as early as possible, despite the fact that she knew as well as I did how beautiful and peaceful Wickley was in the early morning.

As she started the engine, I rolled the window down and let the morning breeze, crisp and playful, caress my face. It was invigorating, and drove away the last remnants of sleepiness that lingered in my eyes.

As I had predicted, we arrived at the school well before eight o'clock. I pouted in annoyance; being early was one of my pet peeves, as much as being late was one of Jasmine's.

As we headed toward the school building, I smiled at the thought that we were *finally* entering as seniors. Only one year remained before I could break free into the world of university, and I couldn't wait for that taste of freedom and independence.

The main school building faced the student parking lot and was separated from it by a small circle drive that was used for pickup and dropoff. I glanced at the trees toward the left side of the main school building, the leaves just beginning their change to dazzling fall colors of amber, red and yellow. Behind those majestic sentinels was the cafeteria and the gym, and further on behind that was the soccer field. All three sides of the school property were fenced.

Jasmine parked in the student lot, and we crossed the road to enter the large glass doors of Wickley High School.

The first day of school meant that everyone gathered at the cafeteria to find their friends—not that we hadn't been running into each other all summer anyway. With an average of 150 students per grade, we had only around 600 students in the high school. Most of us had been together since preschool and knew each other's families as well, which was frustrating at times as there was no anonymity at all. If anyone made a mistake in school, the whole town talked about it until the next scandal broke out. But as provincial as Wickley was, I loved it. There was a sense of comfort and security about small town life that made me feel safe and content; I hated the tumult of big cities.

The bell rang, signaling the beginning of the school year and the beginning of the end of my high school career. Picking up my schedule from homeroom, I headed to my first class, hoping that Jasmine would be there.

My first class was calculus, and I settled into a chair in the middle of the room.

"Hey, Towel Head," a voice said from behind me, and I turned around, grinning. The voice belonged to Doug, my schoolmate since preschool. Our dads were professors at the same university, and for all his teasing, he was a good guy. We got along pretty well.

"What are you doing here?" I asked him, curious. "I thought you were still in Canada."

Doug stretched out on his chair, his long legs touching the back of my own. "Yeah, we just got back last night," he yawned.

The class filled up with other students, and we dove into parametric equations and trapezoid rules. The school day wore on, and I was disappointed to see that I didn't have second or third period with Jasmine, either. Fourth period was art—my least favorite subject. I hated it and had managed to avoid it for three years, but now I had to take it to graduate. Glancing around, I saw that I was the only senior among a throng of freshmen and sophomores. I shrank in my chair with embarrassment, wishing that class was already over.

Lunch was after fourth period, which meant I could finally see Jasmine. Our school had a system of giving each grade the same lunch break, so all the seniors enjoyed lunch in the 5th period.

The cafeteria was big enough to hold the whole school, so it was often used to hold seminars and assemblies. It was tradition that on the first day of school, someone from our class would get up on stage and welcome everyone.

I groaned a little as Trisha and her brother Colby stepped up and tapped the microphone, testing it. Trisha and Colby were known school-wide as the show-offs *and* the good-looking ones. They had their cliques and, although we weren't enemies, we weren't friends either. Trisha's best friends were Stephanie and Nicole, whose association with Trisha and their sense of fashion led to most of us covertly referring to the three of them as 'the Trashies.' I usually avoided them, and they stayed away from me as well.

Trisha—blonde, blue-eyed, and wearing a black mini-skirt with tube top and high-heels—made a show of welcoming back all the seniors to school.

A tall blond with green eyes, Colby got up next and took the microphone from his sister to make an announcement.

"We've got a new senior joining us from Maryland," Colby's voice was smooth, just like his reputation, and the first row of senior girls giggled in response to the winks he threw them. "He's already made it to the soccer team and is now our new captain," he continued. "Seniors, I give you... Jason Connor!" With a flourish, Colby pointed to the newcomer, who was sitting at one of the cafeteria tables closer to the stage.

Six feet tall and fair skinned with golden-brown hair, the new kid stood up with a self-conscious grin and waved to everyone before sitting down. He looked a bit taken aback by Colby's theatrics. Although I only glanced at Jason when he stood up, I wasn't surprised by the girls who giggled and whispered amongst themselves, fluttering their eyelashes at him a little too obviously. No one could deny that he *was* strikingly attractive.

At the end of the day, I walked through the door and mumbled a *salaam* to my dad. Kicking my shoes off in the foyer, I headed straight to my room, promptly jumped onto my bed, and closed my eyes.

3

My nap didn't last long; it was soon time for the *Asr* prayer, and I got up, rubbing the sleepiness out of my eyes. My bathroom was inside my room, so I changed into my favorite pair of jeans and threw on a comfortable t-shirt. Taking out my contact lenses, I made ablution. The splash of water on my face, arms, and feet was just what I needed—a freshening-up that left me feeling both physically and spiritually alive.

After prayer I headed downstairs, following the curious but delicious aroma that had floated up the stairs. Paula was preparing dinner in the kitchen. I couldn't remember a time without Paula, who'd always treated me just like her own daughter. She'd spoiled me as a kid by always cleaning up my messes instead of making me do it, and clearly now regretted it. I left more mess for her to clean than Dad and Adam put together, and she let me know it.

She lived in Pittsburgh with her daughters, but came over three days a week to clean the house and keep us fed and in line.

"What's cooking, Paula?" I asked, joining her at the stove.

"My friend taught me one Thai dish, so I try today," she replied in her soft Brazillian accent. She gestured at the pot on the stove, and I inhaled the tempting aroma. Paula smiled, her warm hazel eyes crinkling, her plump cheeks pink from the heat of the stove. "I put more in chili for you."

Over time, Paula had learned a variety of international recipes, using us as her guinea pigs. She was so good at it, we never minded.

Paula was a busy woman. Not only did she take care of our house; she also cleaned Wickley's small mosque and occasionally ran errands for Dad's stores.

"I guess I'll just eat now," I decided, and together, Paula and I sat down to a comfortable dinner.

When we were done, I walked to Jasmine's house—it was my second home, and I never had to think twice or call in advance before going over. Jasmine's parents were African American converts, and she had two younger brothers. They'd settled in Wickley when she was only a year old, just like me.

Her father, Uncle Dawud, was a cardiologist in Pittsburgh, and he'd met my dad at a seminar at the university. Uncle Dawud fell in love with Wickley when my dad introduced him to our town, and the rest was history.

"Hey, *salam alaikum*," I smiled at Aunty Elisha, Jasmine's mom, as she opened the door for me.

She smiled back, "*Wa alaikum assalam.* How was the first day?"

I sighed, "Boring, as usual! I can't wait to graduate."

She headed back to the kitchen where she was helping her sons with homework, calling out, "Don't get ahead of yourself, you have a whole year left."

"I know," I moaned as I headed upstairs to find Jasmine.

I chilled with her for a while before heading home, so they could eat together. By the time I got home, Paula had left and Dad was waiting for me. We had a 'family dinner' every night; even if we weren't hungry, we were still obliged to sit together and talk about our day. Dad had religiously enforced this rule since Mom had passed away, and though we sometimes groused about it, Adam and I both appreciated it.

I looked for Adam, but he wasn't home yet. I frowned as I slid into my seat and started piling food on my plate. The new Thai recipe was a hit with me. "Where's Adam?" I asked Dad, who had already started to eat.

"He's still at the university. I don't think he'll be joining us often this semester." Dad took a bite, making a bewildered face as he chewed. "You know he's trying to graduate by this winter, so he's loaded himself with extra classes." Dad's facial expression made me laugh as he finally swallowed. "What *has* she tried to cook this time?"

I giggled and finished my own mouthful. "I thought it was pretty good."

We finished dinner, chatting about which teachers I got and how few classes I had with Jasmine. Then, my plate empty, I got up and stretched.

"Dad, I'm going to bed, it's been exhausting today." I picked up the plates and headed toward the kitchen. "Should I fix you some mint tea?"

He shook his head. "No. I have to run by the café. Alex called." Dad owned one of the oldest cafés in the town, *Café A&S*. For Adam and Sarah. Mom had selected the name for it.

Other than the café, Dad also owned a couple of convenience stores. He'd specifically looked for a job as a professor close to a dry county, so he could invest the money he'd inherited from his parents in stores without having to deal with alcohol. I hugged Dad and gave him a good night kiss. Knowing that Jasmine would be in my doorway and yelling at me to get up before I'd even opened my eyes, I tried to get everything ready for the next day before I slept.

The following week, I had to make a few trips to the counselor's office. The counselor, Mrs. Smith, looked happy to inform me that, based on my GPA, I was on track to become the valedictorian—assuming, of course, that my grades didn't fall. The school administrators still had to vote before the decision was finalized, though, and Mrs. Smith informed me a bit condescendingly that whe was particularly concerned about my public speaking skills.

Apparently, she believed the scarf on my head might interfere with my oratory abilities. I knew she wasn't necessarily discriminating against me, and that she was just genuinely concerned, but since she was an older woman with deep-rooted stereotypes, it was sometimes difficult to get through to her.

After talking to her, I went to see the principal, Mrs. Tanner, whom I held in high esteem. She was a dedicated principal with true leadership skills, always available for each and every student regardless of their race, background or academic status; she truly inspired me. I knocked at her door, although it was already halfway open.

"Mrs. Tanner, do you have a minute?" I called through the open doorway.

"Sarah," she smiled, looking up from her computer screen, "Come on in."

Mrs. Tanner, a middle aged woman with a no-nonsense attitude, brown hair pulled up in a severe ponytail, and sharp but compassionate brown eyes, was a regular customer at my dad's café. Actually, most of the teachers were our regular customers, but Mrs. Tanner had moved to Wickley even before Dad, and knew my mom before she passed away.

"I wanted to talk to you about something that sort of bothered me," I explained.

"Is everything okay?" she asked, looking concerned.

"Well, I was with Mrs. Smith, and she was telling me that I might make it as the valedictorian this year..." my voice trailed off.

"Yes, I know!" Mrs. Tanner exclaimed enthusiastically. "Is that a problem?" She raised her eyebrows, laughing good-naturedly.

I fidgeted slightly. "Ummm, not really... but she was saying that the school admin still has to vote based on my social and leadership skills."

Mrs. Tanner frowned, not understanding what it was that was bothering me. "Yes...?"

I finally spat it out. "I was wondering if my head covering would be problematic in any way?"

Mrs. Tanner looked baffled. "Sarah, your dress code and religious values would never prevent the administration from giving you what you rightfully deserve!" She was emphatic, and looked a little wounded that I could ever think such a thing. I felt oddly guilty.

"No, no, I didn't mean it that way! I was just trying to make sure that the admin realizes that my dress code doesn't stop me from speaking in public," I explained.

She leaned back in her chair, smiling as she finally understood what I was getting at. "Oh, Sarah, we all know that," she reassured me. "You've been actively participating in major school activities. Let's see...you are in MUN, HOSA and you're even on the debate team, and I'm sure I'll find more, once I open your records!"

I looked down at my hands, uncharacteristically nervous. "I know... umm... it's just that Mrs. Smith seemed a bit concerned, and I didn't know how to tell her that I'm perfectly capable of speaking in public." I said hesitantly.

"I'll speak to her," Mrs. Tanner tried to assure me, but I shook my head quickly.

"No, no; it's okay." I didn't want this to become a problem for Mrs. Smith. "I'm sure when the admin votes, if the issue comes up, you can clarify it for them."

She nodded sympathetically, and I left her office feeling much more excited about the possibility that I, Sarah Ali, actually had a chance at becoming valedictorian!

4

It had been a couple of weeks since school started, but I still hadn't exactly caught the school spirit yet. Instead, I was focused solely on graduating so I could make valedictorian and move on to college.

At dinner one day, Dad asked me how school was going. "Well, my Advanced Placement classes are okay, but they're a bit harder than I expected," I said, stabbing a piece of chicken with my fork and probably looking vexed.

Adam, who had managed to join us for dinner that night, wagged his own piece of fork-impaled chicken at me. "Make sure you don't drop your grades just because of AP classes," he warned.

I grimaced. "I'm trying, but they make it so unnecessarily hard!"

"If you think your grades will be affected, then switch to regular classes. It's better that you graduate as valedictorian, and you can do that without AP classes, as long as your grades remain strong." Adam always looked out for my best interests, and was particularly concerned with my education, but he didn't usually engage in much conversation. Dad said he'd been a lot more talkative when Mom was alive.

Eager to take advantage of Adam's conversational mood, I asked, "How're *your* classes?" I was always fascinated by his college activities.

"Harder," came his normal abrupt answer.

I rolled my eyes at him, "Obviously, you've loaded yourself with classes. What's with the rush to graduate early?"

He glanced at me and made a face back. "I want to move to Houston for my masters."

Adam loved Houston, not only because his best friend Zain lived there, but also because he'd spent a lot of time there with our grandmother. Every time Mom had been hospitalized, Adam was sent to Grandma's.

"Yeah, but you have to get married before that!" I laughed, pointing my fork at him.

He ignored me, but I was having fun and wasn't about to drop the subject. "Do you like any girls in the MSA yet?" I teased.

"Shut up, Sarah," he said in annoyance. He hated it whenever I brought up the topic of girls, which I thought meant that either he really liked someone already, or he was truly a gentleman. As much as I liked to tease him, I believed he was the latter; his focus and dedication to his studies, as well as his quiet personality, meant that he was able to keep himself away from the 'distractions' that most of his peers fell into.

I never did understand how he made it out of high school without slipping even a little bit; I knew from friends that girls had often tried to hit on him. And why wouldn't they? His olive complexion made him seem exotic; his height and muscular, athletic build instantly placed him in the 'so hot it's almost hard to believe' category, and his silence, interpreted as either shyness or mystery, had half the girls vying to see who would be able to coax him out of his shell.

Nonetheless, as far as I knew, he always kept himself aloof from even the most attractive girls at school, and had thrown himself into his university studies with the same quiet, ferocious dedication that he had graduated high school with.

"When he likes someone, I'm sure you'll be the first person to find out," Dad assured me. No matter what the topic was, my dad always made sure we communicated very openly, and his loving, friendly manner meant that we were always comfortable sharing even personal details with him.

"Yeah, right!" I protested, "You'll be the first person to know... and I'll be the last, trust me." I pouted at Adam, who ignored me. Sometimes Adam acted more like my dad than my older brother.

He got up and grabbed his plate. "You know what? I don't think either of you will find out," I crowed with laughter. "Oooooh, that means there *is* someone!" I put on the sing-song voice that I knew would bug him like crazy. "Is she pretty? What's her name? Where did you meet her?" I loved pulling his leg, and his expression of irritation just made me crack up even more.

Pointedly ignoring me, Adam left the room, and I stuck my tongue out at him as a parting shot. Most of the time he acted like he had the spirit of a sixty-year-old, even though he was only three years older than I was.

Dad always said that Adam had been really close to Mom and didn't take her death very well. He withdrew into himself for a while, which is probably why his high school years were so isolated. He even graduated almost a year and a half early by taking extra classes during the summers. After Mom died,

I think he tried to get over his grief by immersing himself in his studies.

University life at Carnegie Mellon had brought about a change in him, though; he'd become involved with the Muslim Students Association—MSA—and made some really good friends. Perhaps the change of atmosphere was good for him—away from memories of Mom.

Even with his busy schedule, though, he was always responsible when it came to family. Dad never asked him, but Adam made a point of volunteering to help take care of Dad's business responsibilities. It was his way of expressing his love and appreciation for everything Dad did for us.

5

At Wickly high school, second period was a bit longer than the others because we had school announcements. One of the seniors, usually from the debate team, volunteered to make the announcements over the PA system. I'd been dying to be a senior so I could do just that, and finally, I had my chance! I'd signed the volunteer list the first week of school, and eagerly awaited my turn. When my week finally arrived, I had to go to the main office during the last 20 minutes of second period. My incorrigible sense of humor meant that I ended up saying more than I had to, and I was told off by our grumpy old receptionist more than once. My friends' compliments and the laughs that my comments received boosted my confidence more than I needed, though, and it became the highlight of my day to finish off the announcements with a wisecrack and a laugh.

On Thursday, after making all the announcements without straying from the script, I had one more thing to broadcast: the upcoming soccer match. Leaning into the PA system, I flipped the ends of my peach hijab over the soft beige cardigan I wore and continued, "This season's first soccer match is coming up! We'll be playing against the Bronzers, and you can all show your school spirit by purchasing tickets at the front desk for your family and friends. Hopefully, we'll do a lot better this year, with our team in the capable hands of our *gorgeous* new captain!"

The receptionist's head whipped around and she gave me a glare to rival all the ones she'd previously thrown at me combined. It took me a minute to realize... oh *snap*! Did I just call the new soccer captain *gorgeous*, and broadcast it to the *whole school*? I spent a few seconds stunned by my slip of the tongue, then I winced. Jasmine was going to kill me!

I dashed into my third period psychology class, desperately trying to avoid eye contact with anyone. Ashley, a freckled redhead with sparkling brown eyes, leaned towards me and whispered, "Oh my God, I can't believe you actually said that!"

I slunk down further in my chair, groaning quietly. "What are the Trashies saying?" I asked her, keeping my voice low so Mrs. Howard wouldn't call me out.

Ashley paused for a minute before quoting them, complete with Trashy attitude: "Sarah finally hit puberty!"

Great. I so didn't want to go to lunch after that... How could I do that to myself? Argh!

Jasmine caught me outside the cafeteria, "What was that about?!" she demanded, mortified.

I frowned at her, "You think I did that on purpose?" I asked.

"Purpose or no purpose, everyone's talking about it," she warned me, fixing me with a stern glare.

I grimaced. "I don't want to go inside. I'm going to the library." I turned around and started walking. I turned back to see if she was following. "Comin'?"

She bit her lip, looking conflicted. "I'm hungry!" Jasmine had low hunger tolerance, which meant that she was usually the first person in the cafeteria as well as the first person to get to school.

I smiled, "Go. I'll be fine," and made my way to the library.

I walked over to the main desk to ask Mrs. Harold, our librarian and one of the sweetest women on earth, about a book I'd put on hold. She told me to wait by the counter and went somewhere in the back to find it.

As I waited, resting my elbows on the counter, someone walked in and stood next to me. Glancing to my left, I did a double-take—lo and behold, there stood Jason! The *gorgeous* soccer captain, for everyone who didn't get the memo.

Standing straight and not even looking at me, Jason said, "Thanks for the compliment."

I wanted to make myself disappear, but it wasn't my style to show that I was nervous. Flippantly, I answered, "Well, thanks for taking good care of our soccer team."

"Here we go, Sarah, I found your book!" Mrs. Harold was back just in time, and I would've grabbed her and kissed her wrinkled cheek in thanks if I could've.

"Hi, Mrs. Harold," Jason said, and she smiled at him, her eyes twinkling from behind her glasses.

"Oh, hello, Jason," she beamed back at him. "You seem to be getting along quite well here already!" She winked at me. "You got some nice compliments this morning from a girl who *never* compliments boys." She handed me my book, and I took it from her, wishing that someone would just shoot me already. Seriously, why were old ladies so cheesy?

"So I've been hearing all morning..." Jason sounded indifferent as he gave the librarian his own book to scan. I bristled;

my ego was stung. He must be used to girls losing control around him, and he must have mistaken me for one of those types—because of my own stupidity.

Not one to let my reputation suffer, I collected myself and said, "It's a good omen." I smiled coolly. As confident as I sounded, I was dying of humiliating on the inside. "To say positive things before a game," I finished, silently congratulating myself on the good save.

Mrs. Harold raised her eyebrows and smiled. "Since when did you start believing in omens?"

"Since they let me make announcements," I picked up my book and waved them good bye.

6

On Friday after school, Jasmine came home with me to hang out. After a snack, we headed up to my room so Jaz could take off her scarf and relax. From the pile of unorganized books on my table, I managed to pull out a couple of magazines.

Fashion magazines were my guilty pleasure, and although Jasmine pretended she wasn't interested in shallow, empty-headed 'style advice,' we both flipped through the pages together. She sat cross-legged on the floor, leaning against the frame of the bed, while I lay across the bed on my stomach, my chin resting on Jasmine's soft, cropped hair. I loved her naturally tight curls, and wished my own string straight hair was curled like hers. "Can you do corn rows for me?" I wheedled, yet again, as Jasmine snorted at the ridiculousness of the latest fashion trends on display in the magazine.

She shook her head absent-mindedly, trying to shake off my chin. "I told you before, Sarah, your hair is too *desi* to stay in corn rows!"

"But you look so pretty when you get yours done!" I protested, tugging gently on her hair to emphasize my point.

She swatted at me jokingly, then saw the time on the clock. "I'm going to be late for the game!" she exclaimed, jumping up. We usually spent Friday nights together, but the school's first soccer game was tonight, and Jasmine was a hard-core soccer fan. During soccer season I often wound up staying home or going to the mosque without Jasmine. I liked to go to the mosque on Friday nights, especially since Dad and the rest of the board went to so much trouble to organize activities that catered to all the different age groups, which was hard in such a small town mosque. Wickley's population barely reached six thousand people, and that was after a twenty percent increase since we had moved there 16 years earlier. And regardless of his schedule, Dad made the mosque and its community a priority.

Although Dad had been the first Muslim to settle in Wickley, he had initially convinced two of his friends from Pittsburgh to move to Wickley as well, and then Uncle Dawud moved in. Gradually, as the general population of our town began to increase, so did the number of Muslims. Now we had twelve Muslim families living in town, some in the original inner part of the town, and some in the extended outskirts on the east side.

The families had started off praying in a rented shop, but eventually they were able to build a small mosque next to the First Presbyterian Church. We shared the same parking lot, and even had one common community hall between the church and the mosque buildings that we shared for our respective events.

Growing up in Wickley, I never felt strange or different. Our neighbors had been settled here for years, and regardless of our religious differences, we never had any conflicts;

we were all respectful and accepting of one another. My dad owned the oldest and most well-known café in town, which had helped us become a real part of the community. Almost everyone came to the A&S at sometime or other, since the café served as a central meeting spot for older people during the day and a younger crowd in the evening.

Although the mosque was tiny, it was still an active community center for the Muslim families. Every night after *Isha*, the night prayer, one of the dads gave a small inspirational talk. Aunty Elisha held a Qur'an circle for teaching *Tajweed*, and lectures for the women and girls. Friday nights were family potluck nights, along with spiritual discussions or youth activities. Once a month, the mosque's management invited a speaker to hold a weekend seminar.

My father pitched in to cover the financial costs for most of the events. He firmly believed that God had blessed him with money so spending it in His cause was his duty, and that taking care of his community and the good upbringing of Muslim children was part of his responsibility.

Dad also realized that raising his children in a place with an extremely small Muslim community could have negative side effects. To make sure that we were getting opportunities to grow spiritually, he took Adam and me to different Muslim activities in Pittsburgh. We'd also taken road trips and mini-vacations throughout the States for Islamic conferences and seminars that we might otherwise miss out on. Dad didn't want us to remain secluded and isolated from the larger Muslim community just because we happened to live in a small town. Most of the time Jasmine would come along if her parents weren't available to travel themselves.

"Jasmine, you aren't coming with us?" Dad asked when he noticed Jasmine heading down the driveway.

"Not this time, Uncle Omar, I'm going to the soccer game," she said, embarrassed, shoving her hands in the pockets of her cardigan.

"Leaving knowledge for games?!" Dad teased her. Jasmine was the biggest soccer fan I'd ever seen in my life. Dad turned to me, asking, "You want to go with her?"

"No way! I'm not missing Fun Friday for some stupid soccer game!" I yelled, jumping into the comfortable front seat of Dad's SUV.

After the evening lecture, Brother Sulaiman got up to make a small announcement. Sulaiman lived in Pittsburgh with his family, but he often attended our mosque's activities and was an active member of the MSA at the University of Pittsburgh. He was also good friends with Adam, although they attended separate schools.

"We have recently discovered that the Anti-Islamization of America organization, the AIA, is scheduled to hold a seminar in Wickley. Unfortunately, Mayor McNeil has been invited to attend the seminar and address their members. We encourage all local residents to write to the mayor conveying strong disapproval of AIA's agenda of hate and divisiveness."

The AIA? In Wickley? They claimed to be working for human rights and 'freedom of speech', but it was painfully obvious what their real goal was. It wasn't enough for them to wallow in hate themselves, they wanted everyone in America to loathe Muslims as much as they did.

I knew they had become active in Washington and Philadelphia, but I was shocked and angry to discover that their hatred was about to hit home.

Later that evening I had a brief conversation with Br. Sulaiman about how I could help with the AIA issue. He gave me a few tips on how to approach the matter within my community and offered to provide more help if I needed it. By the time we climbed into the car, it was after 11:00.

"Dad, can I hold a protest in front of Community Hall the day AIA has its seminar?" I asked on the car ride home, trying to suppress a yawn.

"Why would you do that?" Dad questioned, focusing on the road.

"To show my disapproval!" This time I couldn't hold back the yawn. I was struggling to stay awake despite the fact that the conversation was important to me.

"We'll see," Dad answered casually. I was too sleepy to nag him, and when we got home, I stumbled upstairs and into my bed, all thoughts of Islamophobes and protests fading away into peaceful sleep.

7

I was doodling henna designs in my AP psychology notebook when I heard my name being called. "Sarah Ali?"

I looked up. Professor Dan, my Chemistry II teacher from last year, was at the door. "I'm sorry for the interruption," he apologized to Ms. Murray. "I was just wondering if I could borrow Sarah for a few minutes?"

Ms. Murray frowned at the professor through her glasses, which were perched precariously on the tip of her nose, before turning around to frown at me as well. What did Doctor Dan want? I wondered. Although his class was usually taken by seniors, I excelled at chemistry and had been able to take it in my junior year instead. I was probably his best student... maybe he wanted me to teach his class!

I brightened up, excited at the idea, but Ms. Murray's scowl only deepened. "Fine," she snapped, and then turned back toward the class to ignore me. Ms. Murray was one of the most unpleasant teachers at school; my theory was that she was so busy analyzing everyone's statements and moves that she forgot to smile.

"Sarah, do you mind?" This time Mr. Dan addressed me directly.

"Should I leave my stuff here?" I asked.

"Yeah, yeah..." He seemed to be in a bit of a hurry, but excited as well. The whole class was looking at me, and I glanced at Ashley on my way out. She seemed to be wondering the same thing I was—what did the professor want? I shrugged and followed Mr. Dan into the hallway towards his class.

As we hurried through the halls, he asked, "Do you remember the bonus question I gave you guys for mid-term last year, and no one got it right but you?"

Of course I remembered! He had given us a college level problem for a mid-term bonus, but whereas most of the other students had attempted to solve it and failed, I'd solved it with relative ease. He'd been so amazed.

"Yeah, I do," I told him, feeling a bit smug.

"Well, guess what—no one could solve it this year, so I'm taking you to solve it for them on the board!" The professor was an enthusiastic man, and I grinned.

"Okay!" Far be it from me to turn down a chance to show another reason I deserved to be the valedictorian! Entering the Chemistry II classroom, Professor Dan grinned at his students and asked if any of them had managed to solve the question yet. He was greeted by a unanimous "NO!" Most of the students looked frustrated and annoyed.

"Why is she here?" someone asked, eyeing me suspiciously.

Mr. Dan's grin grew wider. "She's the only student of mine who has been able to get the right answer so far," he explained. "As a *junior*! And right now, she's going to solve it for you all."

I was standing by the board at the head of the class. As I looked around the classroom, someone caught my eye. It was

Jason, sitting all the way towards the right side of class. We stared at each other for a couple seconds, but then I quickly looked away and started writing out the question on the board from the exam paper Mr. Dan had handed me. Having my back towards the class made me feel suddenly uncomfortable, knowing that everyone was watching me closely. Trying to appear casual, I tugged on my cardigan with my left hand, making sure it was loose enough to cover me properly.

It was hard concentrating on both the problem and worrying about whether my clothes were revealing my shape or not, but I couldn't help it. Concern over modesty was something ingrained in me. As I got to the lower end of the board, I had to bend down. I had a special way of bending my knee so that my whole body went down, instead of leaning over so that everyone could get a good look at my behind. An older lady at the mosque had taught me this method, and though I hadn't fully understood at the time why she was so insistent about it, I had followed her advice regardless. Later, when I saw young men ogling other girls' backsides like they were on a buffet, I was glad I'd made it a habit.

When I finished the last part of the answer, I turned around, mock-curtseyed, spread my arms and announced, "Ta-da!" I smirked, enjoying my moment in the limelight.

The class clapped, and the professor thanked me before I left. On the way back to psych, I thought of Jason and the way he'd held my gaze. Wincing as I recalled how I had embarrassed myself so thoroughly before, I hoped that this time I'd left him with a much better impression.

During lunch that day, I sat with my regular crowd—Jasmine, Scott, and Ashley.

"I can't believe this is happening!" I vented. I'd brought up the topic of the AIA, which hadn't stopped bothering me since I'd first heard about it. No one really seemed interested other than me and Jasmine, even though there were at least a couple other Muslim kids at school.

Zara, a quiet girl of Syrian origin, had joined the school this year as a freshman; Adnan was a Pakistani whose parents had settled in Wickley a few years ago after leaving New York. Zara was pleasant enough, and her family was active at the mosque, but Adnan was another story entirely. He was the kind of guy who needed to be avoided because he didn't know his limits—actually, I wasn't sure if he *had* any limits. The way his mother praised him, though, you'd think he was an angel on earth.

Nonetheless, neither one of them seemed to care about the AIA coming to our little town when I'd talked to them about it at the mosque. "Don't worry, Sarah, we won't hate you," Scott tried to reassure me. He'd been part of our group since junior high; he was a tall, lanky white guy whose dark hair was always cropped short, and he was one of the most caring and compassionate people I'd ever known.

"That's not the point," I snapped. "Mayor McNeil shouldn't have accepted the invitation to speak at the seminar to begin with!" My youthful indignation didn't understand the political ambitions of a small-town mayor.

Ashley was a bit more practical. "Who knows, he's probably getting some funding from them," she commented, digging into her salad.

"Wickley needs money to fix a lot of things."

Scott disagreed with Ashley. "It doesn't work like that, does it?" He shook his head.

"Well, then, maybe he received campaign money from them?" Ashley insisted.

"I hope nobody goes to their seminar," I growled, ignoring their speculations, and got up to get a smoothie from the juice shop in the cafeteria.

I was standing in line, thinking of the AIA, when Jason's voice came from next to me, "That was quite impressive how you solved the problem."

Jolted out of my deep thoughts, I looked up and saw him standing next to me in line. He was wearing jeans and a red checkered shirt, the sleeves rolled halfway up his muscular arms, his piercing grey eyes focused on me. For a moment, all I could do was stare.

"Thanks," I said smoothly, smiling coolly, my controlled voice not belying my inner reaction. I picked up my smoothie and walked off hastily, thankful that I was able to keep my composure, outwardly at least. After school, I dove into researching the AIA. I emailed some of my mentors in Pittsburg and New Jersey, whom I had met during different Islamic and leadership conferences, for advice. Most of them emailed me back quickly with helpful tips on how to ensure the preservation of peace and understanding, while not allowing hatred to spread.

Sitting back in my chair looking at all my notes, I felt confident that I knew what to do next.

8

I decided to write a letter to the editor of our local newspaper, Wickley's Daily, as some of my mentors had suggested. Although writing wasn't my strong suit, I figured this was worth it. Staring at the screen of my laptop for hours, I was finally able to get the words to flow.

Our forefathers fought for this land to be free, in order to secure people from injustice and discrimination. The pillars of our country are fairness and equality regardless of race, color, or religion. I proudly brag about the American constitution—how it gives Americans the freedom to live their lives the way they want and choose their faith and lifestyle without fear of persecution.

Yet there have grown people and organizations amongst us who want to destroy us from within by tainting our unique constitutional values. They want to exploit the situation and create division. I believe in freedom of speech, but when some people's speech starts spreading hatred for our own people, when the freedom that was meant to secure us starts being used to threaten Americans, then we should all have an issue with that speech.

I have lived in Wickley all my life, and I have felt nothing but safe and secure. But when I heard that the hate mongering, trash-spewing AIA was allowed to hold their malicious conference in my town, I felt I lost a piece of trust. Nothing can divide people or weaken a united country more than fear. I wish our elected representative had considered the consequences of allowing the AIA to bring their hatred to our peaceful Wickley.

Wickley has always been a community of peace and security. Let's not allow ignorance and cowardice to divide us with hatred and fear.

I worded the letter strongly, trying to show my disapproval of such a group's infiltration amongst us. When Adam came home early, I begged him to proofread it, since his writing skills were much better than mine. Although he was swamped with his studies, he agreed to help me out, and edited it for me then and there.

I emailed the letter to Sandra Williams, the editor of Wickley's Daily. I'd heard of her before, but didn't know her personally; luckily, Sandra published my piece in the newspaper the following week, along with a tiny picture of me that she'd requested. I'd sent her my junior yearbook picture.

Mr. Thomas, our AP English teacher, made a passing comment about the letter in class. As I was heading out, he called out, "Sarah, do you have a minute?"

"Yeah, sure," I answered, turning back and walking up to his desk while Jasmine headed on out.

Mr. Thomas took a sip from his coffee mug. "Your letter was good, but if you don't mind me giving you some advice for the future, I'd like to point out a few things." He suggested a few alternatives to the writing style I'd used, offering me helpful tips on how I could make it even stronger and more succinct. I listened carefully and thanked him. His advice would come in handy when I put together my valedictorian speech.

As we talked, I didn't notice that his next class had already taken their seats, some of them whispering to each other, others finishing up homework or reading the latest vampire novel... and more than a few of them looking at me. Mr. Thomas finished up and offered to write me a note so I wouldn't be counted tardy in my next class.

I shifted from foot to foot as Mr. Thomas rummaged through his desk drawer for his pink late slip notepad. More than a few Trashies were in the class, all of them looking at me with unreadable expressions, but I couldn't care less. From the corner of my eye, though, I noticed Jason sitting next to David, a tall, lanky blond. David wasn't stuck up, regardless of his popularity through the soccer team. We'd had a few classes together in the past and maintained a courteous relationship.

As I waited for Mr. Thomas, Nicky, one of the Trashies, flashed a smile at me. "I like your dress, Sarah," she commented, and I blushed a little when I realized that everyone—including Jason—had turned around in their seats to look at me, probably all wondering how I'd react to Nicky. Would I think her comment was snarky or sincere? High school was a crazy balancing act, but I was a senior, not a nervous freshie, and I knew how to handle myself.

I smiled back at her without any maliciousness. "Thanks, Nicky," was all I said, and quickly but confidently left the classroom, grabbing the note from Mr. Thomas.

My letter was featured in Wickley's Daily, and was later picked up by our local radio host, Brian Welch. His show was too lame for any of the teens to bother listening to, but almost every elderly person in Wickley tuned into his show. Wickley being Wickley, whatever Brian talked about usually became the talk of the town, no matter how dull the topic, and was discussed the next morning at the café. That week, though, Brian advertised the AIA seminar during his talk show, and mentioned my piece in Wickley's Daily. I figured this was the first real controversy that Wickley had had in years, and it was a juicy one for him.

Trying to spice up the show, Brian aired an open-call session that he titled, "Are our Muslim neighbors a threat to our future safety?" The public was invited to call in, and I made sure that I was one of the first ones on the line.

"So the fact that we've been living here for more than two decades and practically built this community doesn't mean anything?" I demanded. "All of a sudden, because of some Muslim-haters' false propaganda, you're going to sow the seeds of enmity and doubt among our neighbors and destroy the peace of your own community?" I was all fired up, and so glad I'd been on the debate team. My speaking skills far outshone my writing.

Brian tried to defend himself. "I'm not destroying anything! I'm just asking a simple question that all Americans have the right to ask: Are Muslims a threat to us or not?"

I cut him off. "Some questions are only asked to spark the fire of hatred!" Brian tried to answer with some recycled vitriol, but he didn't have anything concrete to say. In a desperate bid to recover himself, he hung up on me and took a few other calls instead. To my pleasure, most callers opposed the sentiments Brian was sharing and had positive things to say about their Muslim neighbors; unfortunately, there were also a few antagonistic callers as well, who voiced their loud support of the AIA.

I wasn't going to let this go. I called Brian again later and gave him a piece of my mind. What he was doing wasn't journalism, it was tabloid radio! He refused to back down and wasn't even ashamed of what he'd said, although he did let slip that the AIA had paid him to host the topic, in addition to paying for the ads for the seminar. Dad flat-out refused to let me organize a protest outside Community Hall, where their seminar was scheduled to take place. He thought if we kept quiet, no one would even find out about it, and after a few days the hype would die down. According to him, protesting would only draw more attention and give the AIA free advertisement.

As much as I disagreed, I listened to him. Maybe he was right; it could just be AIA's tactic to go to small towns and brainwash people, since those in more isolated areas were less likely to interact with Muslims or experience living with Muslim neighbors. Thankfully, the date of the seminar came and went, and we found out that it had had a low attendance, and that most of those who went only did so out of curiosity, rather than because they shared the AIA's views.

Excited by the reaction he had elicited, Brian latched onto the AIA as his new cause. He aired yet another show asking listeners to call in and share their experiences, and I was sure he must have gotten paid for the follow-up show too. To my pleasant surprise, he faced a lot of heat from the other residents of Wickley, who didn't want to lose their common sense to unreasonable hatred.

The AIA's presence and Brian's publicity on their behalf triggered a spiraling chain of events. I approached Brian, asking him to invite me on the show so that I could speak on my own behalf, as an American and as a Muslim. With some reluctance, he agreed, but of course, to add fuel to the fire, he made a point of inviting an Islamophobic guest as well. Tom Clark was a man in his fifties whose sole purpose in life was to point out everything that was wrong with Muslims, and to convince the rest of America that we should be driven out.

After introducing me and giving me a chance to speak **about my sentiments,** Brian gave Clark the microphone. As expected, Clark went on a rant about Muslims being a threat to "his country," and tried to throw in the fear tactic of bringing up Bin Laden's name, reminding the audience that I shared the same faith.

At this point, I couldn't stay silent any longer. "Stop throwing around names, Bin Laden this and Bin Laden that." I spoke with confidence, knowing that I was in the right. "I don't know those people, okay? Extremists exist in every nation, race, and religion. I don't freak out every time I see a white man just because of what Timothy McVeigh or Dylann Roof have done! I haven't stopped going to the movies because of James Holmes, or stopped going to school because of Adam Lanza. It's unfair to claim that every Muslim man or woman is a threat to our society."

Tom Clark interrupted, "We don't know that!"

I glared at him. "Should we start hosting a program called, 'Is Every American Soldier a Threat to Foreigners?' because of Abu Ghraib, the gang rape of an Iraqi teenager, and the burning of innocent Afghanis?'"Both Brian and Tom were silent at that.

"How long have you lived here?" I asked Clark.

He sputtered a bit. "That's irrelevant!"

I shook my head. "No, it's not. I was born here, and in the seventeen years of my life, I've never been a threat to my community, nor has any Muslim I know. If anything, we've been some of the most constructive citizens of Wickley—which is more than I can say for you!"

Things were getting heated, so Brian decided to take a few calls, since we weren't going to resolve anything in less than an hour. I got quite a few calls of support, but some people were full of nothing but hatred.

When I got home, Dad proudly told me he'd received a lot of compliments about my eloquence and courage from people at the mosque. I was glad that not only was I able to stand up to a few bullies who were trying to ruin my community, but that I had the support of most of the people in my town as well. *Alhamdulillah!*

9

Hey, *Mooz-lum*, the school might expel you!" Gerard slipped into the chair next to me at lunch, while I was in the middle of a furious tirade about the rumors of a protest against Muslims.

Apparently, Tom Clark was planning on organizing a protest outside the school because he didn't feel the students were safe with a few "*Moozlum*" kids in attendance. The news was spreading slowly, though nothing was official yet. I guess Mr. Clark couldn't handle being beaten on a radio show debate by a high school Muslim girl, and thought that this would intimidate me and the other Muslims who dared to speak out against the AIA's activities.

"What are you going to do? Will you take off your thing?" Gerard waggled his finger around my headscarf, although he didn't actually touch it.

"Gerard, go find something better to do," I almost yawned. I was less bothered by his comments than by the news of the protest. I'd never imagined that such a small percentage of haters would have the arrogance to actually take that repugnant step.

"So will you finally go back to your country?" Gerard pressed, leaning closer towards me. I felt like pushing him off his chair, but that would've been immature, no matter how repulsive he was.

"Sure, I'll go back to my country. When you move back to England." I retorted, rolling my eyes. He sniggered and swaggered off, his hands stuck in the pockets of his sagging pants.

I went back to brooding over the immediate problem at hand. It was hard to describe my feelings. I wasn't just angry, I was disappointed and hurt.

What was happening to my town? How could this be? This was my home, my country, and I couldn't let haters creep into our distinctive culture of harmony and liberty.

Right then and there, I decided to go to the protest myself and refute their groundless fears. It was impulsive of me, but I had a habit of thinking with my heart instead of my head.

I didn't want to talk about my plans with anyone. I knew Dad would be the first person to stop me, and Jasmine thought we should just let it go and things would calm down in a few days, just like Dad. I didn't agree with either of them. I had paid enough attention in history class to know how the seeds of hatred could turn into endless weeds of injustice, destroying a beautiful garden.

Scott managed to get the details of the exact time and location of the protest through Gerard, since we both knew that Gerard would never give me straight answers. The protest was to be held on Sunday in the faculty parking lot, right outside the library.

I picked up the library keys from Mrs. Harold, who I was glad didn't seem to be aware of the protest. The school building itself was always unlocked on Saturday afternoons, for the convenience of whatever group had weekend practices or rehersals. I parked in the student lot and walked through the echoing halls to the library. A quick peek out the back fire exit and into the faculty parking lot told me that the event hadn't started yet. And that's how I ended up in the library not only trying to take on a group of protestors, but also dealing with resident bullies Leo and Gerard—until Jason Connor showed up and scared them off.

"You okay?" Jason's voice was softer now, and concerned. Not the stern, threatening growl that had so quickly convinced Leo and Gerard to leave the library.

I nodded, fiddling with my sleeves. "Yeah, thanks," I murmured.

He leaned across the table towards me. "You shouldn't have come here today," he said earnestly. "Didn't you know about the protest?" He sounded surprised that I might not have been aware of it.

What was I going to tell him? That I came here without telling anyone because I wanted to encounter the protestors *singlehandedly*? Yeah, that was me—more guts than brains.

Jason was still looking at me, clearly waiting for an answer, but I didn't say anything. Giving up on getting a reply from me, he got up and walked toward the window, where the crowd was beginning to gather outside.

"You should go," he said quietly, turning back to me. "I don't think it's safe for you to be here right now."

"No..." I paused, then stood up. "I have to go out and talk to those people."

Jason looked incredulous. "Do *what*?"

"I have to convince them that they're wrong!" I replied, and had to quell the urge to stamp my foot.

"Are you out of your mind?" His grey-green eyes widened. He looked as though he was searching for something—something that I wasn't telling him.

I couldn't understand why he was so concerned. After all, it wasn't like we were friends or anything; we'd barely even had a full conversation. And I *definitely* didn't appreciate him asking if I was out of my mind!

On the other hand, I remembered grudgingly, he *had* just gotten rid of Gerard and Leo for me. No matter how much I didn't want to owe him any favors, I *did* owe him at least good manners.

I smoothed down the front of my cardigan over my skirt and said in a rather calmer voice, "Thank you for saving me from those two."

I forced myself to glance at him. He was clearly still getting over the shock. I didn't have time to wait around for him to wrap his mind around the concept of a Muslim girl ready to take on a challenge, so I started walking to the fire exit. "But I've got to do this," I said, my hand on the doorknob.

He raised an amused eyebrow at me. "And I'll have to save you from those guys, too!" he teased.

I turned to face him. "This is really personal to me. I *have* to stop those people from spreading hatred!" I couldn't stop my voice from trembling with emotion.

At my words, Jason looked more somber. "With all due respect, Sarah, this isn't the best way to go about it," his deep voice was serious.

He knew my name? *That* was interesting. I met his thoughtful gaze with my own determined one. "I have to do this. I can't let them ruin the peace of my *home*."

There was a moment of silence between us. My opinion was clear, but I had no clue as to what his views were, or if he even *had* any views about Islamophobia. It was strange, though, that our first proper conversation was about such a serious and sensitive topic.

"Sarah, you should fight hatred with love and in a more constructive way," he said decidedly. I gave him a questioning look. What exactly did *he* know about it?

I decided to give him a chance to explain. "You should continue to write for Wickley's Daily with your positive messages," he continued. "Try to get involved in more community work. I don't know much about the people here in Wickley, but going out and talking to those protestors would be completely useless. They've already made up their minds, and they're not here to be convinced otherwise." He looked worried now. "They're here to attack you. If you talk to them, you might even end up giving them bait they could use to propagate more hatred later on, which could be destructive to your cause. You gotta be careful."

I bit my lip, mulling over his words. I didn't know why he knew so much about the issue, but he was quite convincing. The stubbornness on my face must have started to soften, because I could see Jason relaxing a little as he gave me a few more moments to think about things and cool down.

"I'm sorry this is happening here," he said. "I know it must be hard for you." I didn't know what to say. I still couldn't understand why Jason—this hot-shot new soccer captain, classically gorgeous, completely unaffiliated with Muslims—cared so much about looking out for me.

He stood up and gestured back toward the hallway. "Let's go out this way; I'll walk you to your car," he said gallantly. I nodded and headed away from the fire exit door. Jason followed me to the library entrance, but when I tried to twist the doorknob, it was locked! Those two idiots had locked us inside!

Through the glass doors, I could see the end of the key still in the keyhole. Jason frowned and grabbed the door handle, shaking it vigorously. It didn't budge. "Damn it!" Jason swore, frustrated, and then tried to shove his shoulder against the door.

"Umm, I don't think that's really gonna unlock the door," I commented, trying to hide my smile. It was amusing to see him lose his temper at a locked door when, just a few moments ago, he'd faced down two of the most menacing bullies in the school with a maturity and calm that impressed me.

Jason grinned at me ruefully. "You're right," he said, giving the doorknob one more jiggle.

"We should probably call someone," I suggested, and he nodded. I took my phone out of my pocket, groaning when I saw that the battery had died. At my inquiring look, Jason shook his head regretfully. He'd left his phone in the gym locker.

We were locked in the library, and unless someone unlocked that entrance, our only way out was through the back door, walking straight into the crowd of Islamophobes.

I headed back toward the desks with Jason only a few steps behind me. He let out a frustrated sigh, raking a hand through his golden brown hair.

"It's okay," I told him, "You should leave. You can get out through the back door. I'll just wait them out and leave afterwards."

He frowned at me. "And what will you do if Gerard comes back? You don't even have a phone!" he reminded me.

I drummed my fingers on the table, already feeling restless. "But those people might be here for another four or five hours!"

Jason shook his head in agreement. "Yeah, we can't just sit around for that long." He walked back to the window, peering outside. "Okay, here's what we're going to do," he said decisively. "We'll go out together and walk through them. My car is parked in the faculty parking lot, towards the end. We can go in my car, and then I'll drop you off at yours."

He seemed to expect no argument from me, which rankled my nerves. I hated other people telling me what to do or planning things for me unless I asked them to first; Jason obviously didn't know that about me, despite whatever else he *did* know. My inner feminist was stung and wouldn't let the issue go.

I opened my mouth to object, but Jason had noticed the disdain on my face.

"Come on, Sarah, this is the only way we can get out of here," he repeated. "Trust me."

"Why should I?" I demanded. For some reason, I couldn't help but feel a little suspicious. This whole situation was so unlikely. Who knew, maybe the protesters had sent him inside to draw me out? "How did you even know I was in the library?"

I didn't even know what I was thinking anymore, but my doubts were clear on my face.

Jason looked irritated, then took a deep breath and ran his hand through his hair again. There was something awfully distracting about that move.

"I came to the school to practice, but I needed something from my locker first so I came towards this side of the hallway," Jason explained. "I was passing by when I saw Gerard and Leo entering the library, and then I heard them, so I looked inside and saw you, and...and the rest is history." His voice was polite but firm, and nothing if not sincere. In those few sentences, he addressed all my doubts as though he'd been able to read my mind.

I was still hesitant, though.

"Sarah, I'm not going to hurt you! I'm just trying to help." He paused, searching for the right words. He certainly hadn't anticipated being forced to justify why he was trying to help me. "I'm just trying to get you out of here safely, that's all..." he tried to reassure me.

There was something about his demeanor, the way he looked caught off-guard, that gave me the assurance I needed to believe that none of this was planned. Something in his tone of voice, his earnestness, the way his eyes searched mine, almost pleading... It made me *want* to believe whatever he said.

"Okay," I murmured. I suddenly felt upset at myself for doubting him in the first place. And for needing help twice in a row. My ego wasn't ready to handle the onslaught of favors.

Jason waited a few more moments to make sure I didn't have any more objections. When I didn't say anything, he walked to the door and nodded toward me.

"You're not forgetting anything here, are you?"

"No, my keys are in my pocket and my useless phone is right here," I answered quietly.

"Okay," he nodded. "You're going to have to walk through all these people," he warned me. Though he sounded casual, I'm sure he could not have appreciated my initial distrust of his intentions.

"It's okay," I shrugged, "I'm sure I'll make it through alive."

He ignored my joke. "Okay, so I'm going to open the door, we'll exit, and then we'll walk through them... just try to walk right next to me." He put his hand on the doorknob.

"Jason," I blurted out. He stopped and turned to look back at me; his quizzical eyes met my mortified gaze. It wasn't easy for me to say what I was about to say to him.

I felt the blood rise to my cheeks. I blinked a few times, and then I finally forced myself to say, "I'm sorry for questioning you." I paused for few seconds, twisting my fingers nervously, then looked up at him again. The expression of forced seriousness on his face was starting to melt away, replaced by one of good-natured amusement.

"And..." I managed to choke out, "And I really appreciate all your help." I nearly stumbled over the last few words, flushing even more.

Pressing his lips together, Jason's smile was both warm and amused. It made him look even more handsome, bringing out a dimple in his left cheek that I'd never noticed.

Inclining his head to indicate that he'd accepted my apology, he opened the door and held it for me. I followed him and stepped outside.

The fire exit door opened onto a small porch that, in turn, opened onto the faculty parking lot. Taking a deep breath, I looked out at the protesters, who were waving their posters and shouting their slogans. But the moment I stepped outside, they all went quiet.

They must have been shocked to see a Muslim girl in a ruby-red headscarf, a long red skirt, and a cream cardigan coming out to meet them as though she were the president about to address an unruly crowd. The mental image made me smile fiercely—who knew? One day, I *could* be president—and I lifted my head up higher.

There were about fifteen or twenty people, and I could only spot two or three familiar faces.

Jason and I made our way down the porch steps, with me a step behind him. At the end of the staircase, he waited for me to join him, casting a sweeping look at the crowd. Smiling coolly, he headed forward, his pace swift and confident. I tried to keep up next to him, grateful for his presence after all. There was a strange tension in the crowd. The silence gave way to whispers; the whispers got louder and turned into yelling. People shouted, and I could hear more than a few profanities. An older woman pushed forward, coming up to me, screaming "Go back to your country, *b****!*" The crowd started to bear down on me.

A wave of strong emotion made me want to run. Instead, I stopped and looked at the angry old lady, my eyes full of sympathy for her blind, ignorant hatred. I wanted to talk to her, I wanted to tell her that the country she wanted me to go back to was *America*. I was as much an American as she was; I was not a threat to her or to anyone in my school or in my community. In fact, any threat to American soil was an equal threat to my family and me.

The woman was glaring at me with hostile eyes, though I kept my gaze on her steady. "This *is* my country," I told her. *"And Wickley is my home."*

There was a sudden howl of anger, and what happened next took place so quickly that for a moment, I didn't understand what was going on. The old woman had lifted her hand to slap me, when Jason's fingers closed around my wrist and pulled me back quickly. His hand slipped into mine, pulling me towards him, and I found myself slowly moving away from the crowd.

The strong, warm hand protectively holding mine made me feel safe, secure. I felt comforted, buffered from the wave of anger and hate that was facing me. It took a moment for me to pinpoint the other emotion coursing through me.

Jason holding my hand was *wrong*.

I knew he was helping me get out of a perilous situation, but holding hands with a member of the opposite sex was against my moral values. As comforting as his grip was, it was also troubling.

Jason was oblivious to the thoughts chasing each other through my mind; he made a way for us through the crowd, using his left hand to push away anyone who tried to stop us. His right hand held onto mine firmly, a protective shield that never faltered. He didn't let go until we reached his car, where he opened the door for me and made sure I was safely settled in the front passenger seat.

When he came around and got into the car, neither of us said a word until we arrived at the student parking lot. I pointed out my car, and he stopped next to it, his hands on the steering wheel. We sat in silence for a few moments, neither of us sure what to say.

"Don't worry about the library key," Jason said softly. "I still have to go back for practice."

I looked down at my lap. "Thanks," I whispered. "Can you ask Daryn on the soccer team to drop it at Mrs. Harold's house?" In the silence of the car, the enormity of the day's events was catching up with me, and I felt overwhelmed with emotions—too many to identify easily.

"Your hands are shaking." Jason's voice broke through my thoughts, and I looked up at him, blinking back sudden, inexplicable tears. Seeing him watching me with concern made something twist in my chest, and I had to look away before I did something stupid like break down and cry in front of him. I squeezed my eyes shut, willing myself to remain calm.

Suddenly, I felt my hands being lifted and held again, my knuckles being stroked gently. My eyes flew open in shock. I hesitated, then quietly extricated my hand from his. Jason looked startled.

"I'm sorry!" he apologized quickly. "I didn't mean to do anything wrong! It's just... your hand was really cold when I held it earlier, and now they were shaking..."

I shook my head quickly. "No, no, it's okay..." I stumbled on my words. "Just... please don't do that again." I clenched my hands together tightly, refusing to show any more vulnerability.

"Thanks for all your help," I said without glancing back at him, and got out of the car as fast as I could. Being around

Jason was making me feel woozy and uncomfortable, as though I couldn't think clearly anymore. I got in my car and drove straight home.

When I arrived, Adam was taking a nap and Dad was in his room. Usually I would sit by him as he read a book in his recliner, but today I gave him a distracted kiss on the cheek and told him only that I'd been at the school and seen the small protest. I omitted all mention of Jason.

I excused myself quickly and collapsed back onto my bed, staring at the ceiling. I tried to sort through all the thoughts and feelings churning through me; I wasn't even sure if I was upset or excited about what had happened that day. The only thing I could think about was how Jason had held my hand... fierce and protective at first, then caring and gentle. The corners of my lips twitched upwards in a small, bewildered smile.

Should I tell Jasmine?

I pushed the thought away immediately. Even though she knew everything about me, I wasn't ready to share my confused emotions—or this odd happiness—with her quite yet.

10

I joined Dad and Adam for breakfast the next day, and Adam brought up the protest. There had been a small mention of it in the newspaper, and he was alarmed to discover that it had been held at the school.

"Were you at the school yesterday?" he questioned me, looking concerned. Dad must have told him what I'd said last night.

I shrugged and popped some bread in the toaster. "Yeah." I usually didn't mind talking to him about my adventures, but I didn't feel like telling him about the events of the day before.

"You shouldn't have gone there, Sarah. Those people can become violent sometimes." Adam had his serious-older-brother face on as he kept talking. "They could have hurt you or pulled your *hijab* off or something."

"Yeah, I was kinda forced to walk through them in the parking lot," I told him.

"You didn't tell me that yesterday," Dad said, raising his eyebrows.

"No, Dad, I was fine," I hesitated before adding, "Jason Connor...uh...a classmate... rescued me from the crowd. He helped me walk through them." I tried to sound as casual as

I could, although I felt strangely nervous. I had never kept secrets from my family before; we were usually open books to each other, and I *needed* to get it off my chest, or else it would just keep bothering me. I wasn't sure why I was hesitating, though. Was it because he'd held my hand? Or was it something else? I was confused enough by myself; I didn't want to confuse them as well.

Adam looked at me, his brows furrowed, shifting his focus from his breakfast to me. "Why did he have to help you? Did something happen?" His voice was suddenly sharp.

"No!" I said defensively. "There was just a woman who cursed at me, that's all."

"Sarah..." He looked at me with a worried expression. "Why didn't you call me?"

My brother was rarely affectionate, but he *was* always concerned for my safety. "My battery was dead," I explained, then turned to Dad. "My phone keeps dying, I need a new one!" I hoped that the change of topic would distract them. I didn't want Adam to start questioning me about my "classmate." I was sure they wouldn't get upset, especially since Jason was only trying to help, but since I was also sure that saying it out loud would make it seem like a bigger deal than it really was, I kept that part from Dad and Adam.

"You already have the latest smartphone, what newer phone do you want?" Dad asked dryly as he got up.

Adam wasn't so easily distracted. "Who's Jason Connor?" he asked, washing his hands in the kitchen sink. The name must have sounded new to him.

"He's somebody new in school, just came in this year," I said indifferently. "He's the soccer captain already."

"That's strange," Adam said, wrinkling his forehead. "What happened to Joshua?" Joshua had been the team captain last year.

"Pfffffft. Joshua sucked," I grimaced. I had never been a fan of Joshua. Not only was he an annoying individual, but he'd also lacked the leadership skills necessary to keep our soccer team successful. Jasmine was always complaining about him.

"And is Jason any good?" Adam asked. He wasn't passionate about soccer, but he supported the school team.

He's good-looking alright—I had to bite my tongue from saying it aloud. Instead I just shrugged and tried to sound disinterested, "I dunno..."

"Anyway, Sarah, next time you decide to take on protestors, make sure you let me know ahead of time," Adam ended the discussion and I smiled at him affectionately. He was a good brother, and I really did appreciate him looking out for me.

11

I picked up Jasmine on my way to school, and we talked about the protest in the car. I ended up telling her everything that had happened, and, as I expected, she focused on only one thing.

"Why didn't you pull your hand away?" she wanted to know.

I had known she was going to criticize me, but I had never stopped to think about why I hadn't just removed my hand from his once we were away from the crowd.

"Everything happened so fast. I didn't have time to think about it." Not only did this give her an explanation, but I was able to soothe my troubled conscience, as well.

"You shouldn't have to *think* about it Sarah, it should have been your instinctive reaction!" Jasmine was always persistent.

"Seriously, Jaz, why do you only focus on one thing? You should be worried about my safety rather than Jason Connor holding my hand," I snapped. "At least I didn't *intentionally* do anything wrong." I glared at her.

Thankfully, she let it go. "Fine," she shrugged, smiling at me to show that she wasn't upset.

Even with all the guilt Jasmine tried to make me feel, I wanted to thank Jason properly for all his help. I didn't see him anywhere before school, and I didn't have any classes with him either, so I decided to look for him at lunch. But just before lunch, Zara, Jasmine and I got called into Mrs. Tanner's office—all three of us who wore *hijab* at school. I was surprised, but I didn't expect anything negative from the principled principal.

"Hello, ladies," Mrs. Tanner greeted us warmly as we entered her office.

"Hey, Mrs. Tanner," we chorused in reply.

She pointed toward the chairs across from her desk. "Have a seat," she instructed, as she settled herself down in her comfortable chair.

We all looked at her inquiringly. Spreading her hands on her desk, she gave us a serious look. "We are well aware of what happened yesterday," she began, which tipped me off that this was indeed about the protest.

She continued, "We have notified the mayor's office about our property being used without any official approval by the protesters, and I can assure you all that this will not happen again." She paused, then said, "We're filing a complaint with the city against Brian's show for advertising an unauthorized protest that put our students in jeopardy."

Her expression softened and she gave us all a warm smile. "I also want you to know that I am personally responsible for the safety of each and every student in my school, and I will do whatever I can to make sure no discrimination spreads here. Having said that..." she looked at me pointedly.

"Sarah, you should not have been here yesterday; it wasn't safe. Please be careful and don't put yourself in perilous situations like that. I understand that this is a very sensitive issue, but you have to put your safety first." I could tell that she was observing my reaction.

Snitch! I bristled inwardly. It was obvious who had told her about my presence at school yesterday.

"Who told you I was here?" I asked, trying to keep the annoyance out of my voice. Mrs. Tanner pressed her lips together and tried to suppress a smile. "Whoever told me was only doing so to make sure that the school takes proper action to ensure your safety on the premises. It was all done in good faith," she said calmly.

I arched an eyebrow, skeptical, while Mrs. Tanner merely smiled back at me comfortably.

As Jasmine and I walked together after school, I kept scanning the halls for any sight of Jason. Finally, I spotted him standing by his locker at the end of the upstairs hallway. Impulsive as always, I walked over to him before I could think about it more carefully. He needed to know how I felt about him telling Mrs. Tanner about the protest.

"Hi," I said, as I reached his locker.

Jason was packing away some stuff in his locker, his bag slung over one shoulder. He turned around to look at me. I was standing a few steps away from him, my backpack on my back, holding the shoulder straps with both of my hands.

"Hey," he smiled, "How's it going?"

"Pretty good...how about you?" I sounded a lot friendlier than before, when I had been so overtly suspicious of him.

"I'm okay." He was watching me, obviously wondering what I wanted. All of a sudden, I felt lost for words. My sense of awkwardness grew when I noticed David and Matt, two other seniors on the soccer team, standing behind him. I exchanged hellos with them. Though they usually hung out with the Trashies, they had always maintained a respectful attitude towards me.

As I turned my attention back to Jason, all my indignation evaporated. His face was so open and honest. It was obvious he'd had good intentions when he talked to Mrs. Tanner. So that left me standing in front of him completely dumbfounded, with nothing to say. By this time, Jasmine had caught up with me, and I seized her as an opportunity to continue the conversation.

"This is Jasmine, my best friend," I introduced her to Jason. "We've known each other since forever."

"Hey," Jason nodded at her politely, then looked back at me questioningly. I still hadn't gotten around to saying what I wanted to say, and I could feel my cheeks reddening as I realized that I was making a total fool of myself.

I didn't want Matt and David to think that I was yet another girl throwing herself at Jason. I had a reputation at school for being the type of girl who was friendly to everyone, but never got romantically involved with any guys. I wanted to maintain that reputation, so I quickly composed myself.

"I just wanted to thank you for everything yesterday. I really appreciate you watching my back," I said formally, with a polite smile.

He shrugged and smiled back. "It was nothing, really," he said modestly.

"No, it meant a lot to me." I had regained my confidence, "and I really appreciate it." Thankful that I'd gotten it over with, I quickly waved them goodbye and walked away with Jasmine. She didn't say anything about it, and I didn't bring it up, either. We spent the car ride home talking about all the usual things, but we both avoided any mention of Jason.

Jasmine hung out with me until Adam came home. When I finished my homework and joined him in the living room, I told him about what Mrs. Tanner had said. He was pleased.

"That's really nice of her! She's always been an amazing principal." Mrs. Tanner had been principal for all four of Adam's high school years. Who told her you were at the protest anyways?" he asked, leaning back on the sofa. Although he'd joined us for quality family time, the signs of exhaustion were obvious on his face.

I found myself debating whether to tell him the truth, but I wasn't a liar and I had never been dishonest with my family. "I think Jason did, though Mrs. Tanner didn't say." I paused, "But I still thanked him later after school." I felt relieved to admit it openly.

Adam shot me an annoyed glance. "Any decent guy would have done what Jason did." He stretched his legs on the sofa and closed his eyes.

I thought about that for a bit. Somehow, I doubted that many guys at Wickley High would have done for me what Jason did. And certainly not in such a gallant manner. Since Adam had fallen asleep, though, I decided to keep my thoughts to myself.

12

That week, right after one of the second period announcements, we heard Mrs. Tanner's no-nonsense voice come over the intercom.

"Good morning, Wickely High. I wanted to take a moment for an important reminder to all students, faculty, and myself. We at Wickely are proud to hold the highest standards of appreciation and equality for all. Every student in this school, regardless of their religion, dress code, or race is respected and protected. Neither I nor any other staff member will tolerate any discrimination against anyone's race, gender, religion or ethnicity. I especially will not tolerate any racist or hateful comments toward any student of Wickley. Should any such thing happen, I will personally make sure that severe measures are taken against the perpetrators."

In my classroom, I smiled to myself, my heart swelling with pride. My country wasn't flawless, but it was definitely an exemplary place that valued tolerance and equality, and that's what made it an ideal place to call home.

At lunch time, I waited for Jasmine by her locker. She rarely ever brought her phone to the school, and I had no other way to get in touch with her. Our school had a strict no-phones policy; we were all required to turn our phones in at the front desk.

If any student was found using their phone during class, not only would it would be confiscated, but they were also required to visit the principal's office.

Many of us still snuck our phones in, but most of the teachers were quite strict about enforcing the cell phone rules.

When Jaz didn't show up, I contemplated what to do with my lunch break. I didn't want to stay indoors and waste the beautiful late autumn breeze, so I decided to head outside and enjoy some fresh air.

I exited the main building and was making my way to the benches when Scott called out to me, "Hey, Sarah, come here!" Ashley waved me over, and I obediently altered my course.

"What's going on?" I asked, taking a bite of the apple I'd brought along.

"Nothing much," Scott said, "We were gonna watch the practice game, you wanna come?"

"Seriously, Scott?" He knew very well I hated soccer.

Ashley laughed, "Jasmine's definitely there!"

I made a show of looking reluctant. "Well, the weather *is* nice..." I shrugged, "Fine, let's go!" I offered Ashley my arm and we made our way to the soccer field.

Jasmine was standing beside the track that surrounded the soccer field.

"Hey, *salam alaikum*," I accosted her.

"*Wa 'alaikum salam*," she smiled back.

"What happened?" I asked, "No game?" I was relieved.

"No, they were only practicing, not playing, and they just finished," Jasmine explained. "I knew you would show up here to enjoy the weather!" she laughed.

I was immersed in chatting with my friends, completely oblivious to anything else, when I laughed at something Ashley said and glanced around, catching Jason's gaze. His brilliant grey eyes were fixed on me.

Without thinking twice, I spontaneously waved at him; he looked startled and caught off guard. After a moment's hesitation, he waved back, but quickly walked away towards the gym doors. He ran his hand through his hair again, leaving it fashionably mussed.

"What was that all about?" Jasmine asked me as soon as we left Ashley and Scott.

"What was what about?" I asked, confused.

Her voice sharpened. "Why was Jason staring at you?"

"Was he?" I was surprised. "He probably just noticed us all standing in the middle of the field and was wondering what we were doing."

Jasmine wasn't deterred. "No. He was *staring* at *you*."

"Jaz, he just waved hello because I waved at him first," I tried to convince her.

She frowned. "No, before you noticed him he was walking through the field... but as soon as he saw you, he just stopped and started looking at you this...this *way*." She gestured with her hands emphatically.

I laughed, "What *way*?" Jasmine huffed with irritation. "You only noticed him when you waved at him, but he was there for a while. He was just standing there, *looking* at you." Jasmine was a sharp observer who never missed any details, but this time I told myself she was imagining things.

"Sounds like you were noticing *him* more than he noticed me," I laughed, teasing her.

She looked frustrated. "No, I'm *tellin'* you, the way he stopped when he saw you...it was like he was lost just looking at you." She seemed absolutely convinced of her theory, whatever it was.

"I don't know, Jaz," I was starting to get annoyed at her insistence. "I'm sure the only thing he must have been thinking was about how ugly I look in this outfit!" I tried to laugh it off. Jasmine had a habit of reading into things.

In class, though, I couldn't focus on Othello. Why would Jason be looking at me, out of all the pretty girls at school? He had enough Trashies falling all over him, there was no way he'd ever be interested in me. No matter how proud Jasmine was of herself for being a sharp observer, she was definitely wrong this time.

13

Jasmine's mother had scheduled the monthly "Mother-Daughter" lunch at the mosque's community hall over the weekend. I was invited, although I didn't enjoy participating in this particular event. When Aunty Elisha had first started it, the name had bothered me a lot, since I was the only one who had to join without a mother. Jasmine had guessed the cause of my irritation, and quietly requested her mother to change the name. Officially, the event was now known as the 'Monthly Ladies' Luncheon.'

The idea was still the same, though: girls and their mothers hanging out together. Any time there was a new face at the event, I would have to give them an explanation of why I couldn't bring my mother, and put up with their sympathetic looks.

I hated it, but Dad always said that I should be confident and appreciate their sympathy. Dad didn't get it, though. He could never understand how women can turn sympathy into making you feel miserable and ashamed. Like the older aunties who asked younger women if they were married "yet" or newlyweds, if they were pregnant "yet." I got ready for the event and tried a few different headscarves before deciding on one. Leaving a pile of clothes and scarves on my bed for Paula to yell at me about later, I headed downstairs.

Dad and Adam were in the living room. As usual, Dad complimented me on my lilac-and-amethyst color combination of scarf, skirt, and top, and Adam repeated dutifully, "You look pretty, Sarah." It was nice to see him home, since he'd begun to spend weekends on campus as well. I guess he was glad to see me too, because then he added, "You looked the same yesterday, you look the same today, and I'm sure you'll look exactly the same tomorrow, too!" I pretended to gasp with horror, but was really laughing. "I just wish I could write it down on the notice board so I didn't have to say it every day," he teased Dad. I couldn't stop giggling. I knew Adam had been forced to compliment me every morning since I was little, and how much it annoyed him, but I enjoyed every minute of it.

"Dad, I'm going to grab something from your store to take to the potluck, so I don't look like a moocher," I called out to Dad on my way out.

It wasn't the scrutiny I feared, though; it was the possibility of someone explaining to a new attendee, since some people invited family or friends from Pittsburgh, why I was excused from bringing anything—because I didn't have a mother.

"Bring me some leftovers!" Adam yelled from the living room, surrounded by his books.

When I got to the mosque, only the ladies from Wickley were there at the community hall, and I was relieved not to see any new faces that day. The food was good, a bit of variety from several different countries.

Adnan's mother was there. She cooked good food, but her constant praise of her son and daughter really annoyed me.

Her daughter, Mona, was in the 8ᵗʰ grade and had her mother wrapped around her finger. Adnan, on the other hand, tried to hit on me once at school and I'd been giving him the cold shoulder ever since.

"Sarah, how have you been?" Amal, an Egyptian-American mother in her late twenties, who had moved to Wickley the year before, asked.

"*Alhamdullilah*, how about yourself?" I answered warmly. "How are Maryam and Asma?" I referred to her daughters, who were ten and twelve years old.

Amal nodded, "They're good *alhamdullilah*, still just trying to adjust to a small community after living in the big city." She sighed, looking a bit nostalgic; they had moved to Wickley from California. "Listen, Nada told me that you've been a good influence on her daughter and that you're very active in the community."

I smiled, feeling a bit flattered that Nada—Zara's mother— had complimented me to Amal. I shook my head, trying to be modest. "That's so kind of her. Zara herself is such a good girl, *mashaAllah*."

Amal continued, "Well, I was wondering if you could start a small study circle for the preteen girls? I know Elisha does a talk for teenagers, but I think it would be better if a girl like you could teach our tweens. They could relate to you more and they'd be able to have a more realistic role model."

I was glad they thought so highly of me and agreed to think of a plan once my midterms were over. I remembered being a preteen myself, with no study circle or youth group to attend.

Before heading home, I dropped by the church next door to see if Pastor John was in. He was an older man whose white hair, large stomach, and perpetual smile made me think of

Santa Claus. He was always warm and friendly toward the Muslim community, and the good relationship between the church and mosque was, I gathered, not particularly common, which made me appreciate it all the more. I wanted to discuss the protest and the AIA's presence in Wickley, and explore ways for us to raise awareness together, to make sure that their ignorance and hatred didn't plant its roots in Wickley.

"I spoke against bigotry last Sunday in my sermon," he said as we walked away from his office together, toward the parking lot. "In fact, I was thinking that maybe you could come speak one day."

"In the church?" I asked in surprise.

"Yes, why not? Many churches invite Muslim speakers to build bridges, and I think it would be great if you spoke. I heard your interview on Brian's show, and you speak from your heart." He beamed at me, and I smiled back.

"That's very kind of you, Pastor John. I'll think about it and let you know."

"Sure! You know where to find me," he waved goodbye as I got in my car.

I hadn't forgotten to take food home for Dad and Adam, and they gratefully attacked the platter I'd brought back.

"Maybe you should take some cooking classes from Adnan's mom, since we've given up on your cleaning abilities. Maybe there is still hope for your cooking!" Adam suggested. He missed Mom's cooking and was always bugging me to learn how to cook. "No, thanks! I don't have time," I yelled from the living room. *And I can't imagine setting foot in Adnan's house,* I thought.

"Dad will hire you as a cook," he laughed back.

"I'm sure I'll be able to find something that doesn't involve any kind of pots or pans," I retorted. Cooking and I couldn't be put together in the same sentence. "Why don't you get married so your wife can feed us some good food?" I teased him, fighting fire with fire. Dad looked up from his laptop screen and grinned at me. "And what if his wife's cooking is just like yours?"

"Then Adam is going to cook for all of us," I said firmly, stretching my legs onto the sofa and braiding my long hair.

Adam walked in, wiping his hand with a paper towel. "Dad, I'll be coming home really late all week next week, so if you need me to go over the inventory, I can do that today."

Dad shook his head, "No, I can do that, son. Don't worry." His eyes were warm as he looked at Adam, but then they both went back to their laptops.

It annoyed me when our quality family time was compromised by their need to work so hard all the time, so I decided to grab their attention. "Dad, can I dye my hair purple?" Adam rolled his eyes, but I was stubborn. "Just purple hair and a nose ring!" I really wanted to try something different this year. It *was* my senior year, after all—the last year I had to really enjoy myself before I had to act grown up and responsible.

"Sarah, don't you have anything to do? Where's Jasmine?" Dad always got annoyed whenever I bothered him about dying my hair. He didn't understand why I wanted to do outlandish things with it when, to him, it was already perfect. In his opinion, I'd just be damaging my hair for no good reason.

"*Please*, let me just try it once before I'm too old to do such crazy things!" I begged.

"Yeah, Dad, let her... one time won't hurt." I stared at Adam in shock; he really took me by surprise sometimes! He shrugged back at me and smiled, then looked down at his screen again.

Dad pursed his lips. "We'll see when we go to Houston."

I let out a whoop of joy and jumped off the sofa to give him a huge kiss on the cheek. Dad just smiled and shook his head at me, but I raced off to my room to report this latest development to Jasmine.

14

Thanksgiving break was about to start and, as always, we were flying to Houston to visit my mom's mom. Since Grandma had gotten older, traveling wasn't easy for her, which was why she'd stopped coming to Wickley. For the last few years, Dad, Adam, and I regularly visited her in Houston instead.

My maternal grandparents had settled in Houston from Pakistan before my mother was born. My grandfather had passed away when I was very young, leaving Grandma with Mom's younger brother Amir still in high school.

Although Houston was a big city for me, I admired the Muslim community there, and the huge variety of international restaurants. Dad often took us to Islamic activities and conferences there.

Adam loved Houston more than any of us. He'd spent a lot more time with Grandma than I had; whenever Mom went through Chemo, Adam was sent to Grandma's. It was really hard for him to see Mom suffer through the treatments and their agonizing aftermath. I was younger and easier to distract, so I got to stay with Mom and Dad. As a result, Adam developed a really close bond with Grandma, and he loved traveling to Houston. If it wasn't for Dad's business, he would have convinced Dad to move there by now.

We arrived in Houston on a Wednesday night, and Grandma had invited some of the extended family for Thanksgiving dinner the next day. It was always a mish mash of American and Pakistani food. Grandma could make both killer biriyani and a mean turkey.

On Friday, Aunty Elizabeth, Mom's best friend who was also known as Lizzy, invited us over for dinner. She was a convert who lived with her son Zain. Mom and Aunty Lizzy had known each other since their college days. Aunty Lizzy had been married to a Jordanian immigrant, but a few years ago she'd lost her husband—and her ability to walk—in a car accident.

Zain was Adam's best friend. They'd spent a lot of time together at Aunty Lizzy's house when Adam came to Houston while Mom was sick. He was a few months older than Adam, but they bonded really well, and although they lived thousands of miles apart, they managed to stay well connected.

While we were in Houston, Adam and Zain were so busy catching up and hanging out that they didn't join us for dinner on most nights, whether at Grandma's or Aunty Lizzy's house.

The highlight of the trip for me was being able to attend a popular Islamic talk at a nearby Houston mosque. The environment was vibrant, energetic, and spiritually rejuvenating—just what I needed! And it was great to meet new girls my age.

Unfortunately, the trip ended all too quickly. The next day we headed home, and the whole way back I had to listen to Adam complain about not living in Houston.

15

Returning to school meant returning to art class—my least favorite subject. I always tried to avoid the other students as much as possible, especially since the freshmen couldn't seem to get over their various forms of drama. Doodling absently in my notebook, I looked up just in time to see Jason walking in. He scanned the room briefly before catching my eye, then grinned and walked over.

"Do you mind?" He pointed to the empty chair at my worktable.

I shook my head, perplexed. What was he doing in my class?

"Glad to see another senior here," he gave an exaggerated sigh of relief, winking at me.

"You mean you're in this class now?" I was surprised—the only reason *I* was in art class was because I had procrastinated my last arts and humanities credit and needed it for graduation.

"Yeah," he nodded, but then Ms. Lynn closed the door and started the lesson. This week's project was stained glass painting.

After Ms. Lynn finished explaining what we had to do for the rest of the week, she made her way over to our table. "Hey, guys!" she smiled at us. Ms. Lynn was always perky and upbeat, unlike some of the other teachers at Wickley. Not only was she my neighbor, but her daughter Taylor and I had been friends since first grade. "Sarah, this is Jason. He's joining us a bit late, and he needs to catch up on the missed work. Maybe you can help him catch up if you have time during lunch?"

I nodded, "Yeah, sure." There wasn't much to make up anyway, since we'd mostly just done some painting and reading about the history of art. It wouldn't take long to fill him in.

"Thanks," Jason added as Ms. Lynn walked away.

"Wow, you got your schedule readjusted after three months?" It was notoriously difficult to convince the admin to allow any flexibility when it came to our schedules.

"Yeah, it's a long story. I had study hall for fourth period, and then Mrs. Smith realized before Thanksgiving that I hadn't taken any art classes at my previous school. Apparently, I can't graduate without an art credit from here, so she switched my class. I'm glad she sorted this out now, before it was too late," he explained.

"Oh... It must be hard starting out at a new school in your senior year," I said thoughtfully. I couldn't imagine how difficult it must be to leave behind carefully thought-out plans for high school, only to end up somewhere new in the most important year.

He nodded. "Yeah, it is."

"You must hate your parents for moving during your senior year." I would've been furious at Dad if he made me leave Wickley to go to Houston, even though I knew it pretty well.

Jason shook his head. "Nah, they're still back in Maryland... I'm the one who moved."

My curiosity was definitely piqued now, but I didn't want to pry into his private life. What was the urgency of switching schools in the last year?

I said nothing else, but pursed my lips and raised my eyebrows to make it clear how confused I was.

Jason just smiled enigmatically and said no more.

We both looked back up at the front of the class to focus on Ms. Lynn's demonstration. She was explaining how to cut the glass into different shapes; it wasn't hard, but I found it mind-numbingly boring. Jason's attention span must have been just as short as mine, because after a while, he asked me, "So why are *you* taking this class in your senior year?"

I rolled my eyes. "Same reason you are—I hate art and managed to avoid it every year 'till now. I need it to graduate, too."

His smile revealed his dimples, and I quickly looked down to avoid the odd feeling that had started fluttering in my stomach.

The class ended quickly enough, and I gathered my stuff.

"Let me know whenever you're ready to go over the material you need to know about, and I'll show you what we've done so far," I told him and hoisted my backpack onto my shoulder, making sure that my plain black headscarf wasn't tugged off-center by the straps. I had coordinated my *hijab* with a loose black hoodie that covered a grey cotton maxi dress.

Jason got up, too, his forehead creased in thought. "Hmmmm, I usually practice soccer during lunch because I have PE right after that, but if you're free during lunch today, maybe we can do it then?"

"Okay," I agreed. We walked together towards the cafeteria.

"So how long have you been here?" Jason asked

"Where?" I wasn't sure what he meant. Most of the time when people asked me this question, they meant in America—because *of course* being 'brown' meant that I couldn't possibly have been born and raised here my entire life.

"In Wickley?" he clarified.

"Oh," I laughed. "I was born here."

"Really?" Jason was surprised. "So you've lived here all your life."

"Yup, it's my home."

"Wow, what's it like growing up in such a small place?" He was getting pretty inquisitive, but I forgave him—he was the new kid after all.

"I love it!" I said emphatically. "I hate big cities."

His grin was mischievous. "Have you ever *been* to a big city?" I shot him an annoyed look.

"Pittsburgh, for one," I retorted. "My mom was from Houston, so we go there regularly. My dad takes us around the country a lot, but all those big cities are only nice for a visit."

"I love big cities." Jason looked wistful. "Small town isn't really my thing..." He grimaced a little, and I felt irritated that he was so quick to judge our lovely little burg.

"So what brought you here, then?" I said, my voice a little sharp.

"I...uh..." he stumbled on the words, "I had some issues at my old school, and I couldn't finish the last year there. I had to change schools. And Wickley was the only one that would accept me directly onto the soccer team, if..." he paused for a moment to hold the cafeteria door open for me. "If I could start practicing with the team before school started."

I was confounded. "So you've been here all summer?" I asked.

"Not the whole summer, just the four weeks before school started. That's when I started practicing with the team."

I looked dubious. "That's how important soccer is to you?"

"I'm eligible to receive a full scholarship for college as long as I'm on the school team," he boasted, although he was trying to sound casual about it.

I didn't know anything about sports scholarships, so I just mouthed 'wow' and said, "Good for you. I'm glad we took you in!"

He glanced at me with a pleased smile. We found empty seats.

"Do you want to grab something before we start?" He asked, putting his school bag down on the table.

"Yeah, you want to get a smoothie?"

"Okay," he smiled as he got up to walk with me.

We ran into Scott, who was looking for me. "Where you sittin'?" Scott asked.

"Oh, I was sitting over there," I pointed at the table where we had left our stuff. "I have to help Jason out with some stuff."

Scott nodded hello to Jason and told me, "Ashley was looking for you; we're at our regular spot."

I waved goodbye to him and walked on with Jason.

"Have you found any good friends here?" I asked when we were waiting in the line.

"Yeah, a couple," he said, pulling his phone out of his pocket. "Sorry, someone's texting me." He texted back and quickly put the phone away.

"This phone rule here sucks," he complained.

We picked up our drinks and, as we made our way back to the table, David passed by. "Hey man, aren't you coming with us?" he asked Jason. They did the guy's handshake, some weird combination of a fist bump and finger wiggling. I rolled my eyes. Guys are *so* immature.

"Sorry dude, I'll catch up with you next period. I have to go over some stuff with Sarah." Jason explained. I smiled politely at David as he nodded to me.

We spent the remaining lunch period reviewing the material Jason had missed in art class. There wasn't much, so we finished up a few minutes before the bell rang.

"Why didn't you wait for me by my locker?!" Jasmine's voice accosted me just as I started packing up my bag again. I turned around to see her behind me, arms folded crossly. She hadn't noticed Jason at my side, so I quickly re-introduced them, then left him to walk with her to our next class.

"So why was Jason hanging around?" she asked after she'd finished scolding me about not waiting for her.

"He just joined my art class and Ms. Lynn asked me to help him catch up." I explained patiently. It was getting annoying to have to explain my presence with Jason to everyone in the whole school!

Jasmine narrowed her eyes at me. "You mean he's going to be with you in art class?" she repeated.

"That's what I just said," I snapped, feeling irritated. She gave me an unreadable look. "What's the problem?" I demanded. "Why are you so anti-Jason?"

She shrugged, pretending indifference. "Nothin'," she said, and once more, I tried to laugh off her exasperation.

16

The next day during art, Jason and I were outlining our glass pieces so that Ms. Lynn could cut them for us later. She had left it up to us whether we wanted to try cutting them ourselves or have her cut them for us. I wasn't in any mood to use the cutter again, and Jason didn't seem interested either.

"So who do you live with?" I asked him, continuing the conversation we'd started the day before.

"I'm old enough to live alone," he said, focusing on his glass.

I glanced at him with a raised eyebrow; he smiled and said in answer to the unspoken question, "I turned 18 in September."

"You left home as soon as you turned eighteen?" I couldn't help asking more questions; I was truly curious at this good-natured, good-looking athlete who would clearly be the pride of any school he attended.

"I wasn't planning on it, but I had to." His answer was a bit more abrupt now, and I hoped that I hadn't annoyed him with my snooping. We both fell silent. I couldn't think of any special shape for my glass, so I absent-mindedly drew a heart.

Jason surprised me by talking some more. "I was expelled from my previous school in Ellicott City. It was best if I relocated by myself, rather than having my whole family move. It's only for a year anyway. My dad rented a small house on the edge of Wickley for me. We were lucky to find a rental in this area, otherwise my dad would have had to buy a place here." The whole time, he avoided looking at me directly.

It was too much information for me to grasp immediately. Expellled? Wow, what did he do? I hope he wasn't involved with any gangs or drugs—or guns!

Still, I wasn't the type of person to react over another's overwhelming confessions or personal information, so I kept myself focused on my glass and tried to act casual.

"Expelled? What did you do?" I asked off-handedly. His hands paused in their drawing, and he gave me a searching look. "I had some rivals at school. One day after a game, they set me up for a fight. I was alone," he paused and pressed his lips together, "the next day they filed a complaint against me."

I was taken aback. "Why didn't you tell the principal what had happened?"

"I did! But they were the ones who were injured, so I had the weaker defense."

My jaw dropped. "Wow, you took on more than one guy, and sent them all to the hospital?" I asked naïvely.

Jason laughed, looking amused. "No, two other guys from my school helped me take them down."

"So didn't *they* tell what happened?" Injustice always upset me.

Jason frowned pensively. "The committee was a bit prejudiced against them. They were *Moozlums*, Muhammad and

Hassan. The fact that they were present at the fight didn't help my case at all."

I wasn't sure if he was complaining about them ruining his case, or if he appreciated their help. I wanted to make sure, so I said cautiously, "I'm sorry that their presence ruined your case."

"Oh no! Don't get me wrong! If they hadn't shown up, I'd probably be dead. I owe them. They tried to help me and, as a result, they were expelled, too. I owe them a lot." The expression on his face was distant, mingled with emotions I couldn't read. It must have been painful for him to recall.

I had an epiphany. *This* was why he'd helped me on the day of the protest! He was trying to repay the act of kindness that those brothers had done for him. That made sense, I thought to myself, tapping my finger against my lips.

Art period was almost finished. We handed our glass over to Mrs. Lynn so she could cut it for us. I didn't expect that Jason would walk me to my locker, but he strode next to me, engaged in a discussion about living as a minority in US. Jasmine showed up when we arrived at my locker, and figuring that Jasmine wanted me to go with her, Jason waved goodbye and left.

I wondered if he actually wanted to hang out with us during lunch too, but Jason had already left and Jasmine would probably have objected anyway. She seemed to have an odd grudge against him; Scott, Ashley, and Aaron often sat with us, so boys couldn't have been the issue. I remained puzzled over her disapproval.

At dinner that night, I shared Jason's tragic story with Dad and Adam. They listened with sympathetic ears, and looked rather impressed at his behavior.

"Isn't he the same guy who walked you through the protestors that day?" Adam remarked. He wasn't eating dinner, but he was spending time with us at the dinner table anyway."Yeah, that's him," I confirmed. A prickle of discomfort made me fidget in my seat. Why did I feel so anxious and uncomfortable talking about Jason with my family? I'd never had issues talking to them about other guys at school. The conversation drifted to other topics, and I felt unusually relieved that no one asked me any more questions.

17

The weather in Wickley started to change. The warm summer breezes had turned to chilling wind, and soon enough we'd had several snowfalls.

My weekend was dull, since both Dad and Adam were busy with the stores' inventories. Adam had become even busier during the weekdays, but he always took time during the weekends to help Dad out.

I peeked through the curtains, admiring the shifting clouds as the sun's sharp winter rays pierced through the silvered branches of the trees outside. The world was covered in a blanket of pure, shining snow.

On such a day, the best thing to do would be to go out for a walk. There were few things I loved more than walking through the untouched snow. Bundling up in a warm black jacket and a creamy hijab that complimented my dark grey A-line skirt and combat boots, I walked through the fresh snow towards the mosque, which wasn't far from my house. I loved sitting inside and going through the small library filled with Islamic books that Dad and others had donated. The soft carpets, the smell of incense, and the soft recitation of Qur'an that was played over the old stereo filled me with a sense of spiritual peace.

After praying at the mosque, I remembered that I hadn't gotten back to Pastor John about the speech he had asked me to deliver at the church. I popped over to his office and apologized for my forgetfulness; we decided to set a date for the talk after Christmas, since at the moment he was swamped with holiday preparations.

I left the church, wandering around absently, leaving behind boot prints as the first evidence of exploration into this new, snow-bound world. My cheeks flushed from the cold wind, and I was so immersed in my own world that I didn't even realize someone had been following me.

"Hey," Jason's voice broke into my reverie. I turned back and saw him jogging his way up to me, rather underdressed for the weather in only a pair of sweatpants and a sweatshirt.

"Hi," I said in surprise. "What are you doing here?"

"Jogging!" He smirked at me, his brilliant grey eyes twinkling as brightly as the sun shining off the snow.

I smiled wryly. "Yeah, I can see that."

Jason laughed, and I couldn't help but notice the way his golden brown hair shone in the sunlight. "There are so many drifts out where I live, I decided to try a run in the inner town." He was still panting slightly from his exertions.

"We call this area downtown," I pointed out.

He made a face. "Seriously? That's an insult to a real downtown! Let's just call it the inner town."

We stood by the side of the curb talking for a few minutes. "Want to grab a drink?" he offered. "There's a nice café just around the corner."

I smiled in amusement. "I'm sure you must have been there before," he remarked, and my smile widened in a private joke. He didn't realize that my father owned it!

"Okay," I agreed. For the first time, someone didn't know my entire life history in Wickley! I was so thrilled by the novelty of anonymity that I didn't even take a second to consider the fact that I'd never gone out alone for a drink with a guy before. Chatting amiably, we walked into the A&S, and as he'd done before at school, Jason held the door open for me as we entered.

Alex and two new girls were working. Alex was a Latino-American college student whose mixed parentage had given him deep blonde hair and sea-green eyes that, combined with his bronze complexion, made him the most exotic-looking guy in Wickley. Most of the high school girls had a perpetual crush on him, but he maintained a dignified distance. Alex used to carpool with Adam to Pitts for a while, but then Adam's schedule became too strenuous for him to keep up with, and he started driving in on his own.

The two girls were new and I didn't know them well. Dad had hired them recently when his other full time employee had requested weekends off.

"Hey, what are you doing here?" Alex glanced at me as he grabbed some drinks to hand to waiting customers, but he walked away without waiting for an answer.

Jason and I waited in the line, going over the menu items placed on the wall. Alex was back by the time it was our turn. "You want to come in and make it yourself?" Jason looked confused.

Before Alex said anything else, I jumped in. "I work here sometimes," I said hastily, eyeing Alex warningly. He got the hint, and his grin grew bigger.

"Nah, I'm off today," I told him as we placed our orders. I noticed Jason pulling out his wallet. "Drinks are on me," I added.

He waved his credit card at me. "Come on, guys are the ones who are supposed to pay!"

I cast him a glare of mock anger. "Since you're new here, I'll forgive your chauvinism—this time!" I picked up both our drinks. "And to soothe your male ego, I get free drinks as part of the employee discount." I grinned at him to let him know I wasn't really mad.

He smiled back, looking a little startled at my vehemence. "Hey, I'm not anti-feminist," he protested jokingly as he put his wallet away. "And I appreciate your hospitality."

We seated ourselves at an empty booth. "I should come here with you all the time so I can score free cappuccinos," he joked.

"Do you come often?" I asked. I popped into the café pretty regularly to run small errands for Dad, but I'd never seen Jason there before.

He shook his head. "I just recently found this place," he said. Jason took a sip of his creamy coffee and turned his eyes on me again. There was something about his open gaze that made me unusually relaxed and eager to talk.

"So you were just out for a walk?" he asked.

I nodded. "Yeah, everyone was busy at home and I was bored, so I decided to get some fresh air. I love walking, especially in the snow." I looked out the window and gave a little sigh of happiness. "Doesn't it just look magical?"

Jason tried to suppress his smile. "Isn't that a bit kiddish?"

I lifted my eyebrows at him. "Why?" I demanded, relishing the taste of hot chocolate and whipped cream. "Come on, don't tell me you don't enjoy it too."

He shrugged, laughing a little. "I did when I was a kid, but not anymore."

My pride was stung. "Whatever," I snapped in annoyance. "I'm not a kid. I'm seventeen."

I had a feeling that he was amused at my irritation. "That's not the whole reason I was out, though," I said, trying to change the topic. "I went to the mosque and then the church."

Jason almost choked on his drink. "The mosque *and* the church?"

I smiled, smug at being able to throw him off-kilter. "Yeah. Our mosque is connected to the church, and we have a really good relationship. The pastor suggested that I give a short talk at the church about Islamophobia, so I had to discuss some stuff with him."

Jason leaned forward, listening attentively and looking intrigued.

"Wow, you're really passionate about this cause, aren't you?" His voice was admiring, and a part of me felt flattered that he had noticed.

I leaned towards him as well, resting my elbows on the table and threading my fingers together.

"I believe in the founding American values of liberty, equality and justice for all, and I *will* fight for them for as long as I can."

Though he was smiling, I could tell he was sincerely impressed

My phone gave a little beep, notifying me that I had received a text. Checking it, I saw it was Dad, asking me to come home.

"I have to go," I apologized to Jason, getting up. "My dad's texting me to head on home." I took a last sip of my drink and tucked my phone away.

Jason got up to leave too. "Thanks for the cappuccino." He held the door open for me and we waved each other goodbye as we parted ways.

I barely made it home in time to catch *Maghrib*, the sunset prayer. At dinner, I briefly mentioned running into Jason while on a walk, but I omitted the details of what happened afterwards. Dad looked thoughtful. "He doesn't have any family around. Maybe you should invite him over to dinner one day." Dad had spent enough time away from his family to be sympathetic toward anyone living without theirs.

Before I could say anything, Adam interjected, "Dad, she can't invite some random guy from school to dinner!" Adam had always disagreed with Dad about letting me interact with boys.

"He's not some random guy; after all, he *did* help her during the protest," Dad pointed out as he took a sip of water.

Adam frowned. "I'll drop off a few gift vouchers from the café for him. That should pay off our debt to him."

Dad smiled gently. "To return kindness with money is really not the best way of portraying an honorable image of Muslims."

The conversation was starting to sound too serious now, so I jumped in. "I've already thanked him." I made a desperate attempt to conclude the discussion.

"It's up to you, but you've invited Scott and Aaron over before," Dad commented.

Dad was right. I could've shown him gratitude by displaying the proper Muslim hospitality, but for some odd reason that I couldn't quite fathom myself, I didn't want to invite Jason over to my house. "I've known them all my life, and you know their families too," I objected. "Besides, every time they came over, it was for school projects."

"I still don't understand why you let her invite them over, even if it was for school projects," Adam added, his frown deepening. Despite the fact that Dad had come directly from Pakistan and Adam had been born and raised in the States, Adam's mindset was extremely traditional about gender interaction. He believed that I should stay away from boys, period, whereas Dad believed that allowing me to interact with boys within the comfort of my own house was not only safer, but was also a good way of weaning me off of thinking about romance *every* time I saw a boy.

Dad took a deep breath. "Adam, we've talked about this before. I want Sarah to be able to interact with boys professionally and not always think in just one direction every time she sees the opposite gender. This is my way of training her to maintain a platonic relationship. I might be wrong, but it has worked so far, and I have no reason to put unnecessary restrictions on her or on *you*." Dad fixed Adam with a pointed look.

When Adam had first started talking about how I should stay away from boys, Dad had told him that if that was the case, Adam shouldn't go to university either, which had a mixed environment of young men and women too.

I was unusually vexed. "Can we please not talk about this?" I begged. "Dad, I really don't want to invite him over right now."

"He's a guest in our town, and you've never protested like this about inviting a friend home before," Dad teased.

"He's not a friend, he's just an acquaintance," I said petulantly. I didn't understand why I was getting so irritated, but I really wished he'd just drop the subject already.

Dad's smile slowly faded and he looked at me for a long moment with an unreadable expression. Then he got up, gently brushed his hand through my long, dark hair, and quietly left.

I looked at Adam, and he just gave me an *I don't know* shrug.

18

ad brought up the subject of traveling to Houston during Christmas break at breakfast.

"Adam, I need to make reservations," he reminded. "You need to give me the dates ASAP."

I couldn't wait to attend the *Texas Dawah Convention* in Houston during Christmas break. It was one of the highlights of my year. I got to enjoy an entire energetic crowd: many long distance friends, active youth dedicated to their faith, and truly inspiring scholars of the West. That convention was like a "spiritual fix" for the whole year.

"Dad, I told you my graduation is on the 23rd and then I have to start my internship soon after," Adam answered with chagrin.

"I didn't know you'd already been accepted for an internship," I scowled. "No one bothers to tell me anything anymore!" I felt unreasonably irked that morning

Both Dad and Adam looked at me with raised eyebrows. "What's wrong with *you?* Are you PMSing?" Adam sneered.

"Your face is PMSing," I snapped back. I didn't want him to spoil our Houston trip. I *really* wanted to attend TDC.

Adam walked around to my chair, standing behind me and putting his hands on my shoulders. "Get your allowance together. You'll be buying me a Rolex for my graduation," he whispered. "Right?" He tilted my head back so I was looking up at him and grinned.

"Whatever," I said sourly, but I felt bad. Adam's graduation was a big event for him—in fact, it was a big deal for the whole family—and I was sure he must have been missing Mom terribly. I had to stop being selfish and let my brother enjoy his once-in-a-lifetime event.

"The conference starts on the twenty-third," Dad mused. "We can travel on the twenty-fourth."

That meant we'd miss the first two days of the conference, but I didn't object. I owed my brother his chance to celebrate.

Adam thought about it for a moment. "Okay," he nodded. "That's fine. But Dad, Zain's leaving for College Station on the twenty-fifth, would you mind if I go with him and fly back to Houston by myself?"

"What do you mean?" I interrupted. "What's Zain doing in College Station?"

"He's in med school there..." Adam replied absently, still looking at Dad and waiting for an answer.

College Station was a small city about 125 miles away from Houston, and had one of the best medical schools in the country.

Dad seemed confused, "I don't understand; you'll stay a whole week with Zain?"

Adam sat down next to Dad and pulled his phone out of his pocket.

"No, Dad," he showed Dad the calendar on the phone. "Look, I'll go with him on the night of the twenty-fifth, stay with Grandma for a few days afterward, and then fly back home myself," he explained. "And you two can fly back whenever you want."

Dad's university started around the same time I had to get back to school, but he had to be back early for his businesses. "You can go with Zain as long as you're in Houston on the twenty-seventh and spend the whole day with me," Dad decided firmly. "Afterwards, you can stay in Houston as long as you want."

Adam wasn't the kind of person to argue with Dad. He took a deep breath and looked away with a frown on his face. It was obvious he didn't like Dad's condition, but he agreed and left for school.

I didn't understand why Dad wanted Adam back so soon from College Station. Dad loved Zain and had always admired his level of maturity. After Zain's father passed away in the accident and his mother became disabled, he took care of the family business and still made it into medical school. It was his father's wish for him to become a doctor, although from what I'd heard, Zain himself didn't have much interest in the medical field. After his father's death, though, he sacrificed his own ambitions and chose to study medicine.

"Dad, why are you making him come back early?" I asked as soon as Adam left. "You know Zain is his best-est friend!"

Dad smiled sheepishly, "Your grandma called last night. She said they've organized a surprise graduation party for Adam on the twenty-seventh!"

My jaw dropped and I gave a small scream of excitement. "That's awesome!" I exclaimed. "And he'll never guess!"

A thought occurred to me. "But Zain will miss the party," I thought of how disappointed Adam would be. I wanted Adam's graduation party to be perfect, which meant that he *had* to have his best friend there.

Dad got up from his chair, saying, "He's in med school now, and his schedule will be extremely rigid, especially for the first two years." He washed his hands and picked up his keys. "But I'll talk to him and see if he can stay longer, or come back with Adam. Otherwise we'll just have to make the best of it."

19

One Wednesday afternoon I had to stay after school for some useless speech workshop. By the time I'd finished, Jasmine had already gone home and I didn't have my car because I'd carpooled with her that morning. Dad was supposed to come home late from Pittsburgh due to a faculty dinner he had to attend that night.

I didn't mind walking home and enjoying the fresh, cold evening breeze. The snow had melted a bit and refrozen, so I veered off the clean sidewalks and crunched through lawns. To my dismay, however, the front door was locked when I got home. We almost never lock our front door, but I assumed that Paula had had to go out for something and decided to take the precaution.

I hadn't brought my own keys either, since my house key was attached to my car keys, and I'd left the keychain at home in my room. I walked over to Jasmine's house, only to find that her house was empty and locked as well.

I let out a huff of frustration and dialed her cell. "Salaamu Alaikum, Jaz, where are you?" I asked plaintively.

"We're out," she said, and I could hear her noisy brothers in the background.

"We had to go to Pitts for some dinner with Dad's friends," she raised her voice over the commotion around her.

"How far are you?" I asked, desperately hoping that they'd be back soon and I could get indoors.

"We're in Pitts," she reminded me. "What happened?"

"Nothing, just wondering where you were. I'll talk to you later," I sighed, and hung up.

Great. I didn't have Jasmine's house key either because it was on the same keychain with all my other keys. I felt a wave of irritation at whoever had locked our front door.

It was getting dark and I didn't want to be stuck outside, so I decided to walk to the café.

Dad had done a wonderful job making the café unique. The menu boasted a wide selection of items not found at other cafés, and the décor featured exotic souvenirs from around the world. Dad's secret was that he had friends all over the world who were able to export various recipes and ingredients, and as a result, the café was famous for its international array of desserts and teas, in addition to sandwiches and snacks made only with organic fruits, vegetables, and whole-wheat flour. The café also served fresh juices and smoothies as well as a huge variety of hot drinks.

The A&S featured a comfortable seating arrangement; booths lined the walls, while the rest of the space was scattered with cozy sofas and coffee tables, and one entire corner was colonized by study tables. The complimentary Wi-Fi did a good job of keeping customers hooked as well.

I settled down on a quiet sofa, looking around at the bustling rush of customers. Alex and Tammy were busy working the evening shift, so they didn't notice me initially. But once the crowd faded away, they both waved me hello.

"Do you want something to drink?" Alex called out from behind the counter.

"Give me something to eat first," I growled. I was really tired, and all I wanted right then was the comfort of my own home.

Tammy laughed, "What happened?" Tammy was an older lady from Pitts who acted as manager. She was the single mother of a young girl, and had been working for my dad for a really long time. "Dad kick you out?"

"Yeah, he locked me out," I said sarcastically, making myself comfortable on the sofa and stretching my legs.

They looked perplexed, but I was in no mood to share the details of my sorry situation. I got up, took out a couple of turkey sandwiches, and asked Alex to make me some fresh fruit juice. If it was after hours, I would have made the juice myself, but since we were open I would have to put on an apron, head cap and gloves to work in the kitchen, as required by the health department. I was too tired to do any of that now.

Alex came by to give me my juice, then sat down on the small sofa-chair across from me. "So what really happened?" he asked sympathetically. I gave in and told him the whole story, and he had a good laugh over it. I smiled grudgingly too, but then he had to go back to work, and I could feel the exhaustion making my head throb.

I took off my camel brown trench coat and lay down on the sofa, using the cushion as a pillow and spreading the coat over my body. My chocolate colored skirt and ivory blouse were loose enough to conceal my curves, but I felt more comfortable with the coat covering me up properly.

That week was finals week in most colleges, and many students were at the café to study or work on projects. I was hoping to get some peace after nine when the café closed, but Alex had plans to stay after hours and work on a project with his friends.

As I closed my eyes, I could hear the door open and close, people going in and out, forks scraping dishes, and the swirl of several conversations, some cheerful and some serious. I must have dozed off for a while, because when I opened my eyes, I saw Jason sitting on a sofa nearby with Matt, David, Stephanie, and Nicole. Stephanie was one of the Trashies—a thin, pale blonde with wide blue eyes.

Should I have been surprised to see Jason with Steph and Nicky, or was it only a matter of time before these girls threw themselves all over him? What I failed to understand, as I rubbed my eyes groggily and glared in their direction, was why it bothered me.

The sofa wasn't nearly as comfortable as my bed at home. I stretched my hand to look at my wristwatch; it was eight o'clock. Still an hour left before Alex closed the café. I didn't want to call Dad because he would have headed straight home upon learning I was locked out, leaving behind his colleagues at the dinner. I wasn't about to drag him away from good company and entertainment. I could suffer a bit longer in the café.

I sat up and stretched my back. My movements caught Jason's eye, and he gave me a delighted smile. His friends turned around to see whom he was smiling at, and I waved back at him, pointedly ignoring the others.

The café had quieted down, leaving only Jason's group and Alex's friends. Even Tammy had left, although she always left a little early because she had a long trip back to Pitts. Dad was pretty easy-going with his employees.

My eyes felt gritty, and I wanted to take out my contacts. Luckily, I always kept my glasses and a contact case filled with solution in my bag, so I went to the bathroom and freshened up.

Leaving the restroom, I passed by Jason and his friends on my way to the counter. It was only polite for me to say hello to them all; even if we weren't all friends, we still knew each other. They were spread out over two sofas. David was sitting with Nicky on one couch, his arm around her shoulders, while Stephanie was cozily sandwiched between Matt and Jason on the adjacent sofa.

"You look nice with glasses, Sarah," Jason commented. He was leaning back on the couch, one leg crossed over the other.

Reflexively, I retorted, "What, and I don't look nice without them?" It was the same snarky question I always asked to anyone who complimented me on my glasses. I wasn't trying to squeeze a compliment out of Jason, much less anybody else.

Jason paused for a second, and then without changing his posture, he said quietly in his deep voice, "You look gorgeous without glasses." His sparkling gray eyes, as brilliant as polished metal, looked straight into mine. "And I'm not saying that for any *good omens*."

Our eyes locked, and I felt as though someone had just run an electric current through me. The air seemed to vibrate and shimmer, and I only dimly registered the way Stephanie and Nicole's jaws dropped, Matt's low whistle, and the knowing smile that David gave as he looked back and forth from me to Jason.

Abruptly, I realized that we were still in the café. My cheeks turned bright red, and I bit the corner of my bottom lip to stop the embarrassed smile on my face from turning into a full-fledged grin.

I wasn't blushing because of Jason's compliments. I was flushing because of his reference to 'good omens'—I was surprised that he remembered my flippant comeback at the library during our brief first meeting, if it could even be *called* a meeting.

Of course, none of the others knew what he was referring to, and they immediately interpreted my reaction as being related to his flattery. I didn't realize then how my innocent, unconscious reaction would come back and haunt me.

David shot Jason an admiring glance. "Wow, dude, she hasn't kicked you out of the café yet!" He had a point. Had anyone else been so blatant with me, I would have drawn upon the Sarah Ali power and inflicted them with my outraged wrath. Instead, I had just turned red—out of embarrassment, but others interrupted it as a blush from Jason's compliments—and I said absolutely nothing; a change that those present noticed immediately, and that I was forced to admit to myself.

The tense moment was diffused when Alex called out from the cash register, "Hey, Sarah! Can you take the checks with you?"

Phew, Alex to the rescue! I turned around, feeling almost faint with relief. Before heading towards Alex, I said casually, "I'll see you guys around," and walked away quickly before anyone had the chance to say anything else.

"Why do people still use checks?" I groused to Alex, who just rolled his eyes. Dad was the one who usually collected the checks to deposit, but since I was already at the café, Alex thought I could save Dad a trip.

"Do you get paid for napping here?" Jason had followed me to the counter, watching as Alex handed me the zippered bag full of checks. Alex and I shared a look of amusement, recalling that Jason still didn't know that my father owned the café. I smirked a little, while Alex winked at me and told Jason, "Her dad kicked her out of the house, so she's going to need some money." Alex's sense of humor was one of the things that my whole family liked about him.

Jason looked bewildered, unable to fathom the connection. "I told her to spend the night at my place but..." Alex shook his head playfully, "Hey man, you have an empty house!"

I felt a frisson of alarm and shot Alex a glare. Now he was taking it a little too far. "Very funny, Alex," I muttered, glancing at Jason. "Don't mind him, he doesn't know what he's saying."

Jason looked skeptical. He wasn't stupid; he could tell that there was something he was missing.

The rest of his friends had gotten up to leave, looking impatient, but Stephanie appeared behind Jason, catching me by surprise. She'd caught the last part of our conversation, and the expression of disdain on her face was clear. "Finally learning to have some fun, Sarah?" Stephanie's sarcasm was obvious, but I was shocked at the bitterness in her voice and the bluntness of her words.

I bristled with anger, but I leaned forward on the counter and gave her a brittle smile. "Oh no, Steph," I smirked. "I already know how to have fun... I'm just *very* selective of whom I have it with." *Tit for tat.*

Her glare of fury made me feel smug with satisfaction. "Let's go guys, we're done here," she ordered the rest of them. Nicky and Matt immediately headed over to the door. David reluctantly followed them, but Jason didn't move. At the door, Stephanie turned around and put her hands on her hips. "Jason, aren't you coming with us?" she demanded.

"Nah, I'm gonna stay," Jason replied, flashing me a smile. Stephanie's face turned red, anger and humiliation warring for dominance. She ground her teeth and walked out, slamming the door behind her.

"Ouch," Alex commented, having watched the whole episode. "I'm going to study... and *you* can explain to him why you get to have all these checks." Alex headed toward his group, the last few students who still lingered in the café.

Jason was watching me with an expression that said, '*Well? Are you going to tell me or not?*'

I pursed my lips, trying to suppress my smile. "My dad owns the café," I explained finally.

"Really? You lied to me?" he growled.

"I didn't lie to you," I laughed, but he didn't look very amused. "I said I work here, and I *do* work here sometimes to cover for the absent employees." My lips twitched in a smile, but when he frowned and didn't say anything, I felt compelled to apologize. "I'm sorry. It was the first time someone didn't know my entire life history here, and it felt good to finally be able to have some anonymity."

Jason folded his arms and finally flashed me his signature smile. "Is there anything else I should know about you?"

I raised an eyebrow, wondering what exactly he meant. His smile made me feel warm. "I don't know," I smiled. "I'm not sure how much you know about me already." A part of me wondered why I was letting myself talk to Jason this way; if it were anyone else, I would have ended the conversation abruptly and walked off.

The trill of a phone's ringtone broke the silence between us, and Jason looked down at his phone. "It's my dad," he said apologetically. "I'm going to have to take this call outside... I'll see you around later." He waved and left the café, leaving me wondering what exactly our entire conversation had been about, and why I felt so delightfully strange.

20

The next day at school, Jasmine was inexplicably furious at me. As we headed out toward the parking lot, she gave me a piece of her mind: she'd heard rumors all over school about me flirting with Jason at the café.

"*I* was flirting with *him?*" I was shocked and defensive. "*He* was the one who said I looked gorgeous!" I was sure that it was either Nicole or Stephanie or both who couldn't keep their big mouths shut.

"He said *what?!*" Jasmine's jaw dropped. "I hope you told him off!"

Great! Now Jasmine would harass me about *that.* "Jaz, it's not the first time someone's complimented me." I dreaded listening to her nag me about this, too.

"Well, yeah... but no one else has held your hand before, and *then* said you're gorgeous," she persisted.

I exhaled noisily. "Stop taking things out of context!" I insisted. I couldn't believe that instead of sympathizing with my plight, she was criticizing me. "It's not as if Nelson didn't call you pretty before, and you blushed and said 'thanks' instead of telling him off," I accused her, remembering a few years before in middle school. "And Tony left you a poem telling you how beautiful you are, and you thought it was cute! You never said anything to him!"

"That was a million years ago," Jasmine reminded me.

"Whatever time it was Jaz, the point is that sometimes these things just happen, okay? And you don't need to be a pest about it." I was still upset. "Sometimes guys compliment girls and they don't mean anything more than a compliment, but girls read more into it than they should!" My words came out in a rush, and my cheeks were getting heated with emotion.

Jasmine slowed her pace and frowned. I stopped to glance at her. "Sarah," she said in a deep, thoughtful way. "You've maintained an sterling reputation, especially for being as pretty and confident as you are, *mashaAllah.*" She paused, giving me a searching look. "Don't tarnish it now."

Her words caught me off-guard. It was so corny and totally unexpected. She usually scolded and nagged, but what she had just said was far too profound to be coming from her. I gave a short laugh and grabbed her hand, pulling her with me towards my car.

The days passed by quickly. Although no one said anything directly to me at school, Jasmine and Ashley kept me updated with the Trashies' gossip, mostly revolving around how I supposedly 'couldn't resist' Jason. I could see their changing attitude towards me; the previous polite smiles were replaced with sneers and scowls, the occasional hellos stopped and I was usually the recipient of rolled eyes or muttered jeers.

Jason started walking me to my locker after art class. It wasn't anything special, really, since he had to pass by my locker anyway on his way to his, but that added fuel to the gossip.

One day, after Jason left me at my locker, I was emptying my books into my bag when someone knocked at my locker door. I jumped, startled and alarmed. Adnan was leaning against the wall next to my locker, smirking at my shock. "Adnan?" My face twisted in distaste.

"Hello, beautiful," he sneered, enjoying my reaction.

I slammed the locker door shut and gritted my teeth. "My name is Sarah," I said coldly, the disgust and disdain on my face clear.

Adnan bared his teeth in a lewd smile. "Don't pretend to be something you're not," he hissed. Just then, his girlfriend Wendy sauntered over and threw herself on him. "Come on, baby, let's go." Wrapping her arms around him, she kissed him, leaving me gagging in disgust at the blatant display. Adnan leered at me one more time, then pulled Wendy closer and swaggered off without saying anything else.

I stood still for a few seconds, trembling with anger and irritation, before I decided to just brush it off. Adnan really wasn't worth my time or energy, and I shouldn't let myself be bothered by anything he said.

The last week of school before the winter holidays was the week of final exams as well. All my teachers told me that if I got an A in their classes, I'd be exempt from taking the finals next semester—except for art, since it wasn't a senior level class. I immersed myself in my studies and kept my mind off the troubling rumors at school.

I met Jason in the school library a few times—once during lunch and a couple times after school, to help him catch up with the art history assignments and a couple projects. I made Jasmine accompany me so she could make sure I wasn't alone with him, and that I didn't say anything inappropriate.

It was hard not to drift away from the topic at hand, though; Jason and I often ended up talking about other things. We shared quite a few common interests, and even on those subjects that we disagreed about, our conversations became lively and were always fascinating. Jasmine took part as well a few times, but she was always formal—sometimes to the point of being abrupt and curt.

On the last day I had to meet Jason at the library, we digressed into talking about my personal lack of interest in the arts.

"I hate all this art history stuff," I closed the book and pushed it toward Jason, "I'm glad Ms. Lynn breezed through it, and we're finally doing more of the craft stuff now."

Jason leaned back on his chair, stretching his hands behind his head. "Yeah, I think I'll enjoy the sketching assignments."

"Why's that?" I asked casually, glancing at Jasmine—my self-appointed censor—to see if I was still in the bounds of acceptable conversation or not. She wasn't paying attention, though, her brows furrowed as she tried to finish off a particularly challenging page of calculus problems.

"I sketch sometimes," Jason said unexpectedly.

"Wow!" I was impressed. "You don't look like the sketching type." Even though I didn't know exactly what the sketching type looked like.

Jason raised an eyebrow at me, his lips quirked in a half-smile that brought out his dimples. "So what type *do* I look like?" he inquired.

I quickly averted my gaze from that distracting smile. "I don't know..." I shrugged. "Someone who plays soccer and rescues people?" I laughed a little, trying to hide the fact that I didn't really know what else to say.

Jason's grin widened. "Superhero?" he teased, and flashed me that smile again.

I rolled my eyes. "Don't get ahead of yourself!" The sharp tapping of Jasmine's pen on the desk told me that I'd strayed too far off-topic, but I couldn't help looking back at Jason, basking in his smile. I figured it couldn't hurt to ask one more question, since this was my last day of tutoring him anyway. "How did you learn to sketch?"

Jason's expression turned wistful. "My mom sketches, and she let me practice with her when I was small," he said. I could hear the homesickness in his voice. "I was always mesmerized by how well she could pen down an exact replica of a person on the paper."

I wrapped a fringe of my hijab around my finger, leaning forward to listen to him. When he was passionate about something, his voice grew deeper, drawing you in and leaving you wanting to know more.

"So your mom gave you sketching lessons?" I asked curiously.

He picked up a pen and fiddled with it. "Sometimes," he said, the pen flitting across a piece of paper. "I can sketch, but not nearly as well as she can." He looked down at the paper and gave a small, private smile.

Next to me, Jasmine stood up and packed away her books, her facial expression stern and implacable. I had no excuse to linger in the library any longer, so I reluctantly followed her out the door, turning briefly to cast a glance at Jason, who was watching us thoughtfully.

21

It was finally time for us to go to Houston for the *Texas Da'wah Convention*! Truth be told, I was more excited to be at the conference than to see my grandma and uncle.

My uncle Amir was several years younger than my mother. He wasn't as religiously-oriented as she had been; in fact, not many of her family members were interested in practicing Islam much at all. My mom had been the only one in her family to truly immerse herself in her faith.

Uncle Amir had had a bit of a troubled life, mostly to do with woman issues—getting engaged a couple different times, breaking them off, and then finally marrying—only to get divorced shortly thereafter. Eventually, he moved back in with Grandma and tried to stay away from any further relationships. He was focused on his work now; he had an important position for some international oil company and had to travel for business a lot.

The day we landed in Houston, we headed straight to the hotel for the convention. We would stay there until the conference was over, then go to Grandma's afterward.

The conference was one of the greatest events I'd ever been to. It was always hard to keep track of my family there, since the convention had more attendees than Wickley's entire population!

Even though we had missed the first two days, there were plenty of lectures I could still attend. The speakers were dynamic and enlightened us passionately on a variety of subjects, including God's attributes of Mercy and Forgiveness, and the importance of repentance. I left every speech on a spiritual high.

One of the themes of the conference was love—and a special lecture was held for the youth, discussing the temptations of the opposite gender. The speaker was well-prepared and held the attention of her audience, using practical, real-life examples that resonated with us all. As her words sank into my heart, I kept seeing Jason in my mind's eye. Was there a connection between the speaker's words and my experiences with Jason? I was surprised and a little confused. I hadn't acknowledged any unusual feelings for him, and kept telling myself that he was just a school friend—someone like Scott or Aaron, whom I'd known for years but never felt any kind of romantic feelings towards. Was my friendship with Jason really that platonic, though? Maybe not. A part of me denied it vehemently—it's not like we had done anything wrong. All we did was study together and meet a couple times, and even that was by coincidence rather than because we planned it.

Why, then, did I feel so guilty?

As the lecturer spoke on, she mentioned that subtle feelings often turn into attachment without us even realizing it, and by the time we became aware of it, we were already too deeply involved to make exiting easy. There was only one solution, the speaker told us, and as she discussed it, I could do nothing but stare at the huge screen behind her, projecting her words.

Tears blurred my vision, my stomach lurched, and I felt an odd sense of dread settle over me, a prickling of my neck and a flush of heat in my cheeks. Was I crying because the speaker's words were that moving, or because of something else? Was I crying because the solution that she offered was impossible in my case? There was only one option, the speaker informed us. Cut all ties with the subject of our attachment.

The lecture was followed by the evening prayer, and the *Imam* recited a heartwarming part of the Qur'an so beautifully that many of the congregants silently wept. My own eyes overflowed throughout the prayer. It was easier to acknowledge my guilt and pray for strength in such a pure and spiritual environment. I made a commitment to myself and to God, and left the convention with higher goals and the determination to carry them out.

The rest of the trip to Houston was fun. Adam's surprise party was even better than we had planned it to be; Adam walked into Grandma's house annoyed and grumpy because of being forced to leave College Station early, but as soon as he entered the living room, we all jumped out to yell, "Surprise!"

Jasmine's family had managed to stay in Houston long enough to attend, but Zain couldn't make it, though he tried his best. Aunty Lizzy refused to miss the party for the world, and arrived with a cheery smile, accompanied by the full-time caretaker she'd hired when Zain had gone off to college. After a while of mingling with the guests, Aunty Lizzy quietly told me she felt tired, so I accompanied her to an empty bedroom. She was one of my favorite people, not only because she'd been Mom's best friend, but also because she had a wicked sense of humor in addition to being extremely wise.

As we sat together and talked, I noticed that her fair skin had wrinkled slightly with age. Nonetheless, her blue eyes sparkled with all the liveliness of someone my age, and her smile remained as refreshing as well.

"Agh...I need to let my hair breathe!" she exclaimed, unpinning her hijab. My eyes widened as her long blonde hair tumbled down. Despite everything she'd gone through, her hair was untouched by any grey strands. Aunty Lizzy's specialty was in braiding hair, so I begged her to do mine.

"Of course!" she beamed at me. "I'd love to, Sarah."

I yanked off my hijab eagerly, shaking out my own dark tresses, and leaned against her knees.

She smiled at my anticipation and ran her soft hands through my hair, gently gathering the strands and braiding them together. Listening to her laughing voice telling me stories about her and Mom during their college days, a wave of sadness washed over me. If Mom were still alive, she would've done this for me every day—listened to me, talked to me, braided my hair. I quickly swallowed down my grief and pushed away the thoughts. My memories of Mom had faded, and I didn't want to indulge in thoughts that would only give me more sorrow.

The day ended, and soon after so did our trip to Houston. I returned home with high spirits and lofty goals.

22

G oing back to school after vacation is never easy, and it was especially difficult in this case, since I had promised myself that I'd avoid Jason when I got back. He wasn't exactly a major part of my school day, but I always looked forward to our conversations, and the mere thought of having to hold myself back and formalize our interactions made me feel anxious.

Art class was the biggest challenge. It was the only time we regularly sat together and exchanged conversation. I considered moving to another desk, but the seats were unofficially assigned; friends all sat together, and since I had made a point of avoiding the other students in the class, I couldn't suddenly just squeeze myself into one of their circles after a whole semester.

I was left with no option but to remain at the same desk with Jason. No worries. I would keep our interaction to a bare minimum, I kept reminding myself.

My agitation was for naught; Jason didn't come to school the first day. In fact, he didn't show up for the whole week. I was disturbed by his absence, and what worried me most was that it wasn't curiosity over why he was away that troubled me, but simply that I missed his presence.

Maybe he was re-accepted to his old school. With that thought, I felt suddenly forlorn. I quickly told myself that it was probably best for me if he'd left for good... I wouldn't have to deal with his 'temptation' anymore. I thought back to the lecturer at the convention, and reassured myself that I was embarking on a fresh start.

Of course, my self-confidence was quickly shaken when Jason was back in his seat the following week, looking even more muscular and relaxed than before. I wondered if he had spent the whole vacation working out. Nevertheless, I resolved to refrain from discussing personal topics with him, pretending to be busy and absorbed in the latest class project. It was hard not to communicate with him, especially since he and I shared a table alone, and the long silences as we worked on our art became awkward.

We ended up sharing stories from our winter break, although I tried to sound as formal as I could. Jason had gone to London with his family, which was why he'd returned to school late. I made a point of telling him all about the convention and its religious environment, highlighting the spiritually rejuvenating prayers and all the serious topics that the lecturers had discussed. I hoped that he'd be intimidated by all the details, but to my dismay, it had the opposite affect—he seemed even more fascinated and bombarded me with questions.

It was hard for me not to slip back into our previous friendly routine. The person I *should* have been trying to avoid was the person I felt the most like talking to.

Desperate, I asked Jasmine to leave class early so she could pick me up from art class, which would mean that Jason couldn't walk me to my locker. I didn't explain my reasons to her because I wanted to keep my struggles to myself, but as it happened, my plan didn't work anyway. Jasmine's fourth hour was calculus and she couldn't leave early every day.

I was glad we sat far apart during lunch, at least. Most days he had soccer practice, and on the days he didn't, I saw him sitting with David. I kept myself safely ensconced in my old group of Jasmine, Scott, and Ashley.

For the next couple of weeks, I congratulated myself on sticking to the terms of my personal pledge. The casual atmosphere of school, though, made it harder and harder to maintain my determination. Soon enough, I'd slipped back into my old habits.

The taxing schedule of senior year meant that I had eight hours of school to get through and way too much homework to complete at home, which left me feeling too tired to put in much effort on my prayers. Naturally, the effects of the spiritual rejuvenation I'd experienced over the winter break began to wear off.

Just when I'd thought that the worst was over and my limited interaction with Jason had become the new norm, he showed up at the library one day, where I was working on an English essay with Jasmine.

"Hello, ladies," he said cheerfully. We looked up together and saw him standing across the table from us, his hands in his jeans pockets and the sleeves of his checkered shirt rolled up to his forearms. Jasmine and I answered his greeting; Jasmine's tone was stiff, while mine was cautious.

Jason must have noticed Jasmine's reaction to him. He smiled at her charmingly. "How are you doing, Jasmine?" he asked pleasantly. The wariness in her expression faded somewhat as she smiled back. *Hah!* I thought to myself. *Even Jasmine isn't fully immune to Jason's charms!*

"I'm fine," she smiled back.

Jason leaned towards me slightly. "Sarah," he said earnestly, "I need some help with chemistry..." he looked a little embarrassed. "I was wondering if you could take some time out to tutor me."

This was it—the moment that I could act on my resolution to be firm and refuse his request. Instead, I rested my elbows on the table and bit the corner of my bottom lip as I thought about it for a moment... and then I nodded in smiling agreement.

Under the table, the toe of Jasmine's shoe stung painfully as she kicked me in the leg, but instead of yelping, I said smoothly, "Of course I can help, and Jasmine will come along, too—if you don't mind."

Jason's smile faltered a little, but he said with forced humor, "Sure, if she doesn't mind chaperoning you!" Jason wasn't dumb. He'd noticed that I made sure Jasmine stayed with us whenever we could have been alone.

I looked down at the books scattered on the desk, feeling both Jason's curious gaze and Jasmine's furious glare.

Jason broke the awkward silence with a light laugh. "Listen, how about we meet here once a week or so, depending on your schedule?"

I paused for a moment, thinking about it. "Maybe we can play it by ear?" I looked at Jasmine, hoping she'd say something to back me up, or maybe even bail me out now that I'd made the mistake of agreeing, but she remained silent. I felt a little nervous—I was definitely in trouble with her now. "I'll let you know in art class," I told him.

Jason looked at Jasmine and then at me, probably sensing that something was going on. "Okay," he said. "Or maybe you can text me?"

Up until now, I hadn't had his phone number... and now I was going to take yet another step that wasn't in line with my pledge. I shook off the uneasy feeling that had crept over me and silently told myself that this was just for necessity. "Yeah, sure," I pulled out my phone. "Give me your number." I sent him a missed call so he'd have mine as well, and then he waved us goodbye and left.

To my surprise, Jasmine didn't say a word about what I'd just done; she remained extremely quiet for the rest of the day. It was strange that when I most wanted her to scold me, she decided to remain silent.

23

Jason and I decided to meet in the library once a week, during lunch. Jasmine wasn't thrilled about missing her lunch, but I ignored her objections and dragged her along anyway.

"So what is it that you need help with?" I asked Jason cheerfully, spreading my hands on the desk. The gold sparkle of my small, delicate ring flattered the pastel blue of my dress, which was covered with a loose white cardigan.

Jasmine and I sat on my side of the desk and Jason took a seat across from us.

Jason's grey eyes looked into my own. He opened his mouth as though to bring up another subject, then pressed his lips together and said instead, "We can start with thermo chemistry. Mr. Dan said the final will be comprehensive, and I didn't do so well on the midterm, so I need to review." He slid the book across the table toward me.

I opened the book and noticed that the first chapter was on thermo. I flipped through the pages, my brows furrowed, and nibbled absently on my bottom lip as I tried to recall the details of those first few chapters. I'd always been good at chemistry, especially since I'd gotten extra help from Dad, who was a professor of chemistry.

Satisfied that I knew what I was doing, I looked back up at Jason to see that his eyes were still fixed on my face. "What?" I asked, slightly alarmed. Was there something on my face?

Jasmine looked up too, her expression suddenly suspicious.

"Nothing," Jason waved a hand in the air dismissively. "I'm just waiting for you to start."

"Okay, so do you want me to explain the whole chapter to you, or do you just need help with some specific problems?" I asked. I hoped that he didn't need to be taught the *whole* chapter.

He took the book from me. "No, I just couldn't figure out this set of problems," he pointed to a couple of questions. I knew the concept well, so I explained them to him patiently and in detail. Jason nodded throughout my explanations, his gaze shifting between me and the textbook.

By the time we finished with those problems, there was hardly any time left to chat about anything else. He thanked me when we finished, but later on, my phone gave a low tinkle. I opened it to see a text from Jason. "Thank you," it said, with a smiley face.

Dad could see all my texts—it was one of the rules he had enforced a long time ago, when I'd first gotten my own phone. I'd never cared before, but for the first time, I felt uncomfortable texting someone back. Still, I reassured myself, I doubted that Dad kept a *regular* check on my messages. And we weren't saying anything inappropriate.

From that day onwards, Jason and I began to meet regularly in the library, always chaperoned by Jasmine. Soon, once a week didn't seem enough, since by the time we got to the library from class and settled down, there was hardly enough time left to cover everything Jason wanted to study. He suggested we meet twice a week instead, or more depending on our schedules. From the frown on Jasmine's face and the way she pressed her lips together tightly, I could tell she hated the idea, but she came along regardless.

As I helped Jason, Jasmine began to pay attention as well, since she was also taking chemistry II and found it a bit challenging.

To be honest, though, our conversations weren't *always* about chemistry. Just as before, we tended to drift off topic. Though I tried to keep things formal, the frequency of the meetings meant that we became comfortable with each other, and our conversations took on a more personal note. It was usually Jasmine who brought us back to chemistry.

We never talked about anything unseemly, nor did our chats ever hint at one person's interest in the other. Of course our continued contact allowed me to get to know him much better—his confident personality, his respectful demeanor, and the way he shared even private thoughts with me. The more I learned about him, the more he stirred feelings in my heart that I'd never experienced before.

But I learned to make myself believe that everything was normal, and the more I pretended, the better I became at it.

As our meetings in the library continued, our communication in art class grew even friendlier and more relaxed. The week we had to make clay sculptures, Jason molded his clay into a soccer field and I made a mosque.

"You're really passionate about your faith, aren't you?" Jason asked, pointing at my clay creation.

I glanced at him. "My faith defines me," I said proudly.

"You know, I used to have a really negative image of *Izlam* before," he said, focusing on his soccer field.

I was taken aback by his confession. "Really?"

He nodded. "I believed everything I saw in the media," he admitted. He couldn't cut the edges of the clay properly, so he rolled it out again.

I grimaced. "So you were one of those bigots?"

"That would be my dad," he said ruefully.

My jaw dropped. "Really?" I repeated.

Jason sighed. "Yeah... those two guys, Muhammad and Hasan... I wasn't really nice to them before." The remorse was clear in his voice. "But when they came to my defense and risked their lives for me..." he paused, recollecting the past, "I was like..." he looked up at me, his brilliant grey eyes earnest and regretful. "I just...for the first time, I saw them as humans... even *more* than humans, actually."

My hands froze as I stared back at him, my attention focused solely on Jason as he recounted what was clearly a painful experience.

"And then throughout the whole disciplinary trial at school, they stood firmly by my side." Jason stared at the table. "I'd never been so embarrassed in my life. They changed my entire perspective on *Muzlims*." He looked back at me with an abashed smile.

My clay lay abandoned on the table, my face cupped in my hands as I watched him, transfixed. "Are you still in touch with them?" I asked.

Jason nodded. "Yeah, of course. We're really good friends now." He smiled at me again, and I felt that strange, pleasant lurch in my stomach.

Suddenly, Jason leaned forward and brushed my bottom lip with his thumb. I could feel the light touch of the pad of his thumb rubbing against my lip, an odd but delightful sensation. The physical contact startled me, and I quickly pulled back, trying to mediate the battle between shock and pleasure.

I stared at him, not sure how to react, indignation warring with other unnamed emotions. Jason quickly pointed to his thumb, showing me a smudge of clay. I must have accidentally wiped the clay on my mouth when I'd put my head in my hands, and he'd just wiped it off for me.

Thoughts clamored in my mind. Why didn't I *immediately* tell him not to touch me again? Why didn't I remind him that there were strict limits of physical engagement with me? Why was I stunned into silence?

Meanwhile, oblivious to the inner turmoil he'd suddenly stirred up, Jason continued speaking about his friends. "When I left, Muhammad and Hasan asked me to get to know a devoted *Muzlim* in person," he mentioned, turning back to his clay soccer field.

Still feeling rather numb, I sat in the same position, considering Jason's words. So *that's* why he was so interested in spending time with me—he'd promised his friends that he would get to know a 'devoted' Muslim. Although I felt a sinking feeling inside, I also felt a stab of relief that now I could make Jasmine get over her paranoia by informing her of his *true* purpose in befriending me.

24

L ife in Wickley went back to being quiet and slow-paced. At home, Adam's schedule had eased up, and though he still had to commute to Pitts for his internship every day, he offered to help Dad out more with the businesses. Dad knew Adam wanted to pursue his master's degree, though, and his internship would go a long way toward helping him get into a good school, so he kept encouraging him to follow his dream. Adam had already applied to several universities, but hadn't picked a grad school yet.

Dad and I both knew that Adam really wanted to go to Houston, but the mere thought of letting his son go that far away depressed my father. Adam understood that Dad wouldn't be too happy if he went to Texas, so he kept putting off the final decision. His deadlines were approaching, though, and we all knew he'd have to commit soon.

The initial uproar caused by the AIA seminar had died down. No other protests took place, and Brian didn't host any more provocative radio shows, either. Since the school administration had made a big deal about the protest and taken action by labeling it an issue of jeopardizing students' safety, Brian must have been forced to take precautions in order to avoid having his show shut down.

My discussions with Pastor John about talking to the church bore fruit: I spoke one Sunday evening to a large audience. I knew most of the people and received an encouraging, positive response. No one was happy about the fact that Wickley's peace had been unnecessarily disrupted.

Someone at the church suggested that we take part in a joint effort to spread positive messages about tolerance and unity. We decided to hand out flyers with shared positive messages, signed by the mosque and the church. Congregants from both religious groups got together in the community hall to design some nice banners, too, which we hung outside both houses of worship. Various volunteers took the responsibility of making copies and distributing the fliers around town, each one assigned a specific area to avoid overlapping.

I was assigned to distribute flyers in Wickley's outer residential area. Knowing that Jason lived in that neighborhood, I casually mentioned it to him during art class, where I'd been keeping him updated about the mosque's and church's joint efforts.

That day, we were working on shaping pots on the clay wheel in class. "Hey, that's where I live!" Jason exclaimed.

"Really?" I said, feigning nonchalance as I leaned forward to hold my clay pot steady.

"Yeah, I can help you distribute," Jason offered. "Tell me when."

My hands trembled slightly, making the smooth surface of my vase become suddenly uneven as I looked at him over my shoulder. I was unsure of whether to accept his offer.

I thought about walking outside with him in a public area, dropping off flyers door to door. It could be the perfect display of a Muslim and a non-Muslim working together in an effort to spread peace and love.

Love?

I shoved the thought away quickly and composed myself, denying the questions that my conscience hurled at me.

"Sure, maybe after school one day," I smiled at him.

Jason leaned forward to help me hold the wobbling wet clay steady on the wheel, his long, strong fingers brushing against my hand. "Hold it still, or it'll come out crooked," he advised helpfully. His eyes were fixed on the vase and he didn't seem to notice that our hands were touching.

Of course, I told myself. *I* was the only one who was noticing these things—the only one who felt our touch so acutely. Jason was caring by nature; he would have helped anyone else in the class if they needed it. It was only *me* who felt differently towards him.

I pushed back at the irrational pang of emotion that shot through me, and instead watched the way his hands carefully re-shaped my clay vase.

We found plenty of time to talk during art class, and walked together in the hallways, however both of us continued to maintain our own routines during lunch, except for the days I tutored him in Chemistry.

I communicated with Jason very little over text and email, knowing that my dad had access to both. However, I started thinking a lot more about my appearance, occasionally wearing light makeup, which I had never done before.

"Why are you wearing so much makeup?" Adam's question came at breakfast one morning, as he poured himself a glass of OJ. I looked up to see him staring at me, his forehead creased as he studied my face carefully.

I nearly choked on my cereal—I'd never expected Adam to observe me that closely; he rarely even glanced at me on most days. I was acutely relieved that I'd chosen to go with a subtle eyeshadow instead of the brighter shades I had considered risking that day.

"Adam, if you want to compliment me sincerely, then just say it! You don't need to pretend I'm wearing makeup as an excuse to say that I look pretty," I retorted.

Adam made a face at me as he got up to wash his hands. "Trust me, the day you look pretty, I'll let you know," he shot back, grinning. He looked back at me and frowned again. "But there *is* something different about your face."

I rolled my eyes at him, but got up quickly in case Dad noticed something too. After that, I was more careful to touch up my makeup at school instead of at home. Even there, though, I had Jasmine to police me.

I was starting to experiment with my clothing styles as well. Although Dad and Adam were oblivious to the change from loose cardigans to long-sleeved boleros, Jasmine's sharp eyes caught every detail. "Are you gaining weight?" she asked me during lunch one day, looking me up and down.

I shrugged and frowned slightly. "I hope not! I've been using Adam's gym like twice a week." When he was in high school, Adam had gone through a fitness-freak phase and had set up a small gym in our garage. I took advantage of it in spurts to stay fit and healthy.

Jasmine's brows furrowed as she looked over me again, then shook her head. "Your clothes seem to be getting tight on you," she remarked. "You seem a lot more curvy than before."

A stab of guilt shot through me. The truth was, I wasn't gaining weight—I was starting to wear pieces of clothing that were usually reserved for home or ladies-only gatherings. My long, loose blouses and billowy dresses had been replaced with more fitted tops and skirts that outlined my hips, and the cardigans and coats that I used to wear on top had been switched out for more flattering cropped sweaters that just barely covered my arms. Even the headscarves I'd begun wearing covered my hair but no longer draped carefully over my chest.

Feeling defensive, I tried to turn the tables on her, "Pfft, getting jealous Jaz?" I said laughingly, pointedly looking at her own figure. Jasmine was tall but not as curvy. "You wouldn't know how hard it is to cover certain blessings!" I teased her.

Jasmine's face darkened and she narrowed her eyes at me, "Oh shut up, you show off."

Though our conversation ended at that moment, I knew the topic would come up again. Jasmine was not one to give up a discussion that easily, especially if she knew she was right. And it wasn't only her; *I* knew very well I didn't have much to say in my defense.

I quickly changed the topic before she could say anything else.

In the meantime, I continued to attend lectures at the mosque. Dad had been organizing some extra weekend seminars, specifically inviting certain speakers to give lectures on topics like "Gender Relations for Muslims," "How to Overcome Temptation," and other subjects that revolved around improving our relationship with God.

Attending the talks made me feel guilty from time to time, but never for long. After all, I never spoke to Jason in a come-hither tone, and our interactions always took place in public.

Jasmine didn't feel the same way. She continued to pester me, telling me that I was being overly-friendly with Jason, warning me that I should cut down on my meetings with him. The more she nagged, the more I tuned her out. She once even threatened to stop 'chaperoning' us, but I knew she'd never leave me to my own devices with Jason—she was too worried about me.

Jasmine tried different ways of convincing me that I was going too far, including religious reminders and moral arguments. She was never rude or ill-mannered towards Jason, but she knew how to observe the limits...the way I used to before I'd met him.

I started avoiding Jasmine just so I wouldn't have to listen to her preach at me. Her nagging was putting a strain on our friendship, and we could both feel the tension. Then one day at the library, Jason and I were distracted from chemistry as usual. He had mentioned something about his younger sister, Emily.

"When Emily started high school last year, I had to take her and bring her back from school with me every day," he said, huffing in annoyance. "It was a nightmare, so the highlight of my move here was that I don't have to deal with her anymore." Despite his complaints, he smiled fondly at the remembrance of his sister.

I couldn't help but laugh, "I must compliment her for putting up with an older brother all that time."

"Excuse me, younger sisters are absolute *pests*," he shot back.

"Older brothers aren't exactly heavenly creatures either!" I protested.

Jason smirked and pointed to himself, "*Hello!*"

"You are so full of yourself," I rolled my eyes, and he chuckled.

"I should be, older brothers are a blessing to younger sisters," he teased backed.

"When we were young, my dad complimented me every day and he forced Adam to do the same, to boost my confidence," I told Jason, sharing the story of our family tradition. "Adam used to get really annoyed. He tried to get out of it at first, but Dad was adamant, so after a while, Adam would compliment me in front of Dad—then later he'd whisper in my ear, 'You're so ugly!' or 'You're so stupid!' He used to make me cry all the time. So much for the blessings of an older brother!"

Jason laughed, but his expression grew softer as his beautiful greenish-gray eyes gazed at me. "I don't know how anyone could call you ugly or stupid."

I flushed and self-consciously tugged at the sleeve of the short white cardigan that I wore over a navy blue dress, then quickly grabbed his chemistry book before Jasmine could step on my foot again in warning.

"So for your upcoming exam, there's an exam review handbook in the library. Check that out and go over it because it really helped me last year." I flipped through the pages aimlessly, desperately hoping that my cheeks weren't as red as they felt.

Jason leaned back in his chair. "You know, Mr. Dan mentioned it in class, but I couldn't find that book anywhere."

I frowned. "That's impossible, no one ever checks it out."

Jason shrugged. "It's not in the library."

I shook my head. "It's always in the same place, just look for it more carefully."

"Fine," he said, getting up from his chair. "Why don't you come with me and show me where it is?"

I led the way to the correct shelf, going down on one knee, and pointed at the textbook that was always in the same exact spot every time I had needed it last year.

Jason bent over to see, and unconsciously, I looked up right into his mesmerizing eyes. He was so close that I inhaled the scent of his cologne—something musky and expensive, not like the cheap deodorant sprays that most guys our age used. His gaze flickered from the textbook on the shelf to me, and I breathed in sharply. There was something strange, almost intoxicating, about being this close to him. Our gazes interlocked with strange expressions in both our eyes.

"I guess you're right," he murmured softly, his voice husky. "For the first time." The softness in his voice and the sparkle in his eyes made me realize that I was blushing again. I quickly got up, trying to distance myself from Jason, but a sharp tug yanked my head backwards, and I realized that a few of the tassels from my hijab had caught onto his hoodie zipper. I could feel Jasmine's eyes narrowing angrily from across the aisle, where she was watching us.

Hurriedly, I tried to pull the threads from the zipper, but just then, Zara turned the corner into the aisle. I smiled at her nervously, hoping that she'd see the tangled threads, but the disdain on her face was clear when her eyes took in how close Jason and I were standing together. She turned and walked away hastily, muttering something under her breath.

My hands trembled and I felt a ripple of despair and anger. *Why did these things happen to me?* Instead of untangling the strings, I made an even bigger mess of things.

Jason gently pulled my fingers away from the knots I'd created, his strong warm hands covered my freezing cold ones, "Here, let me do it," he said kindly, and in a few seconds he quickly released the threads, freeing me. I almost ran back to the study table, but Jasmine refused to make eye contact and gathered her stuff, getting up to leave.

25

On the way home, Jasmine flipped out at me, as I'd expected. "What are you doing with yourself?" she was furious.

I pushed the passenger seat back, getting ready to tune her out. My attitude irritated her even more. I'd never seen her so angry. Finally, I asked her, "So what is it exactly that I'm doing wrong?" Annoyance laced my voice, making it sharp and sarcastic.

"You tell me, Sarah. You know *exactly* what you're doing wrong," she said, her voice uncharacteristically quiet.

"I really don't have time for your riddles, Jaz," I snapped, pretending to be oblivious to what she was saying.

Jasmine hit the steering wheel in frustration, "Sarah, stop deceiving yourself!" she yelled, glaring at me with a mixture of grief and anger.

I struggled to keep my voice low and even. "What *am* I doing wrong? Huh? I'm sitting in a freaking public place! I'm never alone with him. I don't even talk to him over the phone!"

"You may be in a public area, but all you two ever talk about is personal stuff—everything personal, unnecessary chit-chat." She stopped at a stop sign and turned toward me, "Sarah, I've seen you with other boys, from elementary school to middle school to high school, and I've never seen you act like this before. You're just not yourself around Jason!" she said in the same breath.

I looked at Jasmine silently. She was my best friend. We'd been each other's shadows practically since we were born; every detail of my life was open to her. And at the moment, she was absolutely right—but she was asking me to confess something I'd been consistently running away from even admitting to myself.

"So, your question is?" I said instead.

I knew I was pushing her buttons. "Why don't you stop, Sarah?! Why don't you *just stop?*" Jasmine exploded.

"Stop what, Jaz?" I sat up and yelled back. "*Stop freakin' what?!*"

"Stop hanging out with him," she said bluntly. She was blocking the traffic at the stop sign, so she quickly shifted her attention back to the road.

"I can't, okay? I just can't." I looked out the window. Jasmine pulled the car over on the side of the road and turned to look at me squarely.

"You're doing something forbidden, Sarah," she said harshly. "Damn it! You've been a role model for so many of us, and now you're totally screwing yourself up."

"I am *not* screwing myself up," I said coldly. "I've never even touched him."

"Yes, you have!" Jasmine hit her palm against the steering wheel to emphasize her words. "And what happened today?" she said abruptly.

I looked sullen. "It was an accident..."

Jasmine cut me off. "How many things are you going to keep blaming on *accidents*? How come these accidents never happened before? With the same person? During the same school year?"

We both fell silent and just stared at each other. I had never trusted any of my friends more than I trusted Jasmine. Rubbing my forehead with my fingers, I tried to calm her down. "Look, all of this will end when we graduate. He'll move back to Maryland, and I'll move on," I looked away from her, staring out the window at the trees that lined the road.

Jasmine was shocked. "Move on?" She couldn't believe that I was taking it so lightly. "And what if he makes a move on you?"

"Are you out of your mind?" I couldn't believe she actually thought that. "He's not interested in me. Can't you see? Why would someone like him be interested in a girl like me?" *A hot guy like him and a Muslim girl like me,* were the words I meant but didn't say aloud.

"I'm not even going to answer that." Jasmine shook her head in disbelief.

"Don't answer, then," I said quietly.

Jasmine's voice gentled. "You need to ask yourself... *if* he does—or *when* he does—will you be able to uphold your values?"

I didn't get what she meant. "Your religious values, Sarah!" Jasmine cried out in frustration. "Your chastity. Eventually, this will stain your reputation and your character."

"Why do you always over-dramatize everything, Jaz?" I replied in irritation. "Relax, I'm not going that far." I gave a short, bitter laugh. "All of this will end; all the little conversations that have been bothering you so much will all end when he graduates." There was pain etched on my face that only those who were closest to me could ever see. Jasmine saw it clearly.

"Sarah, you idiot... you'll hurt yourself more than you can handle." She leaned towards me, her expression pitying and anguished with concern.

I pulled myself away, resenting her sympathy. "I don't want to have this conversation with you anymore."

The sternness returned to her face. "I do, and I will," she said adamantly.

"Then talk to yourself, because I'm leaving!" I started gathering my stuff.

Jasmine's voice was sharp. "You're not leaving. You're running away like a coward." She knew exactly what to say to make me stay.

"What do you want to talk about?" I demanded. "I'm not going to listen to your lectures; you just don't know when to stop! You don't know your limits," I ground out. She was really pushing me over the edge, and I was in a foul mood.

"My limits?" Jasmine's jaw dropped. "So now we have limits?"

"Every friendship has a limit." I couldn't have sounded colder and harsher. In a matter of seconds, I had relegated her to being a mere friend, while we both knew that we'd been closer than sisters all our lives.

I saw her eyes welling up with tears and looked away.

"Someone has to tell you this and I will, even if I have to cross my "limits," Jasmine's voice was so full of pain that I couldn't even turn around to face her. "Stop deceiving yourself. Whether you admit it or not, you *have* fallen for Jason," she was firm despite the emotion that shook her voice. "Don't admit it to me, but at least confess it to yourself. Don't run away from yourself, Sarah. Hold yourself accountable and ask if what you're doing is right or wrong. Where will your so-called "friendship"—which is already turning into a relationship—go, and how will it end?" Her voice was tremulous. "You'll either be left with painful memories, or you'll risk everything you've managed to protect so far. Or both."

Her last words made me tense with fury, as though she'd spoken of something forbidden—despite the fact that it was *I* who was playing with forbidden emotions. "Thanks for your advice," I snarled. "Are you done?"

"Aren't my words having any effect on you?" Jasmine's face fell in disappointment.

"We're *not* discussing this again, Jasmine," I said harshly.

Jasmine wiped away the tears that were sliding down her face. "Then we won't speak again until you *are* ready to talk about it," she said sadly.

"Fair enough." Why was I being so cruel to her when she was only trying to talk some sense into me?

Jasmine made one last attempt, "Sarah, this game you're playing, there is no winning...you will lose either way."

I got out of the car and leaned in the window to speak to her for the last time. "If and when you feel like you can talk to me without bringing up this topic, *then* we can resume our friendship." And I walked away, away from my best friend in the whole world.

26

I didn't go straight home. My mind was churning with fury, disappointment, and regret, and I felt the urge to run as far away from everything as possible. I went through town instead, across the curving roads, over the soft grass, beyond the "inner town" towards the outskirts of Wickley and into the open fields.

I realized it was time for the afternoon prayer, so I stopped by a tree, dropped my bag on the grass, and prayed. My prayer was empty, without meaning or focus, and though I repeated the words of the Qur'an with my tongue, my mind drifted back to Jason and Jasmine, to everything that had been happening. My prayers had turned into an obligation, a mechanical routine without nourishing my heart or soul.

After my prayer, I sat down, leaning against the tree trunk and trying to wrap my mind around what had just happened. I texted Dad, telling him that I was out for a walk because of a fight with Jasmine. It wasn't unusual for me to tell Dad about our tiffs, though I rarely ever shared the contents, just as I didn't tell him about the details of our argument today.

Restless, I began walking around the beautiful field, which was spread out around a small, clear creek. The more

I thought about our fight, the more my conscience forced me to encounter my feelings for Jason, which was exactly what I had been avoiding all this time, and I still was not ready to face the reality.

I reminded myself again that whatever was happening, it was open and in public; that all of it was temporary and would end with our graduation. Jason would leave not knowing how I felt about him, and I would get over my feelings for him when I didn't see him around anymore. It was that simple, I rationalized to myself, and refused to think beyond it. I decided to head home.

As I passed by the new roads that signified the developing area of Wickley, I ran into Jason. He was jogging down the same road I was walking along, dressed in his sweats and a t-shirt, his earbuds peeking out from his hoodie.

I could see the surprise on his face as he recognized me, and he slowed down, waving. "What are you doing here?" he asked, panting slightly as he jogged on the spot. "Oh, umm..." I didn't know what to tell him, "Taking a walk." I looked down, feeling mentally and emotionally drained.

He raised an eyebrow in disbelief but still asked me, "Care for a drink?" He bent forward a little to make eye contact with me. "In my part of town?" he added, smiling as our gazes locked.

I'd love nothing more than a drink with you right now, I thought to myself, watching him. A deep longing to be with Jason, to just spend as much time with him as possible, stirred within me. My mind flashed back on Zara running into us in the library and the disdain on her face, and then my argument with Jasmine.

I gave a tired laugh. "Thanks...but I can't. Can I get a rain check on that? It's getting dark and I have to head home. My dad's waiting for me."

Knitting his eyebrows, Jason seemed confused at my apprehensiveness. "You sure?"

I nodded, smiling with a wistfulness that I hoped he couldn't see.

"Okay... then let me walk you home?" he asked, unexpectedly. There was a confidence in his voice. To him, he was doing the gallant thing. Nothing to be ashamed of here.

I raised my eyebrow at him, and his lips quirked at me in an innocent smile, gesturing 'what?' with his hands.

It was getting late, already time for the sunset prayer, so I told him to let me pray before we headed back.

As I positioned myself to pray, Jason relaxed on the grass, propped up on an elbow. His eyes were fixed on me as I raised my hands and folded them over my chest, and I could feel the intensity of his gaze while I bowed and prostrated. Instead of concentrating on the prayer itself, all I could think about was what he was seeing and thinking right now. My clothes were not really appropriate for prayer—or for his eyes—no longer as loose as they used to be. They clung to my every curve as I bowed. Sudden discomfort and guilt overwhelmed me as I felt the heat of his gaze; I had absolutely no focus in my prayer... in all honesty, when I was done I didn't even know what I'd recited, or how many *rak'as* I'd prayed.

When I turned my head to my right and left shoulders, ending the prayer, I remained where I was sitting, and Jason smiled at me as he plucked blades of new grass in the fading sunlight.

There was something incredibly magnetic about him, something that made me want to move closer to him. I could pick out the spicy scent of his cologne, the deep musky aroma I had inhaled at the library. There was a fluttering in my stomach, a million butterflies awakening within me. But then there was something else inside me, a tiny voice demanding furiously, '*Sarah, what are you doing here?!*'

Maybe it was the effect of the prayer I had just managed to pray. Perhaps it was the temporary departure of the *Shaytan* from my side, or the presence of angels around me that made me realize just how serious my situation was. Sitting next to Jason, with no one around, in a beautiful valley as afternoon darkened into twilight... it was magical. The way Jason looked at me wasn't anywhere near the way Scott, Aaron, Doug, or any other boy had ever looked at me. I felt a deep ache in my heart, a longing that threatened to make my chest burst. '*He can never like you that way, Sarah... he's **the** Jason Connor... he's just trying to get to know a devout Muslim.*' Maybe I couldn't deny my feelings for Jason, but I *could* still convince myself that it wasn't mutual.

I don't know what Jason thought of me looking at him the way I did—in hindsight, I probably looked lovesick—but I had every excuse to justify the way *he* was looking at *me*.

"We can stay here for just a bit... Maybe watch the sunset together?" Jason's voice was soft, deep and persuasive. With that, the feeling of guilt which had been rising within me vanished at the speed with which I'd prayed my prayer. Did he say '*together*'? Did he mean just sitting next to each other, close enough that our shoulders would touch, that our fingers could rest against each other innocently... or did he mean '*together*' as in wrapping our arms around each other? I felt the overwhelming urge to scoot over towards him, to draw closer to him, maybe rest my head on his shoulder...My breaths came faster, and I had to fight off the increasing temptation and fading guilt. I finally managed to refuse. "No, my dad will be waiting for me... Maybe some other time?"

The snarky voice that I'd come to recognize as my conscience spoke up again in my mind. *Really, Sarah Ali? "Some other time"? In seventeen years, you've never sat with a boy to watch the sunset.*

God, how do I make this voice shut up?! It gets louder the more I wish it would go away, fighting my emotions with criticism and reminders that I'd managed to ignore from Jasmine, but found more difficult to avoid when they were echoing in my own mind.

I was so absorbed in my thoughts that I hadn't noticed how closely I was walking to Jason, until I felt the softness of his hoodie brushing against my hand—and not for the first time, I realized.

"So what brought you to this part of town?" Jason broke through my train of thought again. We had started walking toward my house, which was less than twenty minutes away. "Were you delivering the fliers?"

I sighed, "I had a little fight with Jasmine."

"Were you planning to run away?" he teased.

I rolled my eyes at him. "Yeah, my girlfriend broke up with me, so I ran to the fields."

Jason laughed, and I couldn't stop myself from stealing a glance at him from beneath my eyelashes. The dark amber of his hair glinted in the rising moonlight, and his eyes shone as brilliantly as ever. I swallowed, trying to ignore the insistent fluttering in my stomach.

"Do you usually jog at this time?" I tried to change the topic.

"Yeah, I have to run at least three to five miles a day," he replied as we crossed the road. "Do you work out?" he asked.

"Me, yeah," I stumbled over my words. Jason glanced at me appraisingly, as though trying to gauge my figure, and I felt the heat rising in my face. "I...uh run."

"Really? Where?" He sounded surprised.

"Adam has a whole gym set up in our garage, so I use the treadmill there."

"Nice," he commented smilingly.

We were both walking slowly, taking our time, and I was savoring every moment of it. As we got closer to home, though, I got a sinking feeling in my stomach, thinking about how Dad would react if he saw me with Jason.

My conscience had given up on trying to make me see the immorality of what I was doing, but now it made yet another vain effort, reminding me of my dad's trust in me. I'd never had to give any explanation to Dad for inviting a male friend home because it was always, *always*, for schoolwork. But right now I had no excuse for walking home with Jason.

When we got home, Dad was standing on the porch. His expression was distant as he stared at the last streaks of brilliant ruby and amethyst that colored the sky. He noticed the two of us walking up the sidewalk, and I introduced him to Jason and told him how we ran into each other and he'd offered to drop me home.

"Thank you, Jason," Dad shook hands with Jason, clasping Jason's palm with both of his own hands. "First, you save my daughter from the protesters, and then you bring her home safely." Jason seemed surprised that my dad was so thoroughly informed about my life. I glanced at Dad, but I couldn't make out if he was joking or if he was upset, though I could detect a hint of sarcasm in his tone.

Right then, Adam's car screeched into the driveway. I wondered what brought him home early and why he was driving so erratically. Adam walked towards us with his coat folded over one arm, loosening his tie with other hand; in his formal business outfit, my brother looked quite handsome and somewhat intimidating.

As Adam walked closer to us, Dad said, "Adam, meet Jason," he looked at Adam with a stern expression, instructing him to be polite, "He came to drop off Sarah."

"Since when does Sarah need to be dropped off at home?" Adam asked curtly.

"Since today," Dad answered calmly. "Jason was kind enough to walk her back." Dad's polite smile was fixed on his face. Adam paused, his eyes narrowing at Jason, then said an abrupt hello and walked inside the house.

Dad stayed with Jason and chatted for few minutes before inviting him inside for dinner, but Jason politely excused himself and waived both of us goodbye.

I followed Dad inside the house, relieved that he hadn't interrogated me and had treated Jason kindly. As I walked toward the kitchen, I released my hair from my headscarf, shaking it out. Looking up, I saw Adam standing by the kitchen table, the sleeves of his light blue shirt rolled up over his forearms. He was furious. "What the hell were you doing with Jason?" he snarled.

"*What?!*" The anger in his voice took me by surprise; I'd never heard my brother talk to me that way before.

I heard Dad's voice from behind me, "Calm down, Adam. There's no need to interrogate Sarah."

I turned back and looked at Dad, still shocked and speechless. I couldn't understand what was wrong with Adam.

"It's okay," Dad looked at me calmly, his demeanor in complete contrast to Adam's.

"How can it be *okay*, Dad?" Adam's voice was unusually high and full of suspicions, "You have to ask her what she was doing with Jason!"

I looked back at Adam in disbelief. "I wasn't *doing* anything with him; I was out in the fields alone when he saw me and offered to walk me home!" I didn't usually give Adam explanations about my activities, but I also knew he was overprotective, and I didn't want him to have any doubts about me.

Adam stepped nearer. "Really?" It was clear that he didn't believe a word I'd said. "And he just *happened* to find you in the field? Since when did you start walking in the field anyway?"

"Adam," Dad tried to interrupt, but I spoke up.

"Since I had a fight with Jasmine and I wanted some fresh air." I was struggling to remain calm in the face of Adam's antagonism. "I even told Dad about it." My words didn't have the effect I'd hope they would. Instead, Adam's dark eyes were even more wrathful.

"And you had a fight with Jasmine because she was trying to keep you *away* from Jason!" Adam yelled, lacing his accusation with a bit of profanity.

"That's *enough*, Adam." Dad finally put his foot down, his tone making it clear that he would brook no argument. "I will not have you address your sister like this."

Adam looked at Dad in disbelief, "What? Are you telling *me* off?" Painful shock registered on his face.

"I am *telling* you to *calm down*," Dad repeated firmly.

Adam ran his hands through his hair, agitated. "Calm down?" He was trying not to yell. "Dad, didn't you read what she's been doing at school?" He looked at Dad, his eyes pleading.

Read? Did he just say *read*? Read *what*? And where? I had to know. "What have I been doing at school?" I demanded.

"Jasmine emailed us this afternoon, warning us to keep an eye on you," Adam said acidly. "She's told us everything—how you've been screwing around."

"Watch your language, Adam," Dad exhaled deeply, looking tired and sorrowful.

"You're telling *me* to watch my language?" Adam snapped. "Shouldn't you be telling your *beloved* daughter to watch her actions?"

I felt a rush of bitterness towards Jasmine, an anger that was even sharper than my vexation at Adam. How *dare* she email my father and brother about this! Now I understood why Adam was furious and had stormed into the driveway.

I glared at him defiantly. "What actions? *Huh?* What actions?!" I took a step toward him, my blood starting to boil. "That I happen to have a class with Jason? Oh my God, Sarah has a class with a boy!" My voice dripped with sarcasm. "And Sarah talks to him because she has projects to do with him! And oh, he needed tutoring for chemistry and Sarah happened to be good at it, as if Sarah has never tutored any boys in her life before!" I spoke breathlessly, my ire making my breaths come in ragged gulps.

"Shut up," Adam growled, his fingers closing into fists.

"Don't you *dare* tell me to shut up!" I screamed back, pouring all my anger towards Jasmine on Adam instead.

Dad walked between us. Looking at me, he said, "Sarah, go upstairs." He turned towards Adam, "Sit down and drink a glass of water."

We both ignored Dad, turning our backs on him. Dad poured some water in a glass and handed it to Adam, but he refused.

"You have always, *always*, spoiled her," Adam pointed his finger at Dad, shaking with the strength of his fury. I couldn't believe he would talk to Dad that way. "She has *always* gotten what she wanted, and now she's ruining her character and you're okay with that, too!"

For the first time, I noticed a flush of anger rising in Dad's face, though he swallowed it and asked quietly, "And you are perfect?"

"Yes." Adam had never sounded so arrogant before.

"Really?" Dad's voice was full of pain. "That's why, without any evidence, without any proof, without even asking her for an explanation, did you just question her character?"

Adam didn't answer. He rested his hands on the kitchen counter and stared at the wall.

Dad shook his head with sorrow. "That's not how I raised you!" He collapsed onto a chair and buried his face in his hands.

"Yeah? And *your* upbringing shines through her actions!"

I was shaking where I stood. I had no idea Adam had so much anger towards Dad, and I really couldn't believe that my own brother doubted me!

The argument was going nowhere, and I didn't have the heart to hear Adam spewing his fury against me, or to see the pain on my father's face. I turned and fled up the stairs, seeking the silence and comfort of my room.

Upstairs, I collapsed on my bed. I wanted to cry, but my eyes felt dry. I wanted someone to hug me, to comfort me, to tell me that it was all going to be okay. Instead, the world was cold and empty of affection. All at once, I'd lost both my best friend and my brother.

I felt a wave of loathing towards Jasmine. She didn't deserve to be my friend. If it wasn't for her email, my father and brother wouldn't be fighting downstairs. God knew what she'd written in that email—she had a terrible habit of exaggerating. After a while, I heard Adam's door slam shut. I wasn't sure what had happened between them, but no one came to my room, and eventually, I fell asleep with a heavy heart.

27

The next morning, I prayed and got ready for school. Opening my door to leave the room, I feared what could possibly lie outside, but no one was in the hallway. Adam's door was closed and the landing was empty.

I tiptoed downstairs, but no one was in the kitchen either, which was unusual in our house unless it was a weekend. My stomach lurched, and I felt my heart constrict with an irrational fear. I went back upstairs, but Dad wasn't in his room either, although his car was parked outside. He must have walked to the mosque, but he always came back by breakfast...I left for school without eating. I was never very fond of breakfast anyway, I just enjoyed my family's company around me. Jasmine didn't come to pick me up... not that I had expected her to. I completely avoided her at school, and didn't even go to the cafeteria during lunch. I spent lunch period roaming around the library absent-mindedly, unable to push the images of Adam's fury and Dad's sorrow out of my mind.

I dreaded going back home that day, but I had no choice. Dad was in his room resting, and I went upstairs to kiss him on the cheek as I always did. I sat on the recliner by his bed quietly, hesitant, not knowing what to say to him.

How odd that overnight, I'd lost the ability to talk to my own father!

"How was your day?" he broke the silence.

I forced a smile. "Good." I was barely able to push the word out of my mouth. Was he going to bring up what happened last night? Was I supposed to say something about it? In those moments of silence, I could feel Dad studying my face.

"What happened?" he asked simply. His voice was free from judgment, but his searching gaze was discerning.

What happened? Didn't Dad know what happened? I looked at him, the shock visible on my face. Wasn't he going to ask me anything about Jasmine's email?

I looked down, nervously playing with my fingers, "I don't know, Dad. A lot happened yesterday. Don't you want to ask me anything about what Jasmine wrote?"

He furrowed his brows. "Should I be asking you anything?" Dad took a deep breath and sat up straight, fixing his pillows against the bed's headboard, then leaned against them. "Her email was blown out of proportion; she just shared her observations." He paused. "Her observation is *her* point of view; it doesn't have to be correct." He looked at me with those same searching eyes, "Does it?"

My father was an intellectual man with a profound sense of wisdom. His questions were always loaded with deeper meanings. I tried to read between the lines, but my mind went blank.

I smiled nervously and struggled to look into his eyes, but the guilt in my chest made it hard to hold my gaze steady. I looked down. "I didn't read her email, so I don't know what to say."

Dad smiled gently as he observed me. He knew there was more to the story, but he was a wise man and knew when to press further and when not to. I didn't know what he was going to ask me next, but I was desperately hoping that he wouldn't question me about Jason. I wished everyone could just forget about Jason and stop asking me anything about him until June, when we'd finally graduate and everything would go away.

Dad didn't say anything else, so I asked, "Where's Adam?"

Dad sighed and closed his eyes, "He's in Pitts. He sent me a message saying that he won't be coming home for a few days."

I felt a wave of irritation toward Adam. He was making a mountain out of molehill. "Let me talk to him," I suggested.

Dad looked at me solemnly, "I wouldn't recommend you talking to him right now." He paused, "Give him a few days and he'll come around, God willing."

After that, our conversation switched to lighter subjects, and then I went downstairs to make some mint tea for him. He didn't look too well; I had to bring the dinner Paula had left simmering upstairs to him, too, and I sat with him until he was about to fall asleep.

Before he slept, he asked me to sit by his side and in a soft, weary voice he whispered, "Sarah, both you and Adam have been the peace of my heart. In my old age, I would like to have both pieces of my heart in peace." His dark eyes, usually so bright, seemed exhausted, the liveliness of his face replaced with dark bags and wrinkles etched deep around his mouth.

I felt a stabbing pain in my chest. My father had always been my advisor, my counselor; I rarely missed Mom because Dad played both roles so perfectly in my life. He'd been my strength throughout the difficulties of adolescence, and I couldn't imagine a day without him.

"Dad," I held his hands tightly and kissed his forehead, "*InshaAllah* I won't let you down. Just keep praying for me." I turned off the light and left with unshed tears in my eyes.

The days passed. I completely boycotted Jasmine at school, and of course Jason noticed that I wasn't picking her up at lunch anymore. I told him that we weren't talking, without giving him the specifics.

I avoided going to the cafeteria, because sitting away from her would raise too many eyebrows. Instead, I sat outside on the benches or some days on the grass, reading books and trying to enjoy the fresh air. Jason asked me to watch him practice one day.

"There's nothing you can do to make *me* watch a soccer game," I said, stubbornly refusing to look up from my book.

"Please?" he insisted. Then he put a finger under my chin and pressed upwards, gently forcing me to look at him. I was momentarily shocked at his boldness to touch me so openly, but I had no desire to stop him, either. He put on a puppydog face, making me laugh at how ridiculous he looked.

I relented. "Fine," I sighed, pretending to be annoyed. "But I'll be reading my book the whole time!" I said getting up.

Jason shook his finger at me teasingly. "I won't let you!"

"Oh yeah? How will you stop me?" I challenged.

His dancing eyes held my own, breathtaking in their beauty and sincerity. "I'll throw a ball at you!" He ran off to the field before I could smack him lightly with my book, so I just stuck my tongue out at his back and found a seat on the bleachers close by.

Of course my book lay forgotten on the bleacher beside me.....

Adam came home over the weekend. He didn't talk to anyone, just said his *salam* to Dad and went straight upstairs. He didn't even look at me.

Later that night, I woke with a start. A strange emotion had settled over me, pulling me out of restless dreams.

I tiptoed out of the room, hoping not to wake anyone up, but I noticed that Dad's door was already halfway open, light spilling out of the doorway. I could hear Dad and Adam's voices, low and serious. I crouched in the shadows, peeking through the open doorway while remaining unseen.

Dad was sitting on his recliner while Adam was sitting on his bed, leaning forward and staring down at his feet.

"What solution, exactly, do you have in mind?" Dad asked quietly.

Adam's answer was immediate. "Take her out of school; don't let her leave the house. Cut off her communication with Jason completely."

Dad took a deep breath, "And then what?"

"She'll be safe." Adam said firmly.

Dad's smile was sharp and sarcastic. "And how will you make sure she doesn't sneak out of the house? Or run away as soon as she turns 18?" The silence was heavy for a moment. "You're asking me to do this when she hasn't really done anything sinful. What would you do to her if, God forbid, she actually does something truly wrong?" Dad's voice was dismayed, full of anguish.

"We'd have to do something more." Adam must have been on an adrenaline rush; his brain clearly wasn't functioning properly. What scared me, though, was the dead calm of certainty in his voice.

"Adam, her desire, although forbidden, seems to be contained; but your anger, although perhaps, justified, is turning extreme. And anything extreme, my son, only becomes devastating and poisonous."

"Dad, she's talking to him every day! Couldn't that lead to something extreme?" Adam demanded.

"She's studying in a public school which happens to be full of boys. Should I remind you that you talk to girls every day, too?" Dad looked at him pointedly.

"Not *that* way, Dad! Can't you understand…?" Adam insisted

"I *do* understand, Adam. What makes it right for you to talk to girls and wrong for her to talk to boys?" Dad objected.

"Because she's a *girl*." Finally, Adam spat out the words. His voice softened a little. "Dad, can't you see? She's a very pretty young girl, simple and untouched. Don't you understand how desirable that makes her to all those guys out there?" For the first time, I heard my brother praise me genuinely. Part of me softened toward him.

I closed my eyes and tried to stop my heart from pounding. What was I doing? What trial was I putting my family through?

Adam continued, "Some idiot is going to fool her, and she won't even know it!"

"And so out of fear of some idiot, I must imprison her?" Dad questioned him.

"No, not imprison her. *Protect* her." Irritation tinged Adam's response.

"There is a difference between protection and imprisonment. What you are asking is the latter." Dad was adamant. "Adam, I have raised both of you, and I have tried my best to instill religious and moral values in you both, but at the end of the day, I can only teach and it is up to you two to choose. I cannot force every virtue on either one of you; there will be decisions you will have to make without me. You kept yourself within your limits, by God's Mercy, and now I have to see what Sarah is going to do. I cannot make these decisions for her any more than I made them for you."

"Dad... I never disappointed you." The pride in Adam's voice was clear.

"No, not in this area not at all, *alhamdullilah*. But we each have our own weaknesses. I cannot lock her down simply because I fear someone might ruin her life. Sarah has to go through these challenges and decide on her own."

"And what if she slips? Then you'll realize how wrong you were." Adam was not pleased with Dad's resolution.

"I am not raising angels, Adam..." Dad took a deep breath, "Every human being makes mistakes, and sometimes those mistakes refine us and change us for the better. So far, she has not given me reason to doubt her."

Adam's temper was hot tonight. "You're just closing your eyes to reality, and you're making a *big* mistake by letting your daughter ruin her life."

I could hear the control in Dad's voice as he strove to remain calm. "There are certain things I cannot teach you in theory; you will only learn them when you become a father yourself."

"I really hope I become a better father than this." I could hear the sneer in Adam's voice. He had truly transgressed the limits of respect. I was furious at him.

Dad closed his eyes. "May God make you one of the best fathers in the world, and bless you with the best offspring and wife."

With that, Dad got up, and I quickly snuck back to my room. But I spent a long time staring up into the darkness, hearing Adam's words over and over again.

28

As upset as I was at both Jasmine and Adam, a part of me knew that what they were saying was true. The problem with acknowledging that truth was that I would have to change my behavior and cut off all communication with Jason. And I wasn't prepared to do that. I felt a surge of resentment towards the two people I had once loved so dearly. Why couldn't they just mind their own business, or at least wait until graduation, when everything would go back to normal?

To avoid the tension at home and my own inner conflict, I withdrew from everything else and sought solace in Jason's company.

He made me laugh, and just being with him eased the unpleasant reality that lurked ever-present in my mind. It was as though I was in a different world altogether with him—one where all that mattered was his smile, his laugh, the intensity of his voice when he'd lean towards me during a particularly deep conversation, the way his eyes held mine, the way I never wanted to let him go.

I felt pinpricks of guilt, but the pleasure of being around Jason was intoxicating. And we had less than three months until graduation—how bad could it be to let myself enjoy a few more weeks?

At school during lunch, I'd taken to watching Jason practice on the soccer field, and on the days he didn't have practice, he sat with me on the bleachers. Sometimes we talked and laughed, and other times we enjoyed our lunch in companionable silence. What I liked best about Jason was that there was no pressure, ever, to do something or not do something. He let me do what I wanted, and he liked who I was, *as* I was... with no demands to change my behavior.

One afternoon I was sitting on the bleachers, absorbed in *Pride and Prejudice* for the hundredth time, sipping on my smoothie as I admired Elizabeth Bennet's fierce principles.

"Still single?" a deep voice laughed, and I looked up, smiling, to see Jason standing next to me, stretching his legs in preparation for his P.E. class after lunch.

"Yep," I answered, knowing he was referring to Jasmine. "It's the best solution to all the problems in the world." I adjusted the pale lilac headscarf I was wearing with a purple floral dress and pastel cardigan. I pretended not to know that the way I had pinned my headscarf meant the elegant ruffle along the neckline of my dress peeked out.

"Need a shrink?" Jason asked laughingly as he tied his shoelaces.

I frowned. "She definitely does, but not me. I'm in no mood to patch up with her."

Jason's eyes darkened in concern as he looked at me. "Wow, that sounds serious. What actually happened between you two? You guys were inseparable."

I stared back at him, wishing I could just lose myself in those brilliant gray depths. What was I to say? That my life had been a mess since he came? That he was the cause of our fight? I must have zoned out, lost in my thoughts, because the next thing I knew, Jason was snapping his fingers in my face.

"Hellooo, Sarah? Where'd you go?"

I closed my eyes and shook my head. "Nowhere." I opened my eyes again and secretly admired Jason's impressive physique as he stretched. "So why are *you* single?" I asked, changing the topic. To tell the truth, it was a question that had been haunting me for a while.

Jason smiled wryly. "As you said, it's the best solution."

I raised any eyebrow at him, intrigued. He sat on the bleachers a few steps away from me, resting his elbows on his knees. "My girlfriend broke up with me when I got expelled," he explained, bending down to adjust his shin pads. "She didn't think I was 'good enough' for her anymore."

"What a loser," I snorted, feeling a streak of unexpected jealousy. How could any girl give Jason up for a dumb reason like that?

Jason's smile was enigmatic. "I learned a lot from that experience, Sarah." He paused thoughtfully. "I was really popular at school, so my head was above the clouds and I hung out with all the wrong types of people." He took a deep breath. "When I needed them most, they all disappeared, and I realized how superficial my friends were."

I watched Jason sympathetically, able to understand his pain. We all had our fair share of difficulties in life. He'd lost all of his shallow friends, but in turn he had found two solid people who happened to be Muslims, who stood by him when he needed it.

"I hope you've made good friends here," I commented, wedging my finger between the pages of my book as a bookmark.

Jason smiled. The sweet, thoughtful one that made me feel weak at the knees. I was glad I was sitting down. "Yeah, I did. I kept myself out of the spotlight and looked for the right crowd."

"Like Stephanie and Trisha?" I hoped he couldn't hear the jealousy in my voice.

"Hell, no!" he exclaimed, and I cocked my head at him quizzically. "Seriously," he assured me, "They aren't my friends. I had some group projects with Matt and David and those two always just tagged along." He sounded defensive, and a part of me wondered if that meant he really cared what I thought about him and who he spent time with.

I laughed off the notion. "So... you didn't find a girlfriend here," I said casually, my heart hammering. Did I want to know the answer? What answer did I want him to give?

Jason's smile disappeared, his expression turning suddenly serious as he glanced at me and then looked down at his soccer cleats.

"I didn't *want* to find one here," he said slowly, "but..."

"But?" My voice was sharp with impatience and I abruptly shut my book. He'd caught my attention now. Oh God—if he *did* have a girlfriend, it would make my life so much easier... yet there was a stab of emotion twisting through my chest at the idea of Jason in love with another girl. I tried to ignore it.

"There *is* this one girl in school," he said hesitantly. "The more I try not to think about her, the more I can't get her out of my mind." He sighed heavily.

"Oh my God!" I tried to sound happy for him. "Does she like you too?" Apparently I enjoyed torturing myself.

Jason gave a lopsided smile at the enthusiasm in my voice. "She doesn't know yet."

I creased my forehead with a frown. "What?! What are you waiting for? Graduation?"

"Yes!" he said immediately. "Should I even bother telling her now? I mean, what's the point? I'll have to leave soon enough." How unfair—being lovesick made his eyes look even *more* attractive!

I had always been good at giving advice. "I believe that if you love someone, you should tell them, even if you have just one day with them," I said decidedly.

Jason stared into my eyes contemplatively. "And make them go through all the pain of separation?" he questioned.

I tapped my finger against my lips. "I think they have the right to know they were loved by someone."

The smile he flashed me was unusually brilliant.

"So, who is she?" I asked quickly, before he could ask me any questions about my own non-existent love life.

He glanced at me laughingly. "I can't tell you that!"

I scowled and muttered an irritated, "Fine!" Jason chuckled and started getting up from the bleachers.

"I'll tell you once I find out if she likes me or not," he reassured me.

"What does she look like?" I was dying to know. Who *was* the mystery girl that Jason clearly cared about so much?

He smirked at me. "You know almost everyone in school... if I tell you what she looks like, you'll know who she is!"

I rolled my eyes as the bell rang, and we both waved good-bye, heading off on our separate ways.

When I went home that day, I found Dad and Adam sitting in the formal living room, which was by the foyer and separate from the rest of the house. I could hear them arguing, with Adam's voice being the loudest; I sighed at my brother and went inside. They both fell silent when they heard me, so I called out a loud *salam*, and headed for the kitchen.

"Adam, you will not do any such thing," Dad continued whatever he was saying as I started to make a sandwich. "On one hand you're upset with Sarah because she is doing something which could be religiously questionable, but on the other hand you're willing to abuse someone with your hands or your tongue, which is definitely forbidden in our religion! How is that okay, Adam?"

Dad's rebuking words made me stop in my tracks and turn back towards the living room.

"I'm her brother, and if you won't do anything to protect her, then *I will*." Adam was obstinate.

It was obvious what they were discussing. Somehow, Dad had intuited that Adam had a plan to threaten Jason to keep him away from me. I didn't think Adam would have told Dad anything specific; their conversation had probably drifted in that direction and Dad had understood that Adam was in such a state he'd resort to severe measures.

I ran into the living room, bursting with indignant rage. "Two Muslim men defended Jason, turning his bigoted views into positive ones about Islam, and here my own brother is planning to abuse him for some crime he hasn't committed!?" I spoke directly to Adam. "Wow, I wonder what kind of impression *you* would leave on him about Muslims."

Adam looked at me spitefully, "You seem to know his entire life story. What else has he told you?"

I didn't want to hear his ranting. "Adam, he doesn't have any feelings for me, okay? He likes someone else at school." I could finally say it confidently, secure in the knowledge that I was out of harm's way, that there was no chance that Jason reciprocated my feelings for him. I narrowed my eyes at Adam. "And I forbid you to go and threaten him! You'll make a total fool of yourself, *and* you'll make my life a living hell at school."

Dad stepped forward and looked at Adam, his gaze stern. "I, your father, am forbidding you from physically or verbally threatening Jason," Dad said firmly. "If you do any such thing, it will be in direct disobedience to me."

Adam's face twisted with anger. "Wow, Dad, you can only side with her! *Always*, you just blindly side with her!"

"Adam, it has nothing to do with Sarah. It's a matter of principle," Dad tried to explain.

"No, Dad, it's not, and you'll *never* understand. That's why I told you it's best if I leave for Houston, because I *cannot* sit at home and just watch her hang out with Jason every day."

"How many times have you *ever* seen me hang out with Jason?" I snapped at Adam.

"Adam, please," Dad's voice was weakening as he pleaded. "Can you leave this matter for me to handle?"

"Yeah, Dad, I know what you want. You want me out of your way, as always. And you can handle it yourself because I won't be around to interfere in your *perfect* parenting." Adam's voice was harsh.

I frowned, my head turning from Dad to Adam. I didn't understand what they were talking about. Adam out of the way? What did that mean? Where was he going?

"Then you can live with your daughter and have the perfect family you always wanted," Adam spat out.

Dad's face was pained as he shook his head and leaned forward towards Adam beseechingly. "No, Adam, no! That's not true."

Adam couldn't stop. "Yes, Dad. It *is* true. It's been happening to me all my life. Every time you had a difficult situation, you sent me to Houston. I've been getting kicked out ever since I was seven. Every time Mom got sick, you shipped me off so you wouldn't have to deal with me." Adam's voice hitched, and there were sudden tears in his eyes that he blinked away furiously.

Dad closed his eyes and held his head in both his hands.

"Adam," Dad raised his head, his own eyes wet with tears. "My child, my son, it was not like that. Your mom was very sick and it was very hard on *you* to see her in that pain. We sent you to your grandmother's so that *you* wouldn't have to see her suffering." Dad's tears slid down his face and wet his neat beard. "Sarah was small, she didn't understand. But your mom's sickness took a big toll on you."

"And that's why, instead of dealing with my struggles, you just threw me out of the house every time!" Adam insisted. It was as though he refused to believe anything Dad said.

Dad pressed his fingers against his forehead, the tears still silently falling.

Adam stood up, his face dark. "I was in your way then, and I am in your way now, between your perfect parenting and your beloved daughter. But don't worry, because by next month I'll be gone and you won't have to be bothered with me." He stormed out of the living room, out of the house, and zoomed away in his car.

29

The night's revelations were overwhelming. Adam had been hurting deeply ever since Mom had gotten sick, but had kept it to himself all these years. The more I thought about it, the more I felt the need to talk to him, but I couldn't bring myself to call him.

Despite the fact that I knew he was suffering, his judgment had wounded me deeply, and my own confidence was shaky with the guilt that sometimes overpowered my justifications for my behavior.

Had Adam asked me once, calmly looking at me straight in the eye, whether I could justify my actions or not, I wouldn't have been able to answer him. And it was the fear that he would do just that that kept me from trying to talk to him.

From that day on, Adam and I didn't talk, and we didn't have family dinners or quality time anymore. Dad and I ate alone, but I noticed that Dad mostly just toyed with his food.

Was I the culprit? Was I the sole cause of all the turmoil in my family? Oh God! The more I thought, the more my head pounded. Eventually I just tried to block out all the family issues, and avoided home even more.

Other than my Friday nights at the mosque, Aunty Elisha's study circles on Saturdays for teenagers, and the Sunday study circle I had started hosting for the preteen girls upon Amal's request, my life revolved around school.

School became my haven, my solace. Art class, which I'd previously loathed, was my favorite class, and lunch was spent up in the bleachers, laughing and sharing my thoughts and ideas with Jason. We'd changed our chemistry tutoring from the school library during lunch to the public library after school to suit our schedules better. Besides, now that I had no one chaperoning me, I wasn't restricted in terms of time or place.

Wickley's public library had a study area upstairs where the college students often hung out. High school students rarely ever went there, so Jason and I staked it out as our study nook. We usually sat at the same table in the corner, close to a large, gilded floor-to-ceiling mirror. Neither of us understood why the library had that mirror. Jason insisted it had to have been donated, but there wasn't a donation plaque on it anywhere.

The week before spring break was full of turmoil at home. Adam had decided to move to Houston earlier than Dad wanted, and although Dad didn't stop him, he did ask him not to stay at Grandma's. I knew Dad was afraid of Uncle Amir's influence on Adam, especially with all the inner conflicts Adam was dealing with and the manner in which he was leaving home. Adam needed a stabilizing, positive environment and someone who could be a good influence on him.

Dad requested that Adam move to College Station and pursue his masters at Texas A&M. He felt a lot more comfortable with Adam being in Zain's company than Amir's, especially at such a fraught and fragile period in his life.

Not surprisingly, Adam agreed. It was obvious that Zain was a major factor in his decision. Over the next couple of weeks, Dad talked to Zain on the phone several times, trying to rent a house in College Station for Adam. When Adam finally moved, Zain helped out a lot.

I wondered if Zain knew what our family dispute was about, and why Adam was moving on such short notice, but I never asked Dad about it, and he didn't discuss it with me either.

Adam left the day before spring break started. Dad wanted to fly with him and help him settle in, but Adam refused. There was so much I wanted to say to Adam, but I couldn't. I couldn't even cry when he left.

Adam didn't make any effort to speak to me either. As he walked out of the house, his laptop bag slung over his shoulder, I stood in the foyer quietly. When he passed by me, he stopped, but refused to look at me. I just stood there, tucking a lock of hair behind my ear, hoping that he'd say something, *anything*, even if it was something mean or rude. All I wanted was for him to say something to me before he left. Instead, he hesitated, then turned and kissed me on the forehead quickly before walking swiftly out the front door.

I stood in the doorway and watched him drive away. What had happened to the family I was so proud of?

While Dad dropped Adam off at the airport, I went to meet Jason at the library to 'tutor' him. He wanted to review everything we had studied because his midterm was right after spring break, and he was going to go home during the break.

As I walked to the library, my conscience began to berate me. *Why are you going there, Sarah? Why don't you just tell Jason you can't tutor him anymore? Isn't it enough that your actions have already led to so much destruction?*

The guilt was surging through me now, stronger with every step I took. I hesitated at the stairs leading up to the study area and wondered if it wasn't too late to turn back...

"Hey, Sarah!" Jason's loud whisper drifted down to me as he waved from the balcony.

Too bad, you're already here now... just enjoy it and worry about it later! The second voice, the one that justified every move I made with Jason, interrupted my guilty conscience.

I smiled back up at Jason, admiring the gold tint in his hair, highlighted by the late afternoon sunlight that filtered through the library windows. His grin made me feel warm inside, a comfort and security that I no longer felt with my own family.

I climbed up the stairs and seated myself at our usual table. "I think you're ready for the exams," I told Jason, since we'd covered the last of the material a few days before.

He skimmed through the book. "You think so?"

I leaned back in the chair, "Yeah. Just go and have fun with your family, and tell your dad Muslims are good people who help you study."

Jason grinned, "I'm finally going to eat my mom's cooking."

I looked at him with envy, "Lucky duck!"

Jason's face quickly became apologetic. "Oh, God, I'm sorry, Sarah," he said sympathetically. I had told him about my mom passing away when I was young. "I'll bring you some back," he offered, his eyes twinkling.

We both laughed, but Jason noticed the shadow of sorrow that had passed over my face.

"Are you okay?" he asked gently, concerned. I nodded, though my heart was cracking at the thought of Adam, and how I hadn't been able to say goodbye to him.

There was a moment of silence as neither one of us knew what to say.

In an effort to change the subject, Jason asked, "What are you going to do during the vacation?"

I took a deep breath. "I'm volunteering at Wickley Hospital on the pediatric ward. I start tomorrow morning."

"Wow, you really are all over the place, huh?" He whistled, clearly impressed.

I shrugged. "I like to keep myself busy... it helps keep my mind off things." The sorrow on my face was too obvious to ignore. "You don't look like yourself today," he said gently. "Everything okay?"

"It's nothing," I insisted. "Really! It's just that Adam is leaving tonight for Houston, for the next two years." I massaged my shoulders and twisted my head from side to side, stretching the muscles that were tense from stress.

Jason tried to cheer me up. "Party, girl!" he joked. "You're free from your older brother's eagle eye!" He didn't realize that though he was joking, he'd unwittingly hit the nail on the head.

I smiled back, and without wasting a second, changed the topic. "So did you tell her yet?"

Jason shook his head, putting his hands on the back of his neck and sighing heavily.

"You should tell her as soon as you come back from vacation. Or *I'll* tell her," I threatened.

Jason flashed me a fond grin. "Oh yeah, and who's going to tell you who to tell?"

I smirked at him.

"You will," I said confidently.

He looked down at his watch suddenly, looking dismayed. "Oh damn, I've got to catch my flight from Pitts!"

"You're flying?" I was confused. "I thought you were driving in the morning." I felt unreasonably disappointed.

"No, my dad told me to fly instead. I have to go, I'm so sorry. I'm going to miss my flight otherwise." He looked genuinely sorry.

I laughed and waved him off. "Go, go, you don't need to apologize!" He waved goodbye and left quickly.

I went back to the empty house and, after praying *Isha*, went to bed. My schedule was going to be pretty tough during spring break. I was going to be volunteering at the hospital for most of the day, and the remainder of the time was to be spent with Dad, either at the store or just keeping him company wherever he went. I didn't want him to feel lonely, but what hurt me most was that his sadness was caused by me.

30

One Friday in late April, after spring break, I had to run a night shift at the café instead of going to the mosque. Dad was short on staff, and he'd asked if I could fill in from six to ten.

Tammy was there when I arrived, but she kept getting phone calls all night, and seemed distracted. When I asked her what was going on, she explained that her daughter was sick, and the babysitter wanted to leave early.

The weather in Wickley had gone from being pleasant to cold again, and kids were getting sick all over the place. She had to drive all the way back to Pitts and it would've gotten too late if she'd had to leave after closing, so I told her to go on and take care of her daughter. Thanking me profusely, she headed out.

After she left, I was overwhelmed with customers for the next hour, and then the rush slowed to a trickle. Another incoming cold front seemed to have convinced everyone else in Wickley to stay at home where it was warm. Whatever it was, I was happy to finally relax. Since no one was left in the café, I turned off the extra lights, leaving just a few of them on. The café took on a soft ambience, and I untied my apron and made some Limeade for myself.

I brought a stool from the back and had relaxed onto it, flipping through a magazine behind the counter, when someone opened the door. Oh gosh, please don't make me get up! I raised my head, ready to be annoyed at whoever had walked in. To my surprise, it was Jason standing in the doorway, looking right at me. He was wearing a black leather jacket with a neat gray t-shirt and dark jeans. It gave him the air of a rakish biker, complete with his charming smile.

"Hi," he said simply.

"Hey," I answered, still astonished. "What are you doing here?"

"I was with friends, but they went to Vertigo, so I decided to come here," he explained, stumbling slightly over the words. I guessed he hadn't expected to find me at the café. He walked to the counter, his hands stuffed in the pockets of his jeans. "I didn't know you were working tonight."

"Neither did I," I shrugged. "I was called in at the last minute. Alex is sick."

"So it's my lucky day then..." Jason's voice trailed off, the tone of his voice strange.

I watched him silently, my heart beating madly, my stomach fluttering in a way that I'd started getting used to lately.

"You can hook me up with a free drink, right?"

"Oh..." "What would you like to have?" I asked, fixing my hijab out of habit. I suddenly wondered if the green-and-white ensemble I'd put on today—a deep jade dress topped with a tight white jacket and a jade headscarf with a white under piece—was too garish in the café's lighting, and regretted not wearing a softer color instead.

Jason settled down on the bar stool across from me. "Depends on what you can give me."

I shrugged. "Anything."

"Are you sure?" There was something different, something strange in the way he spoke to me, the way his metallic eyes searched mine.

I laughed a little nervously. "Yeah..." I didn't understand what he meant, but the way he was looking at me was making me lose focus. "From the menu," I clarified hastily.

I fiddled with a napkin, glancing at Jason from beneath my eyelashes. He was smiling but seemed both happy and confused. There was something peculiar about him—either he was speaking with double meanings, or I was reading too much between the lines. Thanks to my psychology class, I, too, was starting to over analyze what people said. Annoyed at myself, I brushed away my thoughts and shrugged again.

"What can you make best?" Jason gave the menu only a cursory glance before turning his gaze back towards me.

"I'm good at everything I do, make, or say," I joked back, swinging the bar stool around to put my glass away on the counter.

"That you are..." Jason murmured. His eyes had darkened from their usual gray to something closer to ashen.

There was *definitely* something off about him tonight. I hadn't expected him to answer that way; I thought he'd just laugh and make fun of me the way he usually did. Now, though, Jason was leaning forward on the counter, his voice shaking with some kind of unrecognizable emotion. His face was solemn, more serious than I'd ever seen him.

The intensity of his gaze made me freeze, my mind going blank. All I could think about was how strange, how amazing he made me feel just by looking at me like that.

The heated silence was abruptly broken by the loud snap of the café's door opening and shutting. I nearly jumped in my seat, turning around quickly to see Adnan's dad standing inside the café, staring at us coldly.

I quickly recovered. "*Salam 'alaikum,* Uncle," I smiled.

He didn't answer, instead looking me up and down with an unpleasant expression on his face. I flushed, feeling awkward, and I could feel my stomach sinking. Knowing their family, I could only expect him to assume the worst based on what he had just seen.

"Your dad is not here?" he asked, ignoring my *salam.*

"No. Wasn't he at the mosque?" I tried to sound polite, though I didn't like the way he spoke to me.

"That was a long time ago. It is quite late now..." his voice was frosty.

I looked down at my watch. "Oh wow, it's 9:45 already!" I was shocked at how quickly the time had passed; it was only nine o'clock when the café had emptied.

"You should keep track of your time," Adnan's dad said sardonically, then turned and walked out of the café before I could say anything. I stared at the door as it shut behind him, feeling a wave of anger wash over me.

"Who was that?" Jason noticed my face turning red.

I pushed away the thoughts churning in mind and forced a smile. "That was Adnan's dad."

"Oh, really? I saw Adnan at Vertigo's, with his girlfriend," Jason said casually. My smile was bitter.

"Yeah, Wendy... I guess his girlfriend is limited to just school and the clubs. I don't think his dad knows about her." I didn't want to give Adnan's family's hypocrisy any further attention, so I changed the topic. "Anyway, do you want to have something warm or cold?" I pointed towards the big menu board behind me, getting off the stool.

"Something warm..." Jason answered.

"Cappuccino, coffee, hot chocolate...?" I was going to continue rattling off the list when he cut me off and said, "Hot chocolate is fine."

"With whipped cream?" I continued asking, hoping he'd stop looking so serious.

"However you like it," Jason finally smiled back, and I felt relieved that the intensity had dissipated.

"To go or here?" I asked again.

"Well... I don't mind staying...if it's okay with you?"

Of course it was okay with me—I felt a surge of rebellion against Adnan's father and the critical judgment in his eyes.

"I have to stay 'till ten," I said, looking at my watch. It was 9:50. I had every reason to tell him that he could take his hot chocolate to go so I could close and leave.

"So yeah, you can stay. I don't mind," I said instead. A tiny voice in my head started freaking out. *What the hell are you doing, Sarah Ali?!* I ignored it and focused on Jason's smile instead.

"Cool," he grinned at me.

"So your friends ditched you?" I asked as I prepared the hot chocolate.

"Nah... I actually went with them to Vertigo, but it's not really my kind of place. I went out for some fresh air." Jason watched me, looking interested, as I worked the machines.

Clubs weren't his kind of place? Wow... I could imagine all the cute girls falling over him—how could he not enjoy that?

"Is that fun?" he asked, nodding at the machine I was fiddling with.

"What?" I turned around. "Making these?" I pointed to the mugs.

Jason nodded. "Yeah, it is," I admitted. "You want to try?" The crazy idea of inviting him back behind the counter, of teaching him to make his own hot chocolate made my stomach flutter again. Of course it was totally against protocol, but no one was around!

"Sure!" Jason slid off his stool and joined me in front of the espresso machine.

Standing close enough to be brushing against his shoulder, I showed him what to do. It wasn't complicated, he just had to press a few buttons.

As I was showing him how to make a customized drink, our hands brushed against each other more than once. Neither of us made an effort to prevent it. Every subtle touch brought an intoxicating rush I'd never imagined before, tinged with guilt that I tried to ignore. It was a more intense version of the dilemma I fought every time I was around him. What was it about him that made me too weak to turn away, too fragile to cut him off? God, *what was happening to me?*

I was suddenly, acutely aware that we were both holding the same cup, his hand cradling it from below while my fingers wrapped around it from the top. I was holding the cup very close to me. It was as if electricity was flowing through me, and I was reacting in a way I could barely comprehend.

This was a different type of desire; it wasn't just his company that I longed for... I wanted something more. I felt dizzy from the scent of his cologne.

Sarah Ali, be mindful of Allah! The voice that was usually a whisper became a horrified scream in my mind, and I pulled back suddenly, feeling a deep sense of shame and horror flood through me. I let go of the cup, and took a step back from Jason hastily, striving to compose myself, too embarrassed to look up and read his face. I turned around and quickly made myself busy putting the milk away in the fridge.

It took Jason a few minutes to move from his place and find his way around the counter to seat himself there.

I must go home. I thought to myself. This is wrong. This whole setting is so very wrong. '*Sarah Ali go home. Hold on to your values and respect your father's trust in you.*'

"Sarah I have to ask you for a favor." Jason's deep voice broke my train of thought and I turned around to look at him from the side of the fridge behind the counter.

He looked down at his hot chocolate, biting on his bottom lip and smiling just a bit. His eyes lingered on my face, trying to gauge my feelings. "I was wondering if you could find out from the girl at school whether she likes me or not?"

A sour taste flooded my mouth. So *that's* who I was to Jason... I was just a good friend who could help get to his girl. The middle person. Nothing more.

A part of me was relieved at this confirmation of my excuses. He really didn't think of me as anything more than a friend. It didn't matter how much time I spent with him, how I behaved around him... I was just a friend.

Even as I repeated those thoughts to myself, a part of me vehemently disagreed. Every time he talked about this mysterious girl, the one who didn't know he loved her, I felt a twisting stab of fierce jealousy. The thoughts I struggled so hard to shove away were rearing so powerfully that it was difficult to pretend they didn't exist.

"Sure," I choked out, trying to sound encouraging. "Tell me who she is, and I'll find out for you." The guilt that had been convincing me to leave for home began fading away, as I was just a third person—a way for Jason to get to his beloved—and that should make it safe for me to stick around. *You have to help him, just like he helped you through the protest,* something tried to convince me inside. But my conscience still wasn't convinced, so I tried to tempt Jason into leaving, for its sake. "But are you sure you aren't missing out on the fun at Vertigo?"

"Hell, no!" he replied. "I told you that's not my kinda place."

"I can't believe someone like you doesn't enjoy Vertigo!" I blurted.

"Someone like me?" Jason repeated.

Snap. I'd done it again. I was usually careful in choosing my words, but as always, I lost control of more than just my common sense when I was around Jason. How was I supposed to explain what *'someone like you'* meant? Someone who was not only drop-dead gorgeous, but who had a personality so charming, so sincere, so down-to-earth, so *powerful* that a girl like me, who'd never fallen for a handsome face before, simply couldn't resist? Yeah, right!

"I mean, what's stopping you from going to a club? I don't go because of my religious beliefs," I recovered quickly.

"Just because I'm not a *Muzlim* doesn't mean that I can't adhere to high moral standards," Jason retorted, playing with his drink. "I don't like to throw myself at every girl, and I can't stand girls who do that with guys." He was so earnest that just when I thought I couldn't be any more impressed with him, I was.

"Wow," I mouthed, looking at him with renewed admiration. There was an awkward silence for a few more moments. I looked down into my cup, but I could still feel him studying my face.

"Have you ever played thumb wrestling?" Jason asked abruptly.

"What?" I laughed, confused. Was he planning on playing a game of thumb wrestling with me? How was I supposed to turn him down? I could just say that I can't be so informal and lax with guys, especially not to the point of physical touching.

I conveniently ignored that a significant few seconds of physical touching had occurred just a short while before, and that the entire situation—me sitting with him alone in a café, with closed doors—wasn't exactly appropriate either.

"I can't catch your thumb... sorry!" I giggled nervously.

Jason eyed me, a corner of his mouth quirking upwards. "Okay, how about this—we'll use our spoons. If you grab my spoon then I tell you my secret and if I grab yours then you will have to tell me something about you." The look of triumph on his face made it clear that he had it all figured out. "And no lies," he added.

How could I justify playing thumb wresting with him? Well, spoon wrestling, I amended silently. Let's see... we're just friends sitting in a public place (well, at least people could see in from the street); I'm just a friend who wants to help him get his girl. But it didn't wash. Fine, maybe I *was* doing something wrong but it wasn't *that* bad... it's not like we were going to start groping each other or making out... we were just talking..."Okay," I grinned back at him, grabbing my spoon. We started tackling each other's utensils and it quickly became a game of back-and-forth.

"I talk in my sleep sometimes," Jason admitted when I pushed his spoon back first.

"I'm scared of cockroaches," I confessed.

"Aren't all girls?" Jason teased, then said, "I can score a goal with my eyes closed."

"That's not a secret," I objected. "That's a boast-worthy talent!" I paused. "I screen my calls."

"I know my mom's email password," he pretended to look remorseful, but the twinkle in his eye gave him away.

I pretended to think hard. "I fake cry sometimes to get out of trouble."

"All girls do that," he laughed, and I rolled my eyes.

Jason quickly sobered up when I knocked his spoon back. "I haven't held your hand ever since the day of the protest," he said.

"That's not a secret, that's a fact," I remarked, wondering why he'd even remember such a thing.

"The secret is...that...I want to hold it again." Jason was looking intently at our spoons. His spoon had mine trapped, and at his words, I no longer struggled to fight back. My hand froze, my heart beating so fast that I could hear its frenzied *thump thump* clearly in my ears. I felt hot—and I definitely couldn't blame it on the hot chocolate.

I looked into his eyes, and their misty gray brilliance made me catch my breath, nearly drowning me in their depths. The sensations I had almost successfully managed to suppress mere moments ago rose even more intensely, threatening to overwhelm me.

"Give thanks to Allah for the moon and the stars, take hold of your iman don't give in to shaytaan..." the voice of Zain Bhaikha's song disturbed the poisonously magical moment. It was the ringtone I had set for Dad's calls. The perfect ring tone for the moment! Was it a coincidence? Or was Allah protecting me?

The potent, bewitching silence dissipated as I grabbed my phone with shaking hands and fumbled with it, answering the call. I stumbled off the bar stool, looking away from Jason.

"Dad..." my voice was high-pitched and breathless, and I desperately prayed that Dad wouldn't notice.

"Where are you?" Dad's voice was concerned.

I took a deep breath, trying to steady myself against the counter. "I'm here at the café," I replied, trying to ignore Jason's figure in my peripheral vision.

"Still?" He was surprised.

I checked the time quickly. It was eleven o'clock. Oh my God, how could it be eleven already? It had been 9:50 just a few minutes ago! What was I going to tell Dad if he asked me what I was doing? Before I could come up with an excuse, Dad continued, "You don't have to stay there that late. Just close up and come home. I've been waiting for you," he said.

Thank God that Dad had never been the interrogating type. "Okay, I'll be home in few minutes *inshaAllah*," I chirped over-enthusiastically, then quickly closed the phone.

Jason was looking down, fiddling with the spoons.

"I... I have to go," I said awkwardly. It was the best way for me to get out of the conversation that inevitably would have had to continue if I stayed. After all, he *had* just said that he wanted to hold my hand again. What was that supposed to mean? If he liked someone else at school, what business did he having wanting to hold my hand? Except, I realized, with a sinking heart, holding hands probably didn't even mean anything to him. Touching the opposite gender was a big deal for me, but it wasn't for most teenagers.

I didn't want to think about it any further. Instead, I quickly grabbed our mugs, tossed them in the sink, locked the register, and pulled out my keys. "Sorry, my dad's waiting for me. He's really worried and doesn't like it if I stay out this late," I said hurriedly, avoiding eye contact with Jason.

"No, don't worry about it." Jason sounded as awkward as I felt. "Thanks for keeping me company," he added, smiling at me warmly. He walked out with me while I locked the door from outside. I hesitated, wondering if there was something I was supposed to say or do, but then I abruptly turned away from him and walked swiftly towards my car. I had a feeling he was standing there watching me, but I refused to look back and got into my car quickly, driving home.

Dad was waiting for me in the living room. He didn't seem upset, he was only concerned that I had been out this late alone. Pretending that nothing out of the ordinary had happened, I told him I'd simply lost track of time in the café.

Dad looked unusually tired, so I made him some chamomile tea. As I passed by the hallway mirror with his cup, I caught a glimpse of my reflection. Normally, I would've been exhausted after spending half a day at work, but I looked unusually refreshed. And I didn't want to think about why.

Dad and I chit-chatted about random, uninteresting topics as he sipped his tea. When he bade me good night, I headed upstairs to my room and made *wudu*, remembering that I hadn't prayed *Isha* at the café as I usually did. Raising my hands and folding them over my chest, my lips moved in a mechanical recitation, but my mind was occupied with other thoughts. I flashed back to the moment my hand had touched Jason's in the café, and the earnest way he'd told me his secrets. But then a tsunami of guilt made me realize I was standing in front of my Lord. I felt extremely ashamed, completely unfit to be worshipping God in this state, when all I could think about was the pleasure I craved with a boy I should never have been that close to to begin with.

It's a trick of Shaytan, my conscience consoled me, *don't give in. Keep praying.* Struggling to focus, fighting my thoughts and emotions, I fell down in prostration. *Oh Allah, forgive me and protect me from the evil of my own self!* All the pleasure that I'd been reliving disappeared, replaced with a deep, profound remorse. My prostration prolonged, my supplication was a silent, desperate plea, but I knew that the One I asked could hear me. It was the only appeal I could force myself to say, though—because if I were to say more, I would have to ask Allah to change my feelings for Jason, ask Him to cut my ties with him, ask Him to make me leave him. And I could not bear the idea of being without him.

31

I spent most of the weekend in Pittsburgh with Dad while he ran errands. Since Adam had left, I felt obliged to be with my father more so he didn't feel so lonely. I knew Dad missed Adam dearly, especially his weekend company and help with the businesses, not to mention that I felt responsible for Adam moving away in the first place.

Though I tried to avoid thinking about Jason during that time, I couldn't help reveling in memories of that night in the café. I'd catch myself thinking about his eyes, envisioning the way they smiled at me, as though they could look into my very soul. I'd find myself looking in the mirror, smiling absent-mindedly, remembering Jason's dimple and his warm hands. Most of all, I'd think about the words he'd said to me... *I want to hold your hand again.*

It made me both dread seeing him again and unable to wait until I could.

When I got to school on Monday, though, I didn't see Jason anywhere. He didn't show up to art class either. Scrolling through the contacts list on my phone, I was tempted to text him and ask where he was, but the fact that Dad could read all my texts stopped me. Jason didn't show up on Tuesday, either. By then, I was beyond curious to find out where he was. Asking his friends was an option that my ego would never consider, especially not after the way the Trashies had been treating me lately, and asking him directly would be complicated.

To my surprise, it was David who found me during lunch that day while I sat in the bleachers, absorbed in another book.

"Hey, Sarah," he greeted me cheerfully.

I looked up in vague bewilderment, returning to the real world. "Hey, David."

"Where's Jason?" he asked, as if he expected that I'd definitely have an answer.

I frowned, uncertain at his tone. "Uh... I don't know." Why was he asking me? David was Jason's best friend.

David looked at me doubtfully. "*You* don't know where he is?" He didn't seem to believe me.

I looked at him flatly. "No."

David's brow furrowed. "He hasn't been coming to school and he's not even answering his phone. Is everything okay?"

I felt uncomfortable at the way David seemed to assume that I knew what was up with Jason. "I hope so," I said shortly, pointedly glancing at my book.

"Okay, uh..." David sounded confused as he shoved his hands in his pockets. "When you talk to him, can you please tell him to call me?" It was clear that he didn't believe that I hadn't spoken to Jason.

I shrugged and nodded, trying to come up with something that would enable me to text Jason without looking desperate or getting in trouble. In art class, Ms. Lynn provided the perfect cover when she announced that the next week's project was to sketch a classmate. I seized the opportunity and texted Jason's number.

Hey, Jason. We've got a sketching project next week and we all have to pick a partner to sketch. Ms. Lynn told me to let you know.

To my surprise, he texted back right away:

Thx. I'll think of a partner.

That's it? He wasn't going to tell me why he hadn't come to school? I hadn't asked him though, I reminded myself. I spent the next day hoping he'd text or email me to let me know what was going on, wondering if there were any way I could ask without sounding nosy. By evening, I gave up on trying to be distant and finally texted him.

Hope everything's okay.

If Dad saw the text and asked, I could reasonably say that Jason had been absent at school and that we needed to work on a project together. I could also point out that I knew Dad could see my texts. If I'd had any bad intentions, I wouldn't have texted Jason right in front of him, right?

Jason didn't text back for almost half an hour. It was the most difficult half hour of my life as I waited for his answer, worrying about whether he thought I was pining away for him because of his absence. I was torn between feeling humiliated that he hadn't bothered to text me sooner, and agonized because I needed to know where he was. I berated myself mentally. I should have taken this opportunity to put some distance between us. I shouldn't have shown that I cared. Why did I even ask?

My nerves had nearly frayed beyond repair when he finally texted back.

> *All good went to see my family over the weekend but ended up staying longer bc I had to take care of some paperwork from my old school for college admissions.*

The relief I felt was irrational, knowing that he hadn't stayed away from school because of me.

> *Hope everything works out. See you soon.*

I texted back.

Jason was back in school on Friday, but we didn't get to talk much because we had to watch a video in art about sketching live models, and then he had to meet with Mrs. Smith during lunch.

When I got home from school, my phone rang unexpectedly. It was Jason.

"Hello?" I answered cautiously. It was the first time he'd ever called.

"Hey... hope I'm not bothering you," his voice filtered down from the receiver.

"Nah, you're not." I was bemused, wondering what was so important that he had to call instead of text.

"I was wondering if you could come by the library... I have to ask you something."

I looked at the phone in surprise. "Ask me something? Uh, about chemistry?" He'd done so well in chem that he didn't need to take the final exam, so what could it be?

"Umn, no. Not really. Can I tell you when I see you there?" Jason's tone didn't give anything away, and I was intrigued.

"Okay," I agreed. "When?"

He hesitated. "Like in an hour or so...?"

"Okay," I confirmed.

"Great, I'll see you." With that, he hung up.

I stared at the phone for a few moments after the call ended, contemplating what this was all about. Jason had never asked me to meet him at the library without it having to do with chemistry.

Dad was home, so I had to figure out a way to tell him I was going to the library. I knocked on the bedroom door and entered to find him adjusting his tie in the mirror. "Hey, are you going somewhere?" I asked him.

"Yeah, a friend of mine in Pitts invited me for dinner tonight. He's trying to apply for a job at the university," Dad answered, fixing his shirt collar. "I'll miss that interesting panel discussion at the mosque this evening. Tell me how it goes."

I sat down on the edge of his bed. "Nah, I don't feel like going today."

Dad glanced at me. "You want to come with me? I can drop you off at the mall."

"No thanks. Your dinners take forever and I'll be stuck at the mall alone," I said irritably.

Dad just smiled with his customary patience.

"You can take your own car," he offered.

"It's okay, I'll be fine here." I paused, then added casually, "I might just go to the library."

Dad nodded his agreement and kissed me on the forehead as I left his room to go back to mine.

I stood in front of my closet, surveying the rainbow of colors and textures. Even if Jason didn't like me like *that*, I could still look good, right?

I eventually chose a black knit maxi dress that flowed flatteringly over my hips, pulling on a clingy black cardigan and pinning my silky print scarf with a gorgeous gray brooch. Satisfied with my appearance, I drove to the library.

Pinpricks of guilt plagued my conscience as I thought about how I had told my father only half of the truth. The heavy weight of remorse settled around my shoulders, but was joined by the irresistible pull to meet Jason: a magnetic attraction that, even in the moments when I knew I should, I had no real wish to fight.

I will keep my distance and won't let him touch me, I insisted feebly consoling my conscience. I found our regular table, the one with the full-length mirror next to it. I sat down, settled my bag on the table and texted Dad that I had reached the library. I folded my arms on the table and rested my cheek against them, thinking about why I was at the library and what was I doing with my life. I should've been at the mosque. Why didn't I just tell Jason I was busy? I had a commitment at the mosque! What happened to me dying to be at the mosque on Friday nights?

"Hey," Jason's deep voice broke through my train of thought.

I lifted my head to see him standing across the table, wearing dark blue jeans and a black button-down shirt, casually untucked, the sleeves rolled up to his forearms, as usual. He put a small box on the table and dropped his keys next to it.

"Am I late?" he asked, pulling out the chair next to me.

I shook my head silently. He looked even more handsome than I remembered, though I'd seen him at school just a short while ago. The combination of dark jeans and black shirt brought out the color of his eyes, and I whimsically thought that with my grey brooch and black dress, we looked like a color-coordinated couple. I ignored the twinge of guilt I felt at the word *couple*, and continued to admire him.

"Thanks for coming on such a short notice," Jason said as he settled into the chair.

I shrugged my shoulders and smiled.

"Cat got your tongue?" he teased.

I laughed, but still didn't say anything.

Jason's own smile faded as our gazes locked, something that happened more and more often every time we met, I'd noticed. I shook myself slightly to get over my reaction. "So you said you had something to ask me? Is everything okay?"

"Yeah, I did." Jason hesitated. "Remember when I asked you if you could ask that girl at school about me?" he started.

I arched an eyebrow at him. *Obviously* I remembered.

He gave a rueful grin at my response. "So I guess I'm ready to tell you about her. I got something for her, and I was wondering if you'd tell me how it looks, like whether she'd like it or not."

Yup, no doubt about it. I was definitely just the good friend who was going to act as a messenger between him and his lady love. "So what did you buy?" I asked curiously

"I...ummm," he looked down and smiled, then pushed the little box toward me.

I looked at him quizzically.

He nodded at me. "Open it."

It was a rectangular bracelet box covered in creamy white satin, tied with a ribbon of deep ruby. The box looked expensive all by itself. Gently, I lifted the lid to find a beautiful silver bracelet; a delicate chain decorated with small flowers, set with precious stones of sapphire, ruby, and amethyst. It was breathtaking.

"Wow..." I breathed, admiring it in the light.

"Is it nice?" he asked earnestly, leaning forward towards me.

"It's beautiful," I said honestly. I didn't really have a taste for jewelry; in fact, I could usually care less when it came to things like necklaces and bracelets. But this...this was *gorgeous*.

"Do you think she'll like it?" Jason asked anxiously.

"Of course! She'll love it," I assured him.

Privately, I was starting to feel irritated and resentful. Where were we going with this? Was he going to ask me to take this clearly valuable piece of jewelry to the mysterious girl at school and find out if she liked him? If she did, was I supposed to give it to her? I felt suddenly sullen. Shouldn't he be giving it to her himself? It would make such a romantic scene—his declaration of love, the presentation of his ornate gift, and then a magical first kiss... followed by several more passionate ones, I was sure.

"Put it on," Jason said unexpectedly.

"What?" I was surprised. "Me?"

"Yeah, I want to see how it looks on someone's hand." His face looked guileless and I narrowed my eyes at him.

"You could have asked the sales woman to model it for you!"

He shrugged and smiled. "The saleswoman was a man."

A part of me was falling apart. I wished I hadn't come. I wished I hadn't agreed to help him woo the mysterious girl he was clearly so in love with.

"Please?" Jason asked, nodding at the bracelet.

Reluctantly, I took out the bracelet and laid it over my wrist, struggling to put it on. Bracelets were always annoying to wear because it was hard to close them single-handed.

"Here, let me help." He pulled his chair closer to me, gently lifting both ends of the clasp and clicking them closed. When he was done, he held my wrist up to admire the bracelet adorning it. I could feel my senses heightening, sharpening, acutely aware of the way his thumb brushed against the pulse point on my wrist.

I tugged my hand away from him gently, not looking at him.

Jason gestured to the mirror next to me, and I obediently turned towards it. "Do you see the girl in the mirror?" he asked. What was he up to?

"No, Jason, I see my ghost," I snapped back.

Jason leaned forward, his face nearly next to mine. I could feel his breath stirring the delicate folds of my hijab. "Now ask her if she loves me," he whispered.

I blinked, not comprehending his words. "Ask who?"

"The girl in the mirror," he said softly. We were both looking into the mirror, at my reflection.

The girl in the mirror... the realization dawned upon me so suddenly that I felt light-headed. The girl in the mirror was *me*.

Jason reached out with his hand and put his finger under my chin, turning it towards him gently.

"Does she?" he whispered again.

I could say nothing, do nothing except stare at him as he looked back at me, his face so hopeful, so ardent, his smile so sure of my answer. He was so close to me that I could feel the heat of his body, my knees brushed against his. *Do something*, a voice in my mind pleaded. Shaking, I pushed my chair back, stumbling away from him, around the desk.

"Sarah?" Jason's voice was bewildered.

"She can't!" My answer tore from my throat with a firmness that I almost didn't recognize.

"She *can't* isn't the same as *she doesn't*." Jason expressed every word slowly and clearly. I looked at him over my shoulder, then looked away quickly. It made it so much harder to resist when I could see his expression, the heartache that I suddenly understood he shared with me.

"The end result is the same," I said slowly.

Jason got off his chair and came around to face me, holding me by the shoulders. "Sarah," he said urgently, trying to make eye contact, but I looked away and shook off his grip. "Sarah," he repeated, his voice both cajoling and demanding. "Can't you just put all our differences aside right now and focus on me? On us?"

He bent his head forward, tipping my face upward with one strong, gently calloused finger so I was forced to look at him.

There was a storm rising within me, a convulsion of triumph, fierce joy, and at the same time, a tsunami of guilt and a terrible fear.

"Sarah, you don't understand how much I've thought and rethought this over and over again, but I...I just couldn't get you out of my mind. You know how everyone says that love is crazy, changes everything you ever thought you knew about yourself... That's what happened to me, Sarah." Jason's voice was mesmerizing; soft and gentle, deep and compelling, the kind of voice that makes you want to forget the consequences."This entire school year with you was so unexpectedly beautiful. I didn't plan on falling in love with you, but once I spent some time with you, I couldn't control it. I couldn't control what was happening to me, what I felt for you." Jason's words came faster now, almost breathless with excitement. "I know you felt the same way too, Sarah. I know you fell in love with me."

The confidence in his words, the sure knowledge that he had my affection, stunned me. No one ever had the audacity to claim such a thing before. Every word he spoke made me feel distant and dizzy, and by the time I came back to my senses, he was taking my shaking hands in his own.

"Sarah, I can't fight it anymore." Holding both my hands in one of his own, he reached up to stroke the side of my face with his other hand. I inhaled shakily and wondered if I was going to faint.

Sarah, get out of here. The little voice that never truly left me was shrill and urgent, reminding me of who I was and what I held dear.

Oblivious to my internal turmoil, Jason touched my cheek gently. The urge to look back into his eyes was almost overpowering. *Just give in,* the part of me that was madly in love with Jason begged. *Just once. Just a first kiss. Nothing more...*

Sarah Ali, you are a Muslim woman. The One Who has blessed you with so much is watching you right now. Sarah, you're better than this—don't displease the One Who truly loves you and has always been Merciful to you.

The words crashed through my mind, imbued with a strange and powerful aura, drawn from a part of my soul that I had not truly let go of yet. *Run, Sarah. Escape the temptation, the way Prophet Yusuf, alaihi salam, turned away from the temptation of a woman. Be strong, Sarah! So you won't be lost!*

I felt heat rush through my body; not the flush of pleasure that I was so close to giving in to, but a sense of empowerment that released me from the spell of the moment. I don't know if it was my commitment to my faith, or the strength of my father's love for me and his ceaseless prayers for my protection, but I do know that it was only my Lord's protection and His Mercy that inspired me that night.

I stood tall, pulling myself away from Jason, and stepped back. My eyes caught his for the last time, sorrowful but firm. I turned around and fled, stumbling past chairs and tables, nearly falling, but I didn't stop. I didn't stop running until I got in my car, and then I drove, drove as far away as I could.

32

I drove on blindly that night, not knowing where I was going, knowing only that I needed to get as far away from the library—and Jason—as possible. It was only much later, when I glanced at a passing sign, that I realized I had just entered Ohio. I was about to hit the end of the road leading to Lake Erie!

We used to come here sometimes for family picnics. It was about a hundred miles away from Wickley, an hour and a half drive, and I hadn't even realized I'd been driving for that long. I pulled over and stepped out onto the beach.

It was fully dark by now. Out here, on the quiet beach, the orange-purple haze of Cleveland City faded up into an onyx sky scattered with diamond-hard stars. The cold, glittering beach spread out before me, completely empty.

All I wanted right now was to wipe away everything that had happened in the library, to wake up from the nightmare. Wandering down the beach, barely aware of where my feet led me, I realized that it was high time I faced the facts.

The thunder of waves against the shoreline was deafening—a mournful, vengeful growl. Whether it was because of the late spring tides or the relentless tug of the full moon, I didn't know. Neither the water nor my mind were peaceful. My thoughts were as tossed as the waves, and I before I knew it, the hem of my dress was sodden, tugging me towards the silver crests of the waves. I was numb to the ice cold water; the storm within me was so powerful I didn't notice the danger I was in.

I was barely able to process my emotions. My lips turned upwards in an exhilarated smile, even as my eyes prickled with tears. The vain, petty girl within me was smug and satisfied, triumphant that *Jason*—gorgeous, clever, charming Jason—loved *me*, not some other unknown girl at school. So much for the Trashies! I, Sarah Ali—smart, funny, stubborn Sarah Ali—was the one he loved.

But the core of my heart was disappointed and ashamed. How could I have been so weak? I had been raised to believe in higher moral standards, in being honest not only with others, but with myself and God. Instead, I had played a dangerous game—hoping, pretending that the feelings were only one-sided, that no one would get hurt, that I could indulge myself just once and get away with it unscathed. I had convinced myself that Jason could never develop feelings for a girl so visibly different from himself. I had spent more and more time with him, justifying it by saying that we were only together in public, that we were just classmates, and that my beliefs would deter me from feeling any kind of attaction towards him—or at least from expressing it if I did.

What I'd forgotten was that God knows our natures better than we do. I'd forgotten that the Creator, the One Who fashioned our hearts, knew how vulnerable we were to one another, regardless of our religious differences. How easily we could fall into destructive situations.

I had deluded myself into thinking that the headscarf I wore was enough to protect me from temptation, not realizing that more than my *hijab*, it was my actions and the strength of my obedience to God that would protect me. This was where I had failed. This was where I had preferred to think that my actions were harmless, when in fact they had placed me at the edge of a dangerous cliff. If had listened to Jasmine's advice, so long ago when she first noticed my attraction to Jason, I could have spared myself so much of the pain she had predicted!

Jason's confession made me realize just what kind of tangled web I had woven for myself. The questions my conscience had brought up repeatedly, and which I had consistently ignored, came back to me with a vengeance. The feelings I had insisted on denying were impossible to disavow now.

My legs buckled and I collapsed in the cold lake. Icy water splashed over me, turning my entire body numb. I sat with my head bowed, still fighting a battle between faith and temptation.

I didn't know if I was ready to face the consequences of my actions, but I didn't have any other solution to the mess I'd created, either.

The rising tide washed over my knees, splashing my face and, with a start, I realized just how cold I was. I could barely move my limbs.

With difficulty, I pushed myself to a standing position, nearly collapsing again from the weight of my sodden dress and the shaking of my body. I stumbled toward my car and turned the heater on, feeling pins and needles all over my skin as warmth returned. The blinking green numbers on my car clock told me that it was past midnight—oh no! Dad would have been home by now and going crazy with worry, and I hadn't told anyone where I was going.

I dug through my purse looking for my phone, my dismay increasing when I realized that it was nowhere in the car. I'd forgotten it on the library desk, and here I was, in the middle of nowhere, probably in danger of catching pneumonia, and with no way to call Dad.

I blew on my shaking hands and forced myself to drive back home as quickly as I dared, hoping Dad would be okay. He must have been terrified. How could I do this to him, when I already knew how much he was suffering because of Adam's move? Despite my attempt to rush, it still took more than an hour to get home.

Sheriff Bernard's car was parked in the driveway when I pulled up, and my heart was struck as if by lightening with guilt and terror. I took a deep breath. I had dreaded facing Dad, but now I had to face the sheriff as well. I'd never really liked him, especially since he'd made no move to call out the AIA on their illegal behavior.

Oh Allah! My lips moved in a silent plea, a *du'a.* I realized that I hadn't been supplicating much lately, in addition to not concentrating much on my ritual prayers. I tried to think of something else to say, something to ask Allah for, but all that came out was a general cry of desperation.

I got out of the car and opened the front door as quietly as possible. As I passed by the foyer and turned left towards the living room, I saw Dad and Sheriff Bernard. Dad had his back to the door, but the Sheriff was sitting on the couch that faced the entrance, and he saw me first.

"Sarah!" the Sheriff exclaimed.

Dad whirled around and nearly ran to me, wrapping his arms around me tightly.

"Sarah, are you okay?" his voice was quiet but full of worry, his dark eyes brimming with concern. "Oh God, Sarah, what happened?" My dress was still cold and wet; my face and hands red and chapped by the freezing water.

"Are you hurt?" Dad touched the flaking skin of my face. "I'm fine Dad," I said gently, turning my face away from his hands. "I'm sorry I was out so late and didn't even call you." I was so ashamed of myself that I couldn't bring myself to look into Dad's eyes.

He didn't ask where I'd been, or what I'd been doing, or why I was late. I was home safely, and that was enough for him. Dad's heartfelt relief at my safe return only intensified my burden of shame.

The Sheriff stood up hastily, puffing out his chest and trying to seem authoritative. "Sarah, did someone force you to leave? Were you kidnapped? Were you planning to run off?" His mustache bristled with every word.

"No... I... uh..." I stumbled over the words. "I was alone, by myself and nothing happened. I was safe."

"Where were you?" the Sheriff asked again. I wasn't sure if he was just curious, or if it was part of the routine questioning. I looked at Dad helplessly, and he intervened.

"It's okay, Dave. She's home and she's safe," he told the Sheriff firmly.

The Sheriff looked doubtful. "Look, Omar, these are routine questions I have to ask so I can close up the report."

I guessed that I had no choice but to tell the truth. "I was at Lake Erie," I said finally. "I drove there and lost track of time."

The Sheriff's bushy eyebrows rose in shock. "Lake Erie?!"
I nodded.

"Dave, can't you forget about the report?" Dad interrupted. "She wasn't abducted, and she didn't run away. She's home safely and that's enough for me. Why don't you just forget about filing the report?"

I thought the sherriff would object, but there was a decisiveness in Dad's voice that forced him to comply. He nodded and bid us farewell.

After seeing him off, Dad came back to the living room. I had curled up on the couch under the afghan, anticipating the inevitable barrage of questions that he probably had in store for me. He settled down across from me on a chair silently, while I avoided making eye contact. I didn't have the courage to look at him.

There was a moment of silence for a while before Dad finally spoke. "I don't know what you were doing, and I don't want to know what you were doing, either." He spoke slowly, his voice heavy with extreme disappointment. "But whatever it was, I sincerely pray that it did not betray the bond of trust we have shared all your life."

I knew exactly what he meant. "Dad, I was alone. I swear." For the first time that night, I was able to look at him unflinchingly. He seemed suddenly so weary and so old, but there was still no trace of anger on his face.

Dad looked deeply into my eyes and nodded slowly, then got up and kissed my forehead. "Go rest," he said tiredly, and made his way upstairs.

I didn't move from my spot on the couch. That was it? Wasn't he going to ask me anything else? Wasn't this the moment when a parent was supposed to bombard their child with questions, demanding to know the what, where, when, why, and how? Wasn't he supposed to get mad at me, or yell and scream?

In all the seventeen years of my life, there hadn't been a single moment when Dad didn't know where I was. Today, he'd lost track of me for hours. He'd stayed up 'till three in the morning, not knowing where his only daughter was—his daughter who had already been suspected of inappropriate behavior by her own brother. He must've gone through hell, and yet he didn't utter even a single angry word! Wasn't this the moment when fathers were expected to lose all control? Wasn't this the time when the whacked-out media insisted that Muslim fathers had their daughters killed? But Dad's only reaction was to kiss me and tell me to rest.

More than any screams or beating of fists could have hurt me, Dad's quiet, pure love and kindness wracked my conscience with agony. What had I done? There was no need for anyone to 'honor kill' me—I was buried alive in my own guilt.

33

The next morning, I woke up to a stiff back and an aching body. I managed to sit up, but a stabbing pain coursed through my head and shoulders and I felt dizzy. The long night before, the stress, the drive to and back from the lake, and of course the hypothermia I had most likely suffered, had all caught up with me. My body burned all over, and I could barely drag myself up to pray before collapsing back in bed.

Ever since Adam had left, Dad and I had been going out for breakfast on Saturdays. That morning, though, I couldn't get out of bed, and Dad didn't come by to check on me, either. I waited all morning, hoping that he'd stop by, longing for his attention, but he never came. Later in the afternoon, he sent Paula to check on me. When she told him that I was sick, he came to my room silently, touched my burning forehead, and then left without a word. He sent Paula back with food and medicine, but he didn't return.

I didn't want food, and I didn't want medicine—I wanted my dad. I wanted his gentle hands stroking my hair, his quiet voice murmuring supplications of healing and protection over me. I wanted his love.

I spent the whole day alone in my room, shivering and sweating, as broken down physically as I was torn apart emotionally. This wasn't normal, this wasn't how my dad behaved. Never in a million years would he leave me alone when I was sick... right?

Everything and everyone was changing around me, I realized. First, I'd lost my best friend, then my reputation. My brother left, and now even my dad, the one person I loved most in the whole world, had deserted me. All because of Jason.

After Paula had left for the day, Dad came to my room one more time, but only to check my temperature. I was dozing on and off, and was barely able to crack open my burning eyelids, but Dad didn't talk to me or even make eye contact with me, he didn't even kiss my forehead.

The next day, Paula was back to take care of me, and I spent the whole day in bed. On Monday, I had no desire to go back to school, so despite my improving physical condition, I stayed hidden beneath my quilt and tried to block out reality with sleep.

I knew that eventually I'd have no excuse left to sleep in all day. Soon enough, I'd have to get out of bed and face reality.

Sitting up, I noticed that I was still wearing the bracelet Jason had given me. I examined it in the late afternoon light, admiring the delicacy of the chain and the fine handiwork of the flowers with their bejeweled petals. Thinking about how Jason had tricked me into wearing it, I caught myself smiling. Every word of Jason's profession of love came back to me clearly, and I felt a surge of warmth as I recalled how he had said he couldn't fight his feelings for me. Simply remembering his words released an overwhelming surge of emotion within me. Would I ever be able to control my feelings, or was I consigned to being controlled by them instead?

I had always thought that I was strong and aloof enough to avoid this situation, but I guess every girl thinks she's impervious to weakness and vulnerability... until they challenge her. When girls at school had talked about losing control around the guys they liked, I'd laughed it off. I was embarrassed to admit it, but I *had* thought of myself as being better than them, assuming that the only reason they were so weak was because they didn't have a belief system that kept them strong. I always thought that I was more disciplined and sensible, and that simply declaring myself a Muslim rendered me immune to this particular trap. But the truth was that when I was faced with temptation, I had proven just as susceptible as the next person. And now I had to do my best to regain my strength.

34

The next morning, I finally dragged myself out of the bed. It was senior picture day, and I couldn't skip school, especially since, despite a rocky semester, I'd made it to being class valedictorian, and had been specifically instructed to be there for picture day.

Sighing, I stood in front of my closet and debated whether I should even bother dressing up or not. I wore a classy floral peach dress, and chose a matching beige scarf for my hijab. As I pinned it in the style I'd gotten used to wearing for the last few months, I paused and considered my reflection. My conscience, so sharp and warning before, was more gentle now, but just as serious. *Sarah, your Lord protected you on Friday night, not just from your own lust for Jason, but from your father's anger as well. Pull that piece of cloth down over your dress' neckline and show some gratitude to the One Who has shielded you from all harm.* I fixed my hijab so that it draped properly over my chest, and quietly made my way to the kitchen.

I didn't know if Dad was still avoiding me on purpose or if it was just coincidence, but he wasn't home when I went down for breakfast. I was ready at a miraculously early time and, with no reason to linger at home, I went straight to school.

Everyone was in the cafeteria, hanging out before the bell rang. A couple of people asked how my weekend was and where I had been on Monday, but no one showed any sign of knowing what had happened to me. It seemed like the sherriff had kept his word and hadn't said anything about me going missing. Absently, I found an empty seat and sat down, not paying attention to those around me.

"Hey," Jason said from next to me. I jumped, startled. Turning around, I realized with dismay that I had seated myself right next to him. I caught my breath when I noticed that he, too, had dressed up for picture day, in a pair of dark jeans, a formal white shirt topped with a well-fitting vest, and an unexpectedly elegant tie.

"Oh... hey," I answered, awkwardly. This was embarrassing... he must have thought that I *chose* to sit next to him.

"Say cheese!" Scott yelled from across the table, snapping a picture of Jason and me on his phone. Taken unawares, I froze in my seat, blinking in shock.

"Wait, wait, don't move! Let me take a picture!" screamed Ashley, and her phone clicked as well. She shoved her phone into Scott's hands and squeezed herself between me and Jason, laughing as she threw her arms around the two of us. The screams of laughter made me smile too, and as others crowded around to take pictures, I started looking for my phone before I remembered that I'd left it at the libary.

"I have your phone," Jason managed to tell me in between all the yelling and screaming.

"You do?" How?" Sometimes I ask the dumbest questions.

"You left it at the library," he avoided my gaze as he pulled my phone out of his pocket. "It ran out of battery pretty quickly."

What else was new about my phone... it was always dying. I stretched out my hand to take the phone from him, and as I did, my sleeve was pulled up slightly. I heard Jason inhale sharply; following his eyes, I realized that the bracelet he had given me was still on my wrist.

I should have taken it off before; I tried to tell myself that in the flurry of events that had taken place since Friday night, I had simply forgotten to remove it. I hadn't had the time or energy to think about what to do with it. That was why it was still on my wrist.

Our eyes met—Jason's bewildered, full of questions. I didn't want to mislead him, but by the time I opened my mouth to explain that it wasn't what it looked like, Mrs. Tanner had come to fetch me for my pictures. Traditionally, the principal and vice principal took pictures with the valedictorian first. I glanced over my shoulder helplessly as Jason watched me walk away.

School had already started, but the seniors had to get their pictures taken before going to class. The school portraits were taken on the soccer field; it took ages before the photographers were able to set up their equipment properly and re-arrange the students several times in order to get everyone in the frame. The soccer team came next; the players were all dressed up, their hair slicked back. Jason received extra attention, of course. As the team captain, he had managed to lead our team to the state semi-finals.

I couldn't help but admire the fact that, though he was the star of the day, Jason didn't overreact to all the attention.

We had missed more than two periods by the time we were done. Ashley joined me on my walk back toward the school building, but before I could take more than a few steps, I felt a strong, warm hand close around my hand and pull me in the opposite direction.

Shocked, I looked up to find myself staring into Jason's stormy gray eyes. His expression was one I'd never seen before—anger. I tried to shake off his grip, but it only tightened, and I flushed when I realized that others in the field had noticed what was going on. I could hear low murmurs of surprise; everyone knew and respected my rules and limits of physical engagement. Guys who had been friends with me all my life had never broken these rules, but Jason—whom I'd known for less than a year—had the audacity to hold my hand in public... for the *second* time.

Could I blame him, though? Had I ever set boundaries for him? Or had I been allowing him to cross the limits from the very first day?

"What are you doing?" I hissed, yanking my hand away from him.

"I'm *trying* to have a conversation with you!" he snarled, clearly agitated.

"You want to talk?" I demanded. My face was turning red with fury.

"*Yes,* I want to talk," he growled back, letting go of my hand and shoving his into his pockets.

"Fine, then let's talk." I crossed my arms over my chest and glared at him.

"Yeah, let's talk," he repeated sarcastically.

I bit back the acid retort I had in mind, and looked around quickly. We were standing on the side of the soccer field with no privacy, and everyone was turning around to see us, so I jerked my thumb at the gym doors and walked toward them quickly.

"Talk!" I ordered, folding my arms over my chest again. There was no way I was going to let him hold my hand again.

"Me?" Jason snapped. "I think I already *did* all the talking. Maybe it's your turn to tell me something." He breathed in deeply, struggling to calm himself.

"Don't hold my hand next time." Well, he did tell me to say *something*.

Jason's eyes looked wounded. "I don't understand, Sarah. You're wearing the bracelet I gave you, but you won't let me hold your hand?" His bewildered gaze lingered on the bracelet, which glittered under the fluorescent lighting of the gym.

I sighed. "You're right. I'm sorry that I gave you the wrong impression." I figured I may as well land the final blow. "I didn't keep the bracelet on purpose, I just didn't take it off." I kept my voice cold, but that didn't stop the small voice in my mind from saying, *Forgot to take it off for four days? Yeah, right.*

I struggled to slip the bracelet off my wrist, and held it out for him to take back.

Jason didn't make a move to take it. Instead, he looked deeply into my eyes, looking genuinely troubled. "Sarah, why is it so hard for you to admit that you have feelings for me?"

It was moments like these when I lost control over myself. It was the look in his eyes, the truth of the feelings that shone in them... it was my failure to lower my gaze so that I wouldn't have to see that look. That was how it had all started. Taking a shaking breath, I closed my eyes and turned away.

"Look into my eyes and tell me you don't," Jason demanded softly. I felt a rush of bitterness; he *knew* I couldn't do that. I was scared of looking into his eyes; the profound depths of them pushed me towards things I had no right to want.

"It doesn't matter how I feel about you, Jason, because..."
I didn't know what to say. I had never anticipated this conversation occurring.

"Because what?" The hope in his voice was too much for me to bear.

"Because there's nothing we can do about it."

"You mean, because I don't belong to your faith?" he challenged me.

I shook my head hastily, "It's not that...." I hated for anyone to think negatively about Islam, and I especially didn't want Jason, who had just learned to respect Muslims, to believe those things as well.

"If I was a *Muzlim*, then it would have been fine," he scowled, shoving his hands in his pockets.

"If you were a Muslim, we wouldn't even be having this conversation," I corrected him.

"Why? Because Muzlims don't fall in love?" he asked sarcastically.

"Not this way," I objected.

"Yeah they do." I hated to admit that he was right, but he was.

I rubbed my forehead. "You're right." I tried to rephrase. "Practicing Muslim don't..." I was wrong again, and I knew it. Even practicing Muslims make mistakes.

I took a deep breath and made yet another effort, "I was wrong to allow any feelings for you to begin with." I felt like I was engaging in a rational conversation with him for the first time. It was *really* hard not to look into his eyes.

"Can't you just for a second forget about me not being a *Muzlim,* and talk to me?" he pleaded in a tone that tore my heart apart. I closed my eyes again, trying to dig up the last remnants of strength I had within me, lest I suddenly find myself giving up and throwing myself into his arms.

"Okay, Jason. Tell me: what next?" His persistence was aggravating, not least because it was making it harder for me to control the rising storm within me.

"You can't touch me, you can't kiss me, and you can't even hold me. You can't be my boyfriend, and I can't be your girl-friend." For the first time, I looked straight into his eyes, with a strange strength that made *him* look away from me. It was his turn to be silent this time. He didn't have any answers, and I found myself gaining a fraction of the strength that Sarah Ali *used* to have when boys tried to hit on her.

"Do you want to love me without any physical contact?" I pressed, though I knew that even if he agreed to that, I still wouldn't be able to engage in a relationship like that.

"We could get married," Jason insisted desperately. Was he trying to act smart?

"I can't marry you, either!" I cried out in frustration. Why wouldn't he just give up and walk away from me?

"Can't you just put your faith aside when you are with me? Can't you think beyond your religion for once in your life?" Jason pleaded.

"Beyond my religion?" I was shocked that he could even ask me that. Did such a concept even exist for me? My faith *was* me. I believed in my religion with all my heart and soul; Islam shaped me, and it was a core part of my identity.

"Jason, you knew from the beginning that I was committed to my faith," I reminded him. "My religion defines me. It is who I am. I never gave you any misleading impressions when it came to that."

Jason looked agonized. "What kind of religion separates two people who love each other?" he demanded.

"My religion didn't separate us." I said curtly. "My religion made it very clear that I was not allowed to have a relationship outside of marriage or marry a person who was not a Muslim. *I* made the mistake of entertaining feelings from the very beginning."

"Because love is blind, Sarah!" His words were persuasive, making it difficult for me to answer. The clamor of my own desires within me was overwhelming, and I found myself looking into his eyes again as they gazed at me ardently.

Desperately, I whispered a silent prayer. *Oh God!*

An answer came to me suddenly. "If love is blind, Jason, why don't you convert to Islam?" The possibility crossed my mind for the first time.

"What?" Jason looked shocked. "Me, convert to Izlam?" He looked uncertain and uncomfortable, as though I'd just asked him to do something horribly wrong.

I narrowed my eyes at him, wondering at the strength of his reaction. "Yes. If you truly love me, then why don't you change your faith and become a Muslim?"

Jason frowned. "I respect your faith, Sarah, but I don't think that I could ever become a *Muzlim*." He looked away from me.

"Why not? If you respect my faith and you love me, then wouldn't it be easy to accept Islam?" Suddenly, I wanted nothing more than for him to give it a thought.

Jason rubbed his hand through his hair in frustration. "I can't," he said adamantly.

"Why?" I was wounded. What happened to sweet, charming Jason, who had just professed his love for me?

"Because there are issues in your faith I don't agree with," he said decidedly. "Besides, Sarah," he turned back toward me. "Would you really want me to change my religion only out of love for you, and not because of a true commitment to the faith?"

I felt as though my only hope had been dashed to smithereens. "It doesn't matter what I want, does it?" I looked away, my voice weakening and my heart sinking. Jason hadn't entertained the option of converting for even a second.

"Yes, it does," he said, suddenly fervent. "It matters to me." He grabbed me by the shoulders, looking as desperate as I felt, but I stepped back.

"Then become a Muslim!" I demanded, glaring at him.

Jason whirled around angrily, running one hand through his hair and then setting both hands on hips. "Sarah, religion isn't something you switch around just like that! It's a matter of personal faith and belief."

My smile was both bitter and sad. We were so different from each other, and yet so similar. Our principles, our faiths, were important to each of us.

"Then we can't talk about 'us' anymore," I said finally. "This ends here." The certainty in my tone surprised me more than it surprised him.

"Wow," Jason snapped sarcastically. "Some great religion you have." His face twisted in an angry sneer.

I couldn't believe he had stooped to insulting my religion, when he knew how much it meant to me. "I don't appreciate your mockery of my faith," I snarled, overcome with fury.

"Mockery?" he repeated. "I'm just stating the facts." He crossed his arms, still looking at me with the unpleasant expression on his face.

I looked away. This conversation wasn't going anywhere. I needed to hold onto something—a table, a chair, anything. The gym had *not* been a good place for this talk.

"I have to go," I said, turning away. "I need to get back to class." I hoped that I'd finally be able to leave, but Jason grabbed my hand and pulled me back to him.

"Jason, let me go!" I cried out in frustration. "You need to stop holding my hand!" Though I emphasized every word, the strength behind it was nearly not as emphatic as it should have been, and he knew it. His eyes darkened from gray to metallic and he smiled coldly, completely unapologetic.

"I've touched your heart, and you're worrying about me touching your hand?" he murmured. I looked at Jason with desperate desire *and* with anger, and without another word, I fled from the gym as fast as I possibly could.

35

Fourth period had started and I nearly ran all the way to art class. Something must have held Jason back, because he came to class late, while I was arguing with Mrs. Lynn about assigning me a different partner.

"Sarah, both you and Jason were absent yesterday when everyone picked their partners, so naturally you were left to partner up with each other. I'm sorry, but you don't have any other option," Mrs. Lynn explained.

"Can I ask if anyone is willing to switch their partners with me?" I insisted.

"They already started sketching, and today's class is almost halfway over. They've been working on their sketches all along. I don't think it would be fair to ask them to restart," she told me calmly

"I can't draw Jason because I have religious restrictions against drawing human images." I used my final excuse, knowing that it wasn't really valid because there were many opinions on the subject, hoping that she'd let me off the hook.

"That's fine. You can draw any object that you would like," Mrs. Lynn said patiently. "Could Jason draw an object too, instead of drawing me?" I pleaded.

"But I don't have any religious restrictions," Jason's mocking voice came from behind me. "*My* religion doesn't forbid every other thing." I refused to even turn back to look at him; his comments had definitely crossed a line now, and I was seething.

Mrs. Lynn was observing me closely. She had opened her mouth to say something, but closed it with a snap. She knew me well enough to know that I wasn't the type of person who would take such a comment without offence. Furious but trying to keep myself calm to avoid making a scene in front of everyone, I rubbed at my forehead, saying nothing.

Mrs. Lynn seemed confused as she looked from me to Jason. For the whole school year, she'd seen us interact pleasantly in her class, voluntarily working on projects together. Now all of a sudden I was asking her to assign me a different partner, *and* ignoring his offensive comments about my religion.

"Fine," I said haughtily. "He can draw me, and I'll draw something else."

I went back to my table, walking conceitedly and callously, and sat on the chair with my legs crossed. Jason followed me, grabbing a chair and sitting directly in front of me. Since he was the one who had to sketch a live model, he instructed me on how to sit and where to look, which was, of course, directly at him. I stared at him impassively and waited for the bell to ring while he sketched me in silence. I was annoyed that I couldn't pass over this project entirely, but we both needed the grades from the class. As soon as the bell rang, I picked up my stuff and left.

I hid from Jason for the rest of the day, and avoided Dad at home by pretending to sleep. I didn't know what I was going to achieve by avoiding them. Sooner or later, I'd have to face the the music. But first, I had to face myself. My conscience was demanding an accountability of all that had happened in past few months.

Jason continued to sketch me the next day. For lack of anything else to do, I watched him while he drew intently. He sat with one leg propped over the other, his sleeves rolled up to his elbows, and his golden hair unkempt. Immersed in his sketching. His brows were furrowed together, and he looked both thoughtful and intent as he put pencil to paper, glancing up at me only occasionally. He seemed even more strikingly attractive than ever before.

Did I find myself admiring him even more just because he looked good as he worked, or because all of a sudden he was so out of my reach? Although, I corrected myself, he had never been within my reach to begin with.

Jason must have felt me staring at him, because he looked up suddenly, and I found myself once again transfixed by his gaze. I didn't look away this time. Instead, I looked back at him. I don't know what he saw in my own chocolate brown eyes, but in his I saw a deep well of sadness. Maybe we shared the same pain, but the difference was that there was undying hope in his eyes, and an implacable firmness in mine.

Jason looked down at his paper. "You don't have to stay here if you don't want to, Sarah. I don't need to *look* at you to draw you," he said quietly. "I can see your face even with my eyes closed."

I felt my heart twist, almost unbearably. What was happening to my life? None of this was supposed to happen. He was supposed to leave without ever knowing that I had feelings for him. It was so simple in my mind,... how did it all go wrong? But I knew how. It went wrong when I crossed sacred boundaries, thinking I'd repent properly once Jason left.

My head started pounding. I got up and excused myself from the class, going to the nurse and telling her that I didn't feel well. She was kind enough to send me home early.

Later that day, I went to see my dad. All other problems in my life aside, I couldn't handle my father not speaking to me. I would rather have died than have my dad avoid me for so long. This had never happened before; we had spent five days in silence. I realized that I owed him an apology. Impulsively, without any idea of what I was going to say, I burst into his room. He was sitting in bed reading a book when I walked in.

"Dad..." I hesitated, and he looked up from his book. "I'm so sorry about Friday night. I don't know what to say."

Dad gestured to the recliner, and I sat on it obediently. After a few minutes of silence, Dad asked, "Does he love you?"

His question was so unexpected—and so pointed—that I couldn't even bear to look into his eyes. I was overwhelmed by both embarrassment and confusion—how was I supposed to answer?

I nodded slowly. "He says he does." I didn't want Dad to think that I'd been lying to him all along, that Adam had been right to suspect me, so I explained hastily, "He only told me that on Friday, and...and that's why I drove off." I gulped, biting my lip.

Dad nodded. "You drove off to avoid all the mess?" he asked.

I didn't understand exactly what he meant, but I nodded. Dad looked thoughtful.

"Sarah, to jump in quicksand, thinking that somehow you will manage to swim through it, is never the smartest decision to make," he shook his head. "No one ever just swims through the quicksand." He spoke slowly, emphasizing each and every word and giving me time to reflect.

I looked up at him, and it suddenly dawned on me what I had done wrong. It was as though someone had solved a puzzle for me, a puzzle that I'd been struggling to finish for some time. I looked down again. "What if you unknowingly slipped in it?"

Dad sighed deeply, "Sweetheart, you shouldn't have been walking around it to begin with." His eyes, set deep in his wrinkled face, were painfully thoughtful. "You should have followed the warning signs to stay safe, staying on the path and not approaching the quagmire." There was a moment of silence in the room. Dad studied my face while I played with a fraying thread on my dress.

"What do I do now?" I asked, my voice quivering.

"That is something *you* have to decide, my dear. Do you want to come out, or do you want to drown?

My forehead creased with anxiety. "What if I drown?"

He closed his book and put it away. "Sweetheart, if you drown then..." he took a deep breath. "We'll obviously disappear from your sight."

Two tears rolled down my cheeks. Dad got off the bed and knelt on the floor next to me, his big, warm hands on my knees.

"I'm standing right by the side waiting to help you out, but *you* have to decide whether you want to hold my hand or not, Sarah."

"Dad," I whispered, more tears sliding down my face.

"Sarah, sweetheart," he whispered lovingly, measuring out every word of wisdom. "When God asked Abraham to sacrifice his beloved son, it was not the life or the blood that God needed. He is all above that." He paused, cupping my face in his hands and looking at me, his dark eyes filled with love and wisdom.

"Allah wanted to see whether Abraham would choose to sacrifice that love in his heart for His sake," Dad continued, placing his hand right above my heart.

"Whether Abraham's love for God was deeper than the love he felt for his precious son, the son that was part of him, his own flesh and blood, the son who had never disobeyed or disrespected him, and Abraham did prove that even the love of that perfect child remained less than his love for his Creator."

I couldn't stop the flood of tears.

"If you can understand the depth of Abraham's sacrifice, then you will be able to decide." Dad held my shoulders gently and wiped my tears away with his hands.

"Sarah, if there is one thing I can't see in this world, it's tears in your eyes. I don't know what I will do if I have to see you in trouble on the Day of Judgment, God forbid."

Dad squeezed my hands, got up slowly, kissed my forehead and then left the room.

Curled up in the recliner, I felt as though I finally had an idea of what I needed to do. *Oh Allah, please forgive me and give me the strength to do the right thing... I'm in desperate need of Your help.* The silent plea left my heart; the type of supplication that made me hold my breath, and though I didn't move my lips, my heart ached and my body trembled as I prayed sincerely to my Lord, for the first time in what felt like ages.

36

I skipped school the next day, tossing and turning in bed for hours; pondering over the past, occasionally praying for help and strength, and replaying Dad's words from the day before.

I made an effort to keep away from Jason by not going to school. A part of me refused to push Jason out of my heart, but the voice of my conscience had become stronger and more powerful within the last few days. Whereas before I perceived it as snarky and critical, now it carried the gentle forcefulness of authority, giving me the extra push I needed to ask God's aid to ward off my temptations.

I returned to school on Friday, just in time to turn in my assignment for art, and left immediately after the final bell had rung without talking to anyone.

Over the weekend, Mrs. Lynn called my cell. I answered, wondering what she wanted from me, since I had already turned my sketch in on Friday.

"Hello, Sarah?" Mrs. Lynn said cheerfully.

"Hi, Mrs. Lynn," I replied.

"Hon, is it possible for you to run by my house real quick? I want to show you something."

Though Mrs. Lynn had been my neighbor for years and called me over several times, I had a strange feeling about her summons that day. I was casually dressed in jeans and a t-shirt, so I threw an off-white floral dress over my clothes, put on a black cardigan and casually draped a black headscarf over my head and shoulders. I walked to her house, trying to enjoy the late afternoon sunlight and the warm breeze. I found Mrs. Lynn standing on her porch with a sheet of paper. I smiled and greeted her. "Everything okay, Mrs. Lynn?"

She smiled back. "I wanted to show you something," she said, stepping down into the yard. "I didn't know what to make of it when I first saw it, so I thought maybe I should just ask you, though it's none of my business..." Mrs. Lynn seemed slightly anxious, which piqued my curiosity even further.

"It's okay Ms. Lynn, you can ask me. I don't mind." I smiled.

With an unusual expression of trepidation, Mrs. Lynn handed me the sheet of paper she was holding. I glanced at it and froze. It was a sketch of me—an almost perfect sketch of me without my headscarf, my hair drawn beautifully, dark and luxuriant, a few stray curls falling onto my forehead to give me a more exotic look. The only difference between myself and the sketch was that my hair was drawn slightly shorter than it actually was.

I raised my shocked gaze from the sketch to Mrs. Lynn. "Who sketched this?" I demanded shakily.

She hesitated. "There was only one person in class who sketched you."

"But how did he...?" I couldn't complete my sentence. I felt violated, as though he had stopped in the street and ripped off my hijab in real life. "Can I take this?" Leaving the sketch with Mrs. Lynn made me feel uncertain and unsafe, as though I was leaving a hijab-less photo of myself with someone who wouldn't necessarily keep it private and confidential.

Mrs. Lynn looked apologetic. "I'm sorry, dear, I have to grade it. And I can't give it to you, either. I have to give it back to Jason." She paused, and her curiosity finally showed on her face. "I was just surprised because you've always been so adamant about your headscarf. I remember when you started wearing it in junior high." Her assumption, though unspoken, was clear.

I frowned, not expressing the true extent of my rage. "He didn't see me without my scarf. He never did!"

Mrs. Lynn felt my frustration. "Well then, he has a very strong imagination, Sarah." She sounded as though she couldn't decide whether to admire his sketch, or sympathize with my plight.

I took Jason's address from Mrs. Lynn and rushed back home to get my car. Without a second's hesitation, I hit the accelerator and drove off furiously towards his house. Soon enough, I was standing at his front door, reaching out to ring the doorbell. For a second I hesitated, but I'd always been impulsive, and my anger overwhelmed my common sense. I pressed the little button several times repeatedly, not caring that I was being rude.

Jason opened the door, dressed in a pair of worn jeans and a simple grey t-shirt, an expression of shock on his face as he saw me standing on his doorstep. I took a couple steps back, making sure that I was as far from the entrance to his condo as possible.

"Sarah?" Jason exhaled, looking shocked, confused, and ridiculously hopeful all at once. I quickly disabused him of his hopes.

"How the hell did you draw my picture without my *hijaab*?" My voice was thick with fury and loud with outrage.

Jason's frown relaxed and his lips curved upwards in a slight smile. "Didn't I tell you I don't need to see your face to draw you?"

"You drew more than my face," I said sharply.

"That's how I see you in my dreams." His cloudy grey eyes begged me to soothe his heartache, to lessen his agony. For a passing second, the emotions and sensations I had struggled with days ago at home returned, and I trembled slightly. Quickly enough, however, I recalled the reason I was standing there, and my indignation returned in full force. At any other time, Jason's gaze would have made my heart melt, but right now, all I could think about was how he had disrespected not just my headscarf, but *me*.

I glared at him in righteous fury. "Don't you have any respect for my hijab?" I demanded angrily. My voice was unusually high.

Jason's eyes flashed back at me. "It doesn't symbolize anything to me!" He was right. He didn't understand, and he would never understand. My headscarf meant nothing to him, held no value in his eyes.

My ego was hurt, but this matter was beyond my ego. I had to stop worrying about what he would think of my faith or how he would judge my religion; I had to be honest with him, about the real issue at hand.

"This is exactly why we can't be together," I said harshly. "We're two different people with completely different values. Obviously, what I hold dear to me has no value to you!"

The fire in Jason's eyes disappeared swiftly, and he stepped forward with his hands stretched out apologetically. "Look, I'm sorry if it was that symbolic to you! We can talk about this. We can work on our differences."

Unconsciously, I took a few steps back, "And exactly how many differences are you going to work on? Are you going to work on the fact that I can't have any premarital relationships? That I can only marry a Muslim?"

I was an honest person; I had to make it clear to him that although I *did* have feelings for him, I wasn't committed to my feelings—I was committed to God, to my faith. My beliefs and my religion were the highest priorities in my life, and everything else fell by the wayside.

Jason's face darkened. "There's a world out there beyond *Izlam*," he said, emphasizing every word. "A world of love, where people can be with the ones they love." He wanted so desperately to convince me, but he couldn't understand that my reasons held much greater weight than his protests.

"I know," I said gently, my voice quieting. "But that's in this world. My focus isn't this world, Jason. It's the Hereafter."

"No one should ever have to sacrifice their love, Sarah," he pleaded.

I shook my head in frustration. "But people *do* sacrifice love, and they do it for different reasons. How many times do people sacrifice their love for political positions, their career, for their country or their nation, and their sacrifices are always admired? Why is it that *their* sacrifices are considered brave and praiseworthy, but someone's sacrifices for the sake of their religion are so belittled and mocked?" I tried to use rationality as a way of making him see what I was doing and why.

"Because God doesn't need your sacrifices," he answered immediately.

"Really?" I said skeptically. "Your whole religion is based on Jesus Christ's sacrifice!" My temper was about to flare up again when I noticed him biting his bottom lip, pondering over what I had just said. I felt a flash of hope. "Why don't you try to learn more about Islam?" I hoped he'd soften up. "You might end up reconciling the disagreements you have ."

Jason stared at me pensively, then said, "Muhammad and Hasan have told me enough about their religion. I'm not going to convert, Sarah."

"Why?" Some of the inner pain I struggled with crossed my face. Maybe it was my turn to look at him with pleading eyes, asking him to sooth my heartache, to do the only thing that could possibly give us a chance.

"I have my own religion and I'm perfectly satisfied with it. Besides, I have family who have always stood by my side. There's no way I would make them go through that, especially after what they went through last year because of me." He was decisive.

There was a moment of silence between us. I'd backed up far enough that I was leaning against his car on the driveway, and he was standing a few steps away on the small grassy patch just outside his door. It was bitterly symbolic: we were so overwhelmingly attracted to each other, and yet unyielding in our principles. So close and yet so far.

"God, Sarah," Jason groaned, running a hand through his wind-blown hair. "The further you run from me, the more I want you." His voice was husky, layered with emotions that mirrored my own.

I knew it was time for me to leave.

As I turned away from him and walked towards my car, I stopped and look back at him. "Did you ever *really* need help with chemistry?"

Jason's smile was lopsided and melancholy. "No, not really."

"You *lied* to me?" I felt a wave of anger rising within me. "You set me up for this, *knowing* that I was committed to my faith, that I had religious restrictions!" I strode up to him furiously. It was all his fault—I thought of my past, of how I could have contained my feelings for Jason right after I'd returned from Houston, when I could have remained firm to my pledge... if only he hadn't asked me to tutor him. "Why did you do this to me, Jason? Why did you set this trap for me?"

Jason's face mirrored the pain in my voice. He grabbed my shoulders, and though I tried to squirm away from him, he refused to let go. His fingers dug into me, and I desperately tried to control the pace of my breathing, to slow the erratic beats of my heart. I couldn't afford to lose control of my feelings, of myself, again.

"Listen to me, Sarah, listen to me!" His voice was full of anguish. "Yes, I lied to you... I wanted to be with *you,* and no one else, and that was the only way I could get close to you."

"But *I* didn't want to get close to you. You set me up," I repeated, trying to wrench my shoulders out of his grip. Jason didn't let go. He wasn't trying to pull me closer to him, but he wasn't releasing me either. It was as though he was just trying to hold onto me, as if he knew that if he let me go now, he would never be able to get this close to me again. It was his last, desperate attempt to win me over.

"No, Sarah, you *did* want to be close to me. Don't lie to yourself." His words were blunt, imbued with all the confidence of certainty. Distantly, I realized that I was close enough to him to inhale the scent of his cologne, the spicy scent of expensive musk that previously had me reeling. Now, though, I couldn't care less.

Jason's words had me rooted to the spot, dizzy with shock. I stopped squirming under his grip and gaped at him, bewildered and ashamed.

Did everyone around me know about our feelings for each other except me? Was my obsession with Jason so obvious? Was I the only idiot who couldn't see through my own deceptions? I must have been the laughingstock of school the entire year.

"Sarah," Jason's deep voice broke through my haze. "Maybe there's still a way. Maybe there's something in your religion that'll allow us to be together? Maybe it's okay, and you just don't know it?"

His pleading voice was so persuasive, almost convincing. *Maybe there is something, Sarah...* the tiny, weakened voice of my desires tried one last attempt to push me to give in. For a split second, I wondered if there really was another way, hoping that there was an excuse I didn't know about yet... just maybe...

"At least give me a chance, Sarah." Jason's whisper was so enticing, so tempting... I faltered and looked back up at him.

Jason Connor, school hero, gorgeous soccer captain whose personality was unmatched by anyone else I'd ever known, had professed his love for me, telling me how important I was to him, how he was willing to do anything for me... *almost* anything.

It was that stark reminder that brought me back to reality. If he truly loved me, he would have been willing to give Islam a chance, to give *me* the only chance we could ever have of being together. But he wasn't, and that meant that there was only one thing I could do now.

As much as I wanted to fall into his arms, I needed my father's arms more. My father was waiting to help me out of the quicksand I'd stumbled into, and the only way I could get out was if I seized the hand that was trying to pull me to safety, not the one that would drag me deeper. The aching of my heart for Jason was a pain that would be temporary. If I gave in and sacrificed the last vestiges of my strength for such a fleeting pleasure, there would be nothing left of me in the end.

I wrapped my fingers around Jason's wrists and gently but inexorably pulled his hands away from my shoulders. With all my strength, I looked into his anguished eyes and said quietly, "There is no chance for us. Not like this."

37

The time had come for me to make a decision between right and wrong—a decision I should have made a long time ago, before getting myself tangled in this vicious trap and devastating my family with my stupidity and weakness.

I had been praying for help and guidance, but I knew that I would have to take the first step to receive His help. The strength to pull away from Jason would come not from myself, but from the mercy of my Lord, likely as an answer to my Dad's prayers. But as a rule, the first step has to come from us, and then Divine Help pours over us like the purest, most healing rain. Still fortifying myself inwardly, I stayed away from school for another couple of days. I tried to spend more time with Dad, going with him to the university or to his stores. He understood that I needed the time away to refocus myself, and he helped keep my mind off things by assigning me random chores.

Our monthly Saturday seminar at the mosque was coming up soon. It was scheduled for the day before graduation. Dad decided to give me a challenge by handing over all the major responsibilities for the event. I had to make several trips to the different Islamic centers of Pittsburgh for advertisements and recruiting volunteers, amongst other things, and it was overwhelming, especially since I was taking over at the last minute. But it did an excellent job of keeping my mind occupied.

I was lucky to be able to take the days off from school. Seniors were mostly done with their studies and I was exempt from most of the exams anyway. Dad must have given some excuse to Mrs. Tanner, because she was being unusually cooperative with my excessive absences. Maybe attendance didn't matter that much anyway, though, since May was usually filled with fun activities for the seniors.

There were some events, like the prom, that I wouldn't attend because of religious beliefs, but there were others that I deliberately avoided so that I wouldn't have to interact with Jason. It wasn't easy. My heart still struggled with my feelings for him, and there were times when all I wanted to do was run to him, to seek him out and bask in his company. My mind's eye would constantly resurrect Jason's pleading gaze, begging me to find a way for us to be together, and the tantalizing thought that maybe there *was* a way would echo in my mind.

That's when I'd find an escape with Dad, who offered me his constant and unflinching support. He always made me feel as though I was the one who was really in control of my decisions, and that he was just helping me keep firm in my goals. During these few days, Jason texted me several times.

If it's because of me that you're skipping school, then don't. I'd rather see you and not speak to you than not see you at all.

It took all my strength to ignore his messages. When the temptation overwhelmed me, I turned off my phone. Knowing that Dad could read all my messages gave me the boost I needed to overcome the temptation of one last conversation with Jason.

While I was killing time at home, I decided to attend the class that Aunty Elisha held for ladies on weekday mornings. She was happy to see me, and though I was sure she knew that Jasmine and I weren't on speaking terms, she didn't treat me any differently.

After the lecture, Nada, Zara's mom, surprised me by telling Aunty Elisha, "You should hold a class for girls who wear *hijab* and act religious but don't know their limits around boys." She shot me a pointed look as she spoke.

Adnan's mother jumped in right on her heels. "Mona doesn't wear *hijab*, but I am so proud of how she keeps away from boys at school!" she boasted about her daughter

I bit back the sharp retort that leapt to my tongue. If only she knew about Mona's *real* activities at school! And what about her son? Were boys excluded from this particular rule?

"In my opinion, it's worse to be friends with boys than to not wear *hijab*," she persisted, her nose in the air. Aunty Elisha didn't reply. I hoped it was because she was observing good manners or because she knew that arguing with them was pointless, and not because she agreed with them.

I could suddenly feel several pairs of eyes staring me down. Aunty Elisha quickly changed the topic, discussing the next week's class, and I felt relieved.

When I got home, I checked my email and discovered that I'd received an invitation to Honor's Night. As Valedictorian, I knew that I wouldn't be able to get out of this one—Mrs.

Tanner would expect my presence and would not accept any excuse. I showed the letter to Dad when he got back from the mosque after *Isha*. Though I knew he was excited about my academic achievements, he could also see the troubled expression on my face. I loved that I didn't need to explain anything to Dad; he was usually able to understand what I was feeling even before I had fully processed it.

Dad stretched out on the sofa. "You should go," he said kindly. "You've avoided a lot of events, but this is your night, and you deserve it." I looked down, uneasy. "Try to hold your ground, Sarah, and see if you're strong enough to stand firm when you see him." Dad's advice was sound, but he looked as uncomfortable as I felt. Still, he encouraged me to give it a try.

I didn't say anything. Even though I'd managed to fight my temptations the last couple times I'd been around Jason, I still doubted my own strength. I didn't know if I was ready to face him again, especially not at school, where everyone's eyes would be on us. Dad could see that I was unconvinced. "Maybe it's time for you to patch up with your chaperone," he added gently. Unfortunately, I wasn't sure if I was up to that either.

Dad's voice softened even more. "Sincere friends are difficult to find in life, Sarah. Once you find them, you should never let them go."

I shrugged silently and went up to my room. What Dad said made sense, and I knew deep down that Jasmine had done what she'd done because she was looking out for me. But I still wasn't ready to face her.

The next day, I stayed home instead of going out with Dad. I considered what going to Honor's Night would mean, and soon enough I'd relaxed into the idea and even anticipated the thought of going back to school. I was able to acknowledge the part of me that was looking forward to seeing Jason again as well, though I prayed that I wouldn't lose the control I'd been carefully building within myself.

I had ordered a dress online specifically for Honor's Night, ages before I'd even begun to realize the depth of my feelings for Jason. The dress was a deep amethyst chiffon, the dark purple of royalty. It flowed in countless pleats from a slight gather below the chest, emblazoned with a brilliant black rhinestone. I'd had it altered so I could wear it without a cardigan or undershirt, and I chose a black hijab to keep the outfit simple and elegant. It was breathtaking.

Jason will love it. The thought came unbidden and, with difficulty, I pushed it away. *You should wear something else,* my conscience scolded, but as I glanced at my reflection in the mirror, my vanity won out. I had bought *this* dress for Honor's Night, and it was *this* dress that I would wear. I ignored the twinge of guilt and busied myself with getting ready. Leaning toward the mirror, I fixed my hijab carefully, pinning it to the shoulder so that my neckline was covered but the gorgeous jewel was revealed.

I headed straight for the cafeteria, which had been turned into a formal event hall with round tables beautifully decorated with tablecloths, mirrored candle centerpieces, and satin covers for the chairs. As usual, I showed up a few minutes late—most of the students and quite a few parents had already taken their seats.

I quickly scanned the hall, found an empty space at a table, and settled in.

Mrs. Tanner started off with a brief speech about yet another year ending and her congratulations and encouragement to all the award-winning students. Her remarks were followed by a short talk by the vice principal, Mr. Ryan. Mrs. Smith got up next. It was her job to announce the names of the seniors who were graduating with honors.

"Wickley High School proudly presents the first honor's achievement award to our dear student, Sarah Ali! Not only she is graduating with honors, but she's also the Valedictorian of the senior class, and has maintained exemplary behavior throughout her four years of high school."

I had known that my name was going to be amongst the first ones called, but I was still nervous, and my usual self-confidence was a bit shaky. Because I'd ended up sitting at the back of the room, I had to cross the entire hall to get to the stage. I was suddenly and acutely aware of one particular pair of eyes watching me, and though I kept my head down and tried to avoid catching anyone's gaze, I could *feel* the fervent admiration of one individual. I nearly lost my composure and tripped slightly on my dress as I climbed the stairs to the stage.

Fixing a smile on my face, I accepted the plaque from Mrs. Tanner and shook hands with her. A barrage of applause, congratulatory yells, and wolf whistles followed, and I smiled bashfully as I fled back to my seat.

After the academic awards, Mrs. Smith called out the names of those who had received scholarships due to special achievements... *"Jason Connor!"* I'd been expecting it. Jason had received a full soccer scholarship to Duke University, in large part due to the fact that he was about to lead our school into the state finals the following week.

As Jason accepted his own trophy from Mrs. Smith, she said, "All our students are from town, and most will still be around after graduation, but you, Jason, are special. You've come from out of town and will be leaving for good. Is there anything special you would like to say before you lead our Falcons to the soccer championship and then head off into the sunset?"

Jason smiled and took the podium. He looked particularly dashing in a formal black suit with a pale blue shirt and a navy blue tie, his unruly hair tamed for the first time. He flashed his signature grin at the audience, though I could tell that he was pointedly avoiding looking in my direction.

"I have to thank all the faculty and my fellow students for all your kindness. I'm proud to be able to lead the school team to the finals! Let's keep hoping we win next week." He paused and crossed his fingers, grinning, and the hall erupted with whistles and applause.

"It's been an unusually interesting year. Although I came to this school very reluctantly, as I hate small towns, I must say that..." Jason's gaze scanned the hall and settled on me, as brilliant and piercing as ever. "It seems like I'll be leaving my heart right here in Wickley, with a very special girl." The hall went silent as everyone in the room turned around to see who he was looking at.

I flushed furiously, and now the silence broke into a wave of titters and whispers, littered with wolf whistles and low exclamations. From the corner of my eye, I saw Zara whispering into her someone's ear.

Jason's eyes held me rooted to my spot—as powerful as ever, even across the many tables between us. He'd done it again. With only a glance and a few moving words, the barrier I'd painstakingly worked to build between us had nearly shattered. Why couldn't he just stop?

After the event ended, I spoke to a few teachers, giving excuses as to why I'd been skipping school and missing out on the seniors' activities. From my peripheral vision, I could see Jason making his way through the hall, heading in my direction. I knew he would make an effort to talk to me, I just didn't anticipate the intensity of it.

"Hey," he said as he drew closer.

I leaned against the table behind me for support. "Hey," I answered lightly.

He quirked a smile at me. "Congratulations, Valedictorian Sarah."

I tried to receive it gracefully. "Thanks. Congratulations to you on the Duke Scholarship. When do you head back?"

He folded his arms over his chest and shrugged. "The same day as graduation."

"So soon?" The words slipped out of my mouth involuntarily, and the dismay in them was obvious. I looked down quickly, regretting it, and feeling unexpectedly shaken at the news.

Jason watched me carefully. "You look gorgeous today," he murmured, so quietly that only I could hear his words.

I blushed and bit my lip. "I think we have to vacate the hall now," I said, trying to avert his attention and indicating the people leaving.

He nodded. We started walking toward the parking lot together side by side, though there was enough distance between us that we didn't touch. I held my clutch in my left hand and pulled my dress up a little so I wouldn't trip over myself again.

When we got close to my car, Jason said quietly, "I only have a few more days left here, Sarah." He looked sad, his hair glimmering in the moonlight. "Can you just walk with me for a while?" I hesitated and he protested, "How bad could it get?"

The pain and pleading in his voice echoed the turmoil in my own heart. "We can talk right here," I said. I left my clutch on the hood of my car, and opened the driver's side door. Jason leaned against the car, the open door between us. Neither of us said a word. He watched me silently, and I looked down, fidgeting with my fingers I closed my eyes and took a deep breath. I was starting to feel even more emotional than before; it could have been because of what he'd said on the podium, or perhaps it was simply the fact that I realized I'd never see him again after graduation.

Two tears broke free from my eyelids and rolled down my cheeks. Jason reached out with his finger and gently wiped them off my face without giving me a chance to stop him. Then he softly took my hand, lifted it, kissed my palm, and gently let go.

It was too much. I broke down; the tears became an uncontrollable flood, and my shoulders shook with the force of my sobs. I was too enveloped in my own grief to notice those who saw me cry that night.

Jason looked alarmed. "Sarah, please…" he leaned forward, uncertain of what to do. "Please don't cry."

I held my hand up, signaling him to stop before he tried to touch me again. "I've been fighting with myself, Jason, and it is so hard," I gasped, trying to control my tears. "But every time I finally manage to come to terms with myself, you say something that puts me right back at square one." I looked up at him through the tears blurring my eyes.

Jason was overwhelmed. "I'm so sorry, Sarah! Please don't cry," he begged, trying to approach me again.

"Don't. Please don't," I held my hand up, asking him to stay away. "My life was just fine until you came along. If you really care about me at all, then leave. Just leave, and don't ever try to contact me again." I could hardly talk through the emotions thickening my voice.

Jason looked heartbroken. "I never meant to hurt you, Sarah. I love you. I only wanted to share my love with you, to share the joy of it all." His face hardened slightly. "But I know how much your religion would stand between us."

With that, Jason turned on his heel and walked away, disappearing from sight.

I stood in the darkening parking lot feeling the tears dry, and a deep sense of emotional exhaustion set in. Shakily, I climbed into my car and drove over to Jasmine's house. She hadn't attended the event that night; Scott had told me she wasn't feeling well.

It was time for me to clear the air with my best friend. She had been right in every warning she gave me, in every way she tried to watch out for me, and now that I had allowed myself to be torn apart from within, I was only left with pain and grief. It was the pain and grief she'd tried to protect me from, and I'd completely ignored her heartfelt concerns.

I barely managed to say a quick *salam* to her parents before I ran up to her room. Her door was halfway open, so I knocked on it quickly and pushed it open before she could answer.

Jasmine was leaning against the headboard of her bed, talking to someone on the phone. She put it down as soon as she saw me, and I ran to her side, burrowing my face in her shoulder.

"Oh, Sarah," she said quietly, her voice full of sorrow. She wrapped her arms around me, and I broke down again, my sobs wracking my body.

Jasmine didn't ask a single question or say a single word of reproach. She held me as I cried, and as I sobbed away the love, the grief, the heartbreak of it all, my best friend cried with me. My tears were for Jason my vulnerability to him, self-loathing because of my weakness; but Jasmine's tears were solely for me. I had fallen into the trap that she had so desperately tried to save me from.

38

I fell asleep at Jasmine's house that night, and when I woke up, I headed straight home. Her entire family was there, and I didn't feel like socializing. I skipped Aunty Elisha's talk for teenagers that day as well.

When I got home, Dad was waiting to take me out for brunch. I couldn't deny his offer, and forced myself to keep him company. Instead of going into town, we drove about a half hour to try something different. I was quieter than usual, but Dad didn't seem to mind. He kept me amused with inane chit-chat, and I listened quietly with a smile on my face.

After we got home, Dad had to run some errands for the stores, and I decided to prepare for my talk with the preteens the next day. I'd just opened a couple of books when I got a text message. Flipping over my phone, I saw that it was from Amal.

> **Sarah, the girls have asked for a change in speaker, so I will be taking over the study circle from tomorrow onwards. Thank you for your contribution, but no need to come to the mosque tomorrow.**

I sat on the floor stunned and reread her message, trying to decipher her tone. Was she being strict, sarcastic, or sad? I'd never heard the preteen girls complaining about the speaker; in fact, most usually came up to me after the gathering to tell me how much they enjoyed the class. I was too overwhelmed and mentally drained to deal with any other conflicts, though, so instead of replying I shrugged and went to sit outside on the back porch.

My mind drifted back what Jason had said the night before at the podium and then later in the parking lot, his words echoing in my mind again and again. *Maybe there is a way for us to be together...* His dark eyes were brimming with love, begging me to find a solution that could bring us together. My own heart pleaded with me. *Maybe there is a way, maybe there is an excuse, I just don't know about it yet.*

Desperate, I went to the Internet and searched every Islamic website I could find for any and all rulings related to this situation. I found numerous 'progressive' positions that told me that true love was true love, that God would not punish me for simply following my heart, that the prohibition of a Muslim woman to be with a non-Muslim man was a patriarchal, misogynistic interpretation. As much as I wanted to believe them, however, I knew they were completely wrong. Wanting to hear a more reassuring explanation, I decided to call a well-known conservative *Imam* in Philadelphia.

"*Salam 'alaikum Shaikh...* could you please explain to me why a Muslim woman can't marry a non-Muslim man?" There was a plea in my voice, a desperation to hear words that would soothe my agitated heart.

"*Astaghfirullah,* sister! How could you even ask such a question? You need to learn to submit to Allah."

For a second I thought I didn't hear him correctly, but then I answered defensively, "I do."

The *shaikh's* voice was deep and stern. "Then do you think He doesn't know what He was ordaining?"

"I didn't say that! I'm asking if you can explain to me *why* He commanded it. What's the reason behind it?" I was shocked at the curtness and harshness of his tone, especially when I was already feeling so fragile.

The *shaikh's* tone was still strict. "Sister, we do not ask for the reason behind everything in our religion. A good Muslim woman accepts what Allah has ordained for her. She does not question Allah's decree."

I was hurt and taken aback by his judgmental attitude. "No, I'm not questioning His decree! I just need to be reminded of the wisdoms behind it." Frustrated, I gave him one more chance to pay attention to my question and answer it the way I needed.

"First of all, you should not have even had a *relationship* with a man like that..." The disgust in his voice was clear, and I felt suddenly small and shameful. "Secondly, you should remember that Allah has ordained only Muslim men for Muslim women."

His answers were so unyielding and bereft of any kindness that I immediately regretted calling him. I didn't even know what to say anymore.

Already torn by my own weakness, the *shaikh's* brusqueness dried up the last dregs of strength I had, and my eyes overflowed with tears. I barely managed to thank him and hastily ended the call.

I collapsed on my bed, aghast. If I hadn't known better, this conversation would have been enough to turn me away from a complete and perfect faith. I was vulnerable and hurt; what I needed was to hear reassurances, not judgment and criticism.

It didn't take long for Jason's pleading eyes to cross my mind again, and the brimming tears overflowed. I curled up on my bed, crying my heart out. It just wasn't *fair*. Why did life have to be so hard? Wasn't love supposed to be one of the greatest blessings in life? Why wasn't I allowed to experience it, then?

I cried myself out, and eventually I felt numb inside, too weary to process anything else. My eyes were burning and my head was pounding. Eventually, I dragged myself up and stumbled off to the bathroom to wash my face, then returned to bed, staring blindly at the walls.

After a while, Dad knocked on my door and invited himself inside. He'd brought me some mint tea with snacks, and didn't seem surprised at my condition. As he settled the tray on my nightstand, I made a vain effort to hide my face from him, but he smiled gently and touched my hair.

"Sarah, you don't need to hide from me." Dad's loving voice cut me to pieces. I had caused my father so much agony, yet he was always there to share my pain. "You know, your face is imprinted on my heart, so whenever there is turbulence, I feel it right here," he pointed to his own chest as he settled down in the chair next to the nightstand.

I smiled painfully back at him. A thought occurred to me. "Dad, you asked me if Jason loved me...but you never asked me if *I* loved him."

Dad's smile was rueful. "It was written all over your face, Sarah." I watched him as he took a sip of his tea, curious.

"Remember the day when I asked you to invite him for dinner, and you said he wasn't a friend, just an acquaintance?" he reminded me. I nodded.

"I knew there was much more to what you were saying, because you spoke about him differently than you spoke about the other boys in your school. And the fact that you refused to invite him in spoke volumes..." he paused and examined my facial expression. "I've known you all your life, Sarah. You would have happily invited a complete stranger for dinner." Dad took a deep breath, "But I also realized that perhaps you were unaware of your feelings at the time." He leaned back in his chair and sighed.

"Why didn't you warn me, then?" My eyes blurred with moisture as Dad's words made my heart crumble all over again.

"Because you were not ready to be warned back then. You were in a world of your own, and any warnings would have fallen on deaf ears." Dad leaned forward in his chair.

"You could have spared me all this pain..." My voice cracked, and I shuddered with grief.

Dad got off the chair and sat next to me on the bed.

"Maybe I should have, but I was afraid you'd distance yourself from me, and that would have left you with only Jason to turn to."

I buried my face in my dad's shirt, wishing that what he'd said wasn't true.

"And besides," he continued, "What you have learned by going through this pain, I couldn't have taught you. I had to let go and see what decision you would make. You knew right from wrong. It's like being in a battle field; I could equip you with whatever was important before you faced your challenges, but when the time came, *you* had to decide on your own what to use, when, and how. I was using my strongest weapon for your protection—my du'a for you. But *you* had to make the important decisions." Dad sighed deeply and pulled back to look at me.

I laid down and nestled my head on the pillow. "It's over now, Dad," I mumbled.

"It's not over yet, sweetheart." Dad tucked my hair behind my ear, "You gambled with your emotions, and that's like playing with fire—it burns. Now you have to go through the healing, which can be more painful than the burn itself."

I looked up with empty eyes and Dad kissed my forehead.

"You have a journey ahead of you...you have to get over Jason," Dad whispered and left the room, but his words echoed in my mind until I finally fell asleep.

39

A shley called the next day to tell me that Jason wasn't going to return until graduation, because he had to vacate his condo and wrap up some stuff before he left for Maryland. The coast was clear for me to go back to school. My friends weren't dumb; they had figured out why I was skipping. I'd never missed a day of school without a solid reason in 12 years.

That week was the last week of school. Though I walked in with my head held high and a wall of fearlessness built around me, my heart broke afresh every time I thought of Jason. Every hallway, the library, the cafeteria, the soccer field, and even the parking lot held memories of our time together—time that had seemed precious but had poisoned me from within.

I kept zoning out, and I had to fight to stop my eyes from welling up with tears. I didn't laugh or talk as I usually did with my friends; my infamous 'Sarah Ali smile' was replaced with an expression fit for a zombie. Random classmates would stop me as they passed and ask with concern, "You OK, Sarah?"

I couldn't even muster a fake smile in reply. Healing was hell. Everything outside my home had memories of Jason etched into it—the school, the café, the public library... even the paths I took for ambling walks. I couldn't escape him anywhere. Though I stayed at home as much as I could, Jason was there too, etched into my heart.

I worked on my graduation speech for hours, trying to keep my mind occupied. Usually, I'd only prepare an outline of what I wanted to say, and my confidence and wit would be enough for me to wing it in front of an audience. Now, though, I forced myself to write out the entire speech and tried to memorize it. I called Jasmine so I could practice in front her, and though she laughed at me at first, she realized why I was so nervous.

That Saturday was the monthly lecture at the mosque. I got up early and made it to the community hall, making sure that all the arrangements were taken care of. A well-known speaker had flown in, and the MSA of the University of Pittsburgh had volunteered to bring him from his hotel in Pitts. Shaikh Ahmad was known for his eloquence and his ability to relate with the younger generation. His talk was on the miraculous nature of the Qur'an, and I was glad to see that everyone in attendance was enthralled.

When it was time for the question and answer period, I thought about the question I had asked the imam in Philadelphia. This lecturer's style was so different, so full of empathy and compassion, that hope was rekindled within me—maybe he could give me another answer, a different answer, the answer I so desperately wanted.

Hastily, I scribbled my question out on a piece of paper.

"Dear *Shaikh*, before judging me or passing strict verdicts, can you please read my question carefully? Unfortunately, I've lost my heart to a non-Muslim boy at school, knowing that it wasn't allowed for me to be with him. He's one of the kindest, most gentle, understanding and caring people I've ever met, and he has a lot of respect for my faith. The only problem is that he's not interested in converting to Islam. Is there any possible way for me to be with him? Is there maybe a different ruling for Western Muslim women on this matter?"

I could have written an entire essay, but I had to stop. Surreptitiously, I folded the paper and slipped it in with the other questions I was gathering from audience members.

In the community hall, *Shaikh* Ahmad sat at a table in the front, with one side of the hall filled with men and the other with women. Sitting in the back, I felt my heart clench with anticipation when I saw the *shaikh* unfolding my piece of paper and reading it silently. Though a part of me already knew the answer before he said it, my foolish heart beat faster, hoping that maybe he would say something different.

Shaikh Ahmad looked up at the audience and summarized the question without reading the whole thing aloud. "Basically, this question is about a Muslim sister asking if she can marry a non-Muslim man." As the *shaikh* started answering the question, several a heads turned to look at me. Panicked, I wondered if the *shaikh* had mentioned my name, but I hadn't signed the question—he had no way of knowing who had asked. So why did so many of the mosque crowd, especially the women, look at me so pointedly?

I wanted to focus on his answer, not their stares. "Sister, I deeply sympathize with your situation, but you must understand that unfortunately I cannot give you the answer you are looking for. Our religion doesn't allow a Muslim woman to marry a non-Muslim man. I'm sure that it must be very difficult for you to grasp the full understanding of this right now, but please just hold tight to your faith and know that Allah is Just. Perhaps you can talk to me after the lecture, and I can explain in more depth."

I could feel the stares fixed on me, hear the whispers. As if that wasn't enough to make me feel intimidated and embarrassed, an older man asked loudly, "How can a Muslim woman ask a question like that? If someone does, is her faith even valid?"

I wished the earth would swallow me up. *Shaikh* Ahmad turned to look at the man who had asked the question.

"Yes, she *can* ask a question like that, and this question has nothing to do with her Islam. It is *because* she is a thoughtful Muslim that she is asking a question like that." There was a sternness in his voice, with none of the gentleness he had used when answering my question. "Her Islam is valid, and she is just going through a very difficult test in her life."

The *shaikh* would have said more, but the moderator reminded him that we were running out of time, and he concluded the talk.

Since I was the organizer of the day, I had to stay until the very end. When everyone else had left, I was fortunate enough to catch *Shaikh* Ahmad for about five minutes, standing at a distance from the last few people who lingered in the hall. The MSA guys who were going to drive him back to Pitts had gone to get the car.

The *Shaikh* was a kind-looking man, younger than most experienced imams, but still quite a bit older than me, his beard was full but neatly kept, and when I walked up to him to thank him for his time, he kept his dark gaze lowered. "Thank you for the amazing lecture, *Shaikh* Ahmad," I said, and he smiled.

"Do you know the sister who asked the last question?" he asked, concerned.

I hesitated. "Yes, I do."

"If she needs to ask any more, let her talk to me directly," he offered sincerely.

My heart aching, I couldn't help but say, "If there's any special advice you have for her, please let me know and I'll convey it to her." My voice trembled a little, and *Shaikh* Ahmad's face softened in understanding.

"Okay," he said gently. "Tell her that sometimes, we don't understand Allah's decrees, but that is because we are humans with limited intellect. But in His ultimate wisdom and mercy, He has prescribed for us what is best for us, whether we comprehend it or not. At times, it is difficult to see the goodness in His Decree, especially when we are going through a trial, but always remember that Allah is Merciful and what He has forbidden upon us is from His ultimate Mercy. She has to cling to this belief throughout her trial."

This was exactly what I needed to hear—a firm, gentle reminder. *Shaikh* Ahmad's voice was filled with genuine concern and sincerity, and I bit my lip to stop my tears from rising.

"Your father has my contact number; if the sister needs advice, she can contact me later on," the *shaikh* suggested.

I sniffed and wiped my eyes with my hand hastily. "No, she heard what she needed to hear. Thank you, *Shaikh*."

I walked home, the warm June air drying the streaks of moisture on my cheeks. It was dark and quiet outside, which suited my mood perfectly. I didn't want to go home, I didn't want the day to end, and I didn't want tomorrow to start... tomorrow would be the last day I would have to see Jason. The last day I would ever be *able* to see him again.

Morning came anyway, and I had to get up early to be ready for the graduation ceremony. Listlessly, I color-coordinated my outfit to match with my navy-blue graduation gown—a dark blue dress with long sleeves and a lace top, and a light blue hijab with a white piece under it.

As I met Dad downstairs, I recalled the day that Adam had graduated—the photo session before we left, the laughter and teasing of a happy family. Now, it was just me and Dad. When we got to the hall, Dad joined the parents and I went with the staff to be seated on the stage.

After we were called up to receive our diplomas, Mrs. Tanner made the first speech, followed by the Director of Education for our school district. I was called up next. As I stood in front of everyone, I tried not to look at the audience too carefully. It was hard not to miss Jason, though, his piercing grey eyes fixed on me, filled with emotions that had become all too familiar.

My breathing faltered, and I held onto the podium tightly so I wouldn't stumble on the spot. Looking down quickly, I composed myself, looked back up and glanced at Jasmine. She nodded at me encouragingly, giving me a broad '*I know you can do it!*' smile. Reassured, I kept my eyes on her for the duration of my speech.

To our honorable guest speaker Mayor McNeil, our beloved principle Mrs. Tanner, our distinguished teachers, respected parents, fellow graduates and friends, ladies and gentlemen, good afternoon.

Glancing around the big hall, my eyes found Jason sitting in the front row and looking right at me. My voice didn't falter, though, and my confidence didn't shake as I continued:

It's a great privilege to be able to stand here in front of all of you today.

I have mixed feelings of delight and sorrow today, of excitement and grief. I am happy because I can see the elated faces of my fellow graduates. On them I can see the thrill of finally ending four years of seemingly endless homework, quizzes, tests and stressful projects. But we managed to survive without any casualties.

The laughter made me pause and smile back at the audience. My eyes met Jason's but I maintained my demeanor and signature smile.

During the past four years, I've learned a lot—not only about physics and math and biology and the other academic subjects our teachers spent hours trying to make us understand, but also about life. From both my dedicated teachers and my fellow students.

Most of us have lived here all our lives, but we come from different backgrounds. And we came together to form today's graduating class, in peace and in harmony. Life is short and our time is limited. Don't let others dictate your decisions for you and drown your inner voice. I've learned to live a life true to myself and not a life of regret.

I've learned to live with passion, conviction and purpose. I've learned that if you have a dream, you have the right to live it—even if it means going against all the odds.

Don't ever settle for what others try to force upon you. Fight for what you believe in and live the life that you want to live, knowing that there will be trials and obstacles, but that it will be a life worth living.

I know we are entering a new phase of our lives, the real life, the adult life. But these past four years have laid the foundations for what is about to come. Seeing each one of my classmates here gives me flashbacks to many memories that we formed here.

I paused and looked around at the audience, a farewell glance, and my eyes met Jason's. I truly had formed memories with him, lasting memories that had now become a part of my me, a part of my life. I couldn't afford a prolonged pause in my speech, but it had become obvious that I had stumbled, and Jason was still holding my gaze. My voice trembled as I pushed back my tears,

I know we have all shared amazing memories. We have cried on each other's shoulders, laughed together, argued until someone had to break it off for us...but we have formed unbreakable bonds, and that is the most precious gift that the past four years have brought. Hence, my feelings of sorrow and grief overwhelm me today because it is time for us to say our goodbyes—hopefully temporary goodbyes. But every good thing that ends makes way for the next good thing to begin.

After the ceremony, I took pictures with Dad and Jasmine's family. I couldn't help but glance toward Jason, who seemed happily occupied with his parents and a girl who must have been Emily. I wondered if he was doing what I was—smiling outwardly and weeping from within. Impulsively, I turned to Dad and whispered, "Dad, I'm just going to go say goodbye to Jason."

Dad scanned the hall quickly and saw him. He hesitated, then nodded and said, "Okay." He patted me on the shoulder. "Do you want me to come along?"

I shook my head, and Dad gave me a quick, reassuring hug.

Before I could lose my nerve, I broke away and headed across the room. Jason must have noticed me in his peripheral vision, because he turned around and hurried toward me as well. "Hey," he greeted me before I could even open my mouth.

I smiled self-consciously. "Hey, Jason." From the corner of my eye, I could see his family looking at us.

"You were great today," he said warmly, and my smile widened.

"Thanks," I replied, making no effort to look away from his magnetic gaze. After all, this *was* going to be the last time I'd be around him. "Can I talk to you?"

Jason looked surprised and suddenly hopeful. "Yeah, of course!" he exclaimed, and turned to address the older woman who was obviously his mother. "I'll catch up with you guys in a bit." She nodded, and he walked with me to the hallway outside.

Finding a private corner, I leaned against a pillar while Jason stood in front me, looking both eager and uncertain.

I took a deep breath.

"I don't know what to say...I..." My voice shook, and I dug my fingernails into my palms to stabilize myself.

Jason cut me off. "Don't say anything, because what I want to hear you say, you won't."

I had vowed that I wouldn't cry anymore, but it was hard to hold myself to it when he was right in front of me, when the dreaded moment had actually arrived.

"I need closure, Jason," I choked out.

To my shock, Jason's eyes were the ones brimming with tears. "What if there is no closure?" he said hoarsely, rubbing at his eyes.

I looked at him silently. One last look, to engrave his every feature into my everlasting memory... the unruly golden-brown hair, the shining silver eyes, the soft scrub of facial hair that made him look more mature than the other guys at school. Most of all, it was the look in his eyes that shook me. The heart-wrenching pain.

In those moments of silence, our gazes acknowledged a mutual longing, a shared heartache. "Goodbye, Jason," my voice cracked, and I turned on my heel and walked away.

As I sat in my car, it dawned on me that in a matter of seconds, Jason would be out of my life forever. I wanted to get out of the car and find him again; I wanted to tell him how much I loved him, that I would wait for him for the rest of my life, hoping he would convert one day. I felt as though my heart was ready to burst from my chest with the pain of it all.

Rolling down my window, I drove home letting the wind dry my tears.

40

The next morning, a beautiful bouquet of flowers and a big box of Godiva chocolates greeted me as I answered the door. It was a delivery from Adam. A bashful, delighted smile crossed my face—my brother had remembered my graduation.

It had been almost three months since he'd left, and I hadn't spoken to him since. It was time to change that. As soon as I walked inside, I picked up my phone and dialed his number, impulsive as always.

"Hello," Adam's deep voice answered.

"Hey, *salam 'alaikum!*" I said cheerfully.

"*Wa 'alaikum salam!* Congratulations!" Adam didn't sound angry at all; in fact, he sounded relieved and pleased.

"Thanks for the flowers! I love them! And I'm sure these chocolates will ruin my workout for the next month," I laughed.

Adam laughed too, but didn't say anything. A sudden wave of remorse and grief crashed over me. "I'm so sorry, Adam," I blurted out, my voice cracking. I wished I had listened to Adam, I wished I had let him threaten Jason. I wished I had trusted him as my older brother. How many hearts did I break in the process of trying to satisfy my own? And yet I wasn't even able to find that satisfaction... I was left empty and heartbroken.

"Sarah, it's okay," Adam tried to soothe me, but the tears had started leaking down my face, and I began to cry in earnest. "Sarah, where's Dad? Go sit next to Dad." Adam's deep voice was comforting.

"Dad's not home. He had to stop by the Café on the way home from the ceremony," I sniffed. "I'm so sorry you had to leave because of me. I've been the worst sister in the world, and I don't even deserve you as my brother." I didn't even know what to say anymore. All I wanted was to see him.

"Sarah, it's okay, shhh...Sarah, stop crying. It was my fault, too. I should've talked to you more calmly, maybe more wisely." The tenderness in Adam's voice made me feel even worse. "I had to leave anyway. It's not your fault."

Adam had always wanted to see me graduate as Valedictorian, even more so than Dad, and I'd taken that from him. If he hadn't had to leave so soon, he would have been able to watch me graduate. The more I thought about it, the more I cried, and Adam kept trying to calm me down. Was Adam crying too? I couldn't tell, but I knew one thing for sure—that though I hadn't been there for him when he had cried, my brother was always there for me, just a phone call away.

Adam kept soothing me until I finally calmed down, hiccupping slightly.

"Where are you?" I asked, wiping my nose.

"I'm on campus," he told me, then asked, "When are you starting college?" As usual, he was most worried about my education.

"I don't know yet... I think I'll probably take a break this summer," I answered thoughtfully.

"You should start soon," Adam instructed, sounding just like he used to. "Don't waste your time!" I smiled but didn't say anything.

"Listen, I have to go now, but I don't want you to cry like this again, okay?" Adam's tone was authoritative, and I giggled. "And don't forget to send me pictures from yesterday!"

The next morning, I received another delivery of beautiful red roses. At first, I thought Adam had gone crazy with flowers, but then I read the note. It contained a modified stanza of a song.

If I should stay, I'll only be in your way
So I'll go, but I know, I'll think of you every step of the way
Bittersweet memories, that is all I'm takin' with me
But just know that I will always love you.

Jason had sent me the closure I had asked for. I didn't know if I was glad to have the chapter end, and in such a sweet way, or sad because it really meant the end.

My life after graduation changed dramatically. It felt like it came to a halt; every morning at around eleven, when art class and lunch hour would have begun, I thought of Jason.

Every day I faced an avalanche of mixed emotions. I felt angry at myself for falling into the quicksand, disappointed for being so vulnerable, ashamed for putting my father through so many difficulties, remorseful for fighting with Adam, and frustrated for being so weak. And despite it all, I still missed Jason.

Jasmine had started a summer semester at university and scolded me for missing out, but I didn't have the mental strength to tackle Carnegie Mellon's challenging standards just yet. She tried to be patient and hang out with me after she got back from school, but with the long commute and the intensive workload, she rarely had time.

I blocked all calls and texts from Jason so I wouldn't have to think about receiving any emotional messages. I blocked his emails too. Dad suggested canceling Internet service from the house entirely, and I agreed; I wanted to go cold turkey and cut off all avenues of communication—not just with Jason, but with the whole world.

I was heartsick: an illness that no one can cure except God. I couldn't sleep and I would get up in the morning with dark circles around my eyes and a pale, drawn face. I didn't have an appetite, either, no matter what Paula cooked in an attempt to coax me into swallowing more than a few mouthfuls. Everything tasted like ashes. I'd push food around the plate, waiting for Dad to finish his dinner so I could get up and go back to my room.

One weekend, the mosque hosted an event and I decided to go, hoping that I'd return feeling refreshed. Unfortunately, the ladies at the mosque welcomed me by staring me down and returning my smiles with frowns. Instead of talking to me openly, they whispered amongst themselves whenever I was in sight.

After the lecture, I was sitting in the ladies section waiting for the food to be served when I saw Amal across the room. "How's the study circle going?" I asked her, smiling. I'd really missed the preteen girls.

"It's fine," she answered without her usual warmth.

Adnan's mother spoke up. "Amal, I'm so happy that you listened to Nada and took over the circle," she said obnoxiously, looking down at me over her nose. I regretted having sat next to her to begin with, and was about to get up and move when I overheard her whispering to another woman next to her. "...*Kuffar* boys making love confessions about leaving their hearts... How embarrassing for her father."

The other woman, a lady visiting from Pitts, shook her head in sorrow and gave me a pointed look. "*AstaghfirAllah*, who knows what else these boys leave with girls like that!"

I felt like screaming at them both, but I bit my tongue and held myself together. Furious at their hypocrisy, I left before dinner was served.

After the first summer session was over, Jasmine decided to take a break until fall. Instead of registering for the next semester, she registered for a Muslim youth camp for girls in New Jersey. She begged me to come with her, but I kept refusing until Dad quietly asked me to go, his eyes full of worry. I couldn't tell him no. I knew that he was watching me closely, grieving over my deteriorating health and beside himself with worry. Grudgingly I registered, just so that he could get a break from me. He deserved that much, at least.

41

J asmine and I flew to New Jersey and arrived at the camp, which was being held at a rented beach retreat. The beach and its surrounding area were breathtakingly beautiful; the organizers had done a great job choosing the location of the camp and setting it up as well.

The Reflection Retreat was two weeks long, during which there was an inspiring but rigorous schedule and assigned counselors, as well. The organizers were originally going to accept only ten girls, but after they let me in, they decided to include another girl as well. All in all, we were twelve girls and five counselors, with two girls assigned to each room.

I was surprised at how much more peaceful I felt at the camp. The fresh air, beach view, and change of environment—and most importantly, being with people who didn't know anything about my past—made me feel truly refreshed and interested in the world again. I got to know the other girls, took part in the scheduled activities, and paid attention to the heartfelt spiritual talks. Even so, I remained much quieter and more withdrawn than was usual for me.

My counselor's name was Norah, a young woman in her late twenties. She was a Latina from New York whose parents had converted to Islam before she was born, and thus, she'd been raised in a home where Islam was not just part of the culture, but a chosen lifestyle. Her warm, honey-brown eyes sought us all out, and her firm, loving voice captivated us with its words of wisdom. Allah had blessed her with the ability to help her audience truly grasp the concepts she shared with them.

Most of Norah's talks were about finding our connection with Allah, depending on Him in our times of difficulty, and remembering Him in our times of ease. Whenever she spoke about repenting of our past and seeking Allah's help and guidance for our future, I found myself crying again—but these weren't tears born of my memories of Jason; these were tears of sorrow, remorse, and regret. Of shame that I had ever created memories of Jason to begin with.

Every evening, while the girls enjoyed movies with s'mores or Chex mix in the private hall, I found my way to the beach. I'd sit on the sand, hugging my knees and staring out at the crashing waves, reflecting on what I'd done and where to go from here.

"Are you always this quiet?" Norah asked me one morning at breakfast.

I shrugged and smiled slightly. "Staying quiet is always better."

She raised her eyebrows. "Not many young people know that," she laughed.

My smile faded and a shadow of grief crossed my face. "Some experiences teach us hard lessons at a young age." I tried to force a smile, but Norah's searching gaze understood that there was a story behind the statement. I excused myself quickly, feeling my eyes prickle with tears again.

Later that day, I was sitting on the beach enjoying my solitude, when Norah walked across the sand to join me. She tucked her long white cotton skirt beneath her carefully and settled down gracefully, batting away the ends of her pale green headscarf as they fluttered in the salty breeze.

"How come you're so different from the other girls? No phone, no laptop, not bothering us about the Internet, not interested in movies..." Her voice was light, but her question was serious, curious.

"I don't know. I just lost interest in those things." I looked at her from over my shoulder and then looked down again, trailing my finger along the sand.

Norah watched my scribbles as they formed in the sand, then disappeared again as each individual grain fought to fill the void I had created. "That's good... experiences that reform us can actually be a blessing."

I didn't look up. "How do you know if they've reformed you and not weakened you?"

"Do you feel weak?" Norah asked gently.

That's when I realized I didn't. I felt sad and ashamed, but not weak—not anymore. After that night, Norah joined me on the beach more often. One night, I finally confided in her everything that had happened with Jason. I told her about how I had deceived myself, how I had caused so much pain for my father and alienated Jasmine and Adam, and I broke down when I spoke about the disappointment I felt in myself for being so vulnerable and weak around Jason. She listened silently while I poured my heart out.

"Sarah, I'm so impressed with your good character." Her words took me aback and I stared at her in shock.

"What?! I slipped so far!" I was confused.

"Sometimes Allah lets us slip so we can learn to pick ourselves up. Life's a bumpy road, and sometimes the bumps knock us down. But if we learn to get up again, we're stronger when the next bump comes along." She splashed her toes in the tiny waves that licked along the shore.

"Good character doesn't mean being perfect, it means owning up to our mistakes, accepting responsibility and learning from them. That's what repentance means." Norah's eyes were filled with compassion.

That night, for the first time since my heart had broken, I stood up in the darkness of the last third of the night to pray the late night prayer. I recognized and acknowledged the magnitude of what I had done—not just that I'd ignored the rules that I should have followed, but that I had neglected to turn to my Lord when I had first felt the stirrings of emotion and the warnings pangs of my conscience. I had forgotten Allah, the One Who created me and loved me far more than Jason ever could have.

That night, I cried for all the right reasons and my tears fell in the right place—on my prayer carpet—and for the first time, I felt a delicate, comforting cloak of peace fall upon my heart.

From then on, I got up to pray the late night prayer regularly, begging Allah to purify me of my sins and give me strength going forward. I talked to Norah every night as well; her words were reassuring and soothing.

"Don't be too hard on yourself," she advised me. "Countless girls end up in similar situations. Some girls fall harder than others, and some see their relationships become physical as well as emotional. Nonetheless, the doors of return to Allah are always open, no matter how deep the abyss one falls into."

She was sitting cross-legged, using her hands to scoop up the damp sand and fashion it into a sandcastle.

"Others took me as role model," I recalled, thinking of all the girls who had looked up to me before I'd become the community scandal.

Norah raised an eyebrow at me. "Do you think role models don't make mistakes?" She smiled gently. "All of us make mistakes, each and every one of us."

"Thank God for my father," I said. "After God, I have him to thank for the fact that I didn't slip even further. I never had to be afraid of him—I was only afraid of disappointing him."

On our last night at camp, Norah took me by the hand and walked outside with me on the beach. "It's time, Sarah. Let Jason go. Let your past go and move on." We stood in the water, the cool waves lapping at our knees.

"Your past is nothing but a reflection of who you once were. Focus on the future. You have the potential to be a great leader, Sarah—don't let Jason hold you back."

Norah's words were gentle but commanding. "Jason was not meant to be yours. Trust Allah's decree and let him go. Know that what He didn't give you was not best for you. It was just a trial. And remember that if you leave something for His sake, as you left Jason for His sake, He will never let your sacrifice be in vain."

42

I returned home with new resolve and a new outlook on life. After taking a couple of days to recuperate from the strenuous schedule of camp, I decided it was high time I returned to a normal life.

I registered for the fall semester at Carnegie Mellon, which gave me the opportunity to talk to Adam a lot more, getting his advice about classes and professors, rebuilding my connection with him.

Dad, however, seemed a bit drained and quieter than before. I tried asking him what was wrong, but he assured me that he was just exhausted from work. When Adam had been around, he had done a lot of work for Dad, but with him gone, all the responsibilities had fallen on Dad's shoulders. I mentioned Dad's unusual weariness to Adam, and he promised he would try to visit as soon as his summer session ended, even if only to fly in for the weekend.

I tried to be livelier around Dad so he could at least relax about me. I started going out more, hanging out with friends, and even went back to the mosque for Aunty Elisha's talks, trying to ignore the despicable attitude of many of the aunties. Slowly but surely, my life started to feel more positive.

A week before school was supposed to begin, I was at the café enjoying a drink with Jasmine and Ashley. After Ashley left, Jasmine went to use the restroom, and that was when Adnan squeezed himself into the chair across from mine. He leaned toward me, smirking.

"Hey," he leered at me.

I pushed my chair back, trying to get away from him.

"Feeling lonely?" he drawled, making himself comfortable.

I grimaced. "What do you want, Adnan?"

Adnan stared at me, his face hard. "You," he said abruptly. "And I'll be more careful than Jason was."

I stared at him in horror and disbelief, wondering if I had heard him correctly, while he took a sip of my milkshake. "I can taste you already," he winked at me lewdly.

I stood up, my hands shaking. "How *dare* you speak to me like that?!"

Adnan's face twisted, making him look ugly. "And how exactly *do* you talk to a slut?" he spat.

I struck the table with my hands, furious. "Get out."

Jasmine came out of the bathroom and took the scene in quickly, looking shocked. "What's going on?" she asked, throwing Adnan a look of disgust.

I was breathing heavily, anger coursing through my veins. No one had ever spoken to me like that before. Adnan was still in the chair, leaning back and leering at me. "Why, is there a special *Jason* way of getting you in bed?" he taunted me.

"Get the hell out of here!" I raised my voice, pointing towards the door, but he didn't move. "Did you hear what I said? Get the hell out of *my* café!"

By now, we had attracted the attention of almost everyone in there. Alex came out from behind the counter, wiping his hands on his apron and looking concerned. "Sarah, calm down... what happened?"

I glared Adnan. "He can't stay here, tell him to get out!" I screamed.

Adnan didn't move, smiling at me slyly and playing with the straw in my milkshake. Tammy was trying to calm me down, and I kept demanding that Adnan be thrown out.

"Sarah, we can't just kick customers out of the café like that... it can become a legal issue," Alex told me quietly.

The vile grin on Adnan's face only widened, infuriating me further. Overwhelmed with fury, I grabbed the milkshake glass and tossed its contents in Adnan's face, leaving him soaked and blinking in surprise. Then I whirled around and fled.

Jasmine followed me out onto the street, where I leaned against the side of the dry cleaners next door, closing my eyes and steadying my erratic breathing. "Sarah, what happened?" Jasmine asked, putting her arm around my shoulders and holding me close.

I told her what Adnan had said to me, and something in Jasmine's face made me pull away from her, staring at her suspiciously. "Jaz," I had a feeling that something was wrong. "What is it?"

Jasmine tried to shrug and force a smile. "Nothing, let's just go home and make our own milkshakes and watch a movie."

"Jaz," I said firmly, "What are you hiding?"

She avoided meeting my eyes, mumbling an excuse, but I pressed her until she finally admitted what was going on.

"Adnan and Zara's families have spread a lot of rumors about you," she said hesitantly.

I rolled my eyes. "So what's new? I can tell by the way they stare me down, and they make some pretty pointed remarks during your mom's lectures."

Jasmine bit her lip. "No, Sarah... they've taken it too far this time." Jasmine never acted nervous, especially not around me, and now she was making *me* nervous.

I frowned. "Jasmine?" I prodded her.

She paused, then said, "They're saying you and Jason had an actual affair, and..." she finally looked up at me. "And that you got pregnant with his child."

"What the hell...??!" "Sarah, they think they have the facts all lined up. Everyone noticed how your health started deteriorating after graduation, and then you didn't go out much... and then you suddenly disappeared for two weeks with me, for camp. They all assumed that you were pregnant and that Uncle Omar had sent you away to get an abortion."

I grinned at Jasmine suddenly. "Are you pranking me? Because it's not funny, Jasmine." I refused to believe anything she was saying, but when I glanced at her again, her eyes were watery and her face drawn in sorrow.

"Sarah," Jasmine said, her voice trembling, "I'm so sorry."

My jaw dropped and I stared at her in shock. She was serious. Suddenly numb, I turned to walk towards home, but Jasmine grabbed my arms and said in a broken voice, "Sarah, you can't talk to your dad about this."

Why not? I wanted to ask, but it was as though my tongue didn't want to obey my brain.

"He's already taken too much from those jerks," Jasmine answered my unspoken question. "Please, you have to understand... The board is removing him from his position at the mosque," she whispered, burying her face in her hands.

"I... I don't understand," I said slowly. "They can't remove him, he's one of the founders." I knew the mosque's constitution; Dad and Uncle Dawud could not be forcibly removed from the board.

"I know, but he is being forced to resign," Jasmine explained.

I couldn't say anything for a while, my heart sinking.

"Your family knew I was at the camp, Jasmine!" I managed to say.

"Sarah, do you think my family counts? Rumor has it that my dad arranged for your abortion. My dad was going to resign too, but Uncle Omar forced him to stay. Sarah, I wasn't supposed to tell you any of this."

I felt a rush of anger. "You know what?" I snapped. "I *should* have done something with Jason; I should have at least kissed him!"

Jasmine stared at me, her eyes wide with shock. "You mean, you never even..."

I shook my head, "No! Not even once." I closed my eyes trying to suppress an overwhelming pain, but suddenly I felt a ripple of anger emerging through me. "I should get Jason's number from Scott. I could meet up with him and satisfy my desires—do all the stuff they're saying I did! At least then I'd deserve the rumors!" "Listen to me, Sarah," she told me, her voice firm despite its sorrow. "You are *not* going to let those idiots hurt you. You didn't walk away from Jason for those people. Let the One for Whose sake you left him be your witness."

I stared at Jasmine numbly. I hadn't torn my heart apart because of any of those people. I'd left Jason for God's sake, for His Pleasure alone, and I wasn't going to let my intentions become polluted just because of a couple of hypocrites at the mosque.

43

After this revelation, I couldn't lock myself up in my room again, and I couldn't just sleep through it all, like I did before, either. And I was worried about Dad. When we'd have mint tea after dinner, our usual lively discussions were replaced with silence, and my heart ached when Dad would excuse himself, saying that he was too tired to stay up.

When he'd gone, the silence in the room surrounded me; I could hear only the faint tinkle of the wind chimes outside. As I sat by myself, reflecting on this new sequence of events, I realized that, in a way, Adam's absence was a mercy from Allah. His irrational reaction to these rumors would have caused Dad even more stress.

At the same time, I felt ashamed for giving others the opportunity to invent lies against me; a powerful desire for revenge swept over me, but I had to be strong for my father. I had to be his solace and his strength, and for that, I needed to keep my sanity intact.

The next day, I decided to 'invite' Dad for dinner—I cooked the whole meal myself. He tried to show his pleasure, but his eyes were dull, as though someone had drained the life right out of him.

After dinner, I made some mint tea and sat down next to him on the sofa, pulling my knees up and resting my mug on them. After some small talk, I finally gathered the courage to say, "Dad... I'm so sorry for putting you through this whole mess." I didn't look at him. "I'm so sorry that I brought all this on your shoulders..."

Dad cut me off. "You didn't bring any of this on me," he said. "Others did, when they forgot to mind their own business and give excuses to fellow Muslims." His voice was angry.

"They forgot much more than that," I said quietly, taking a sip of my tea. "Now I know how it takes years to build a good reputation, but literally a few seconds to wreck it." I sighed sadly.

Dad frowned, his forehead creasing. "Who cares how people judge someone? As long as a person holds himself accountable in front of his Lord, his life is no one's business."

Staring into my cup, I took a deep breath. "Yes, but we live amongst these people and we have to deal with their judgments."

Dad looked at me seriously. "Sarah, we can leave if you want. We can move to Houston."

A melancholy smile spread across my face as I tucked a lock of hair behind my ear. "The hatred of Islamophobes didn't drive me out of my home. I never even considered that option. But the ignorance of my own people can force me to leave?" I sighed and shook my head, "No, Dad, I'm not going to run away. I'm going to stay right here where my home is."

"Home is where the heart belongs, Sarah." Dad rested his head on the sofa.

I didn't know what to say, what to feel... I didn't even know if I *could* feel anything anymore. My heart was numb; all it did these days was circulate blood, not harbor any emotions, any feelings.

"Dad, you can prove that I was at the camp," I suggested, thinking of my earlier resolution to set aside my ego.

Dad turned to look at me. "It doesn't make any difference to me, to be honest, but if it means anything to you, I can get all the paperwork and post it on the mosque's bulletin board."

"No! Never! I would never do that for my own sake." My voice became bitter. "These couple of holier-than-thou families, claiming to be practicing their religion," my words were acidic with sarcasm, "Don't they know that the burden of proof is on the accuser and not the accused? And that spreading rumors about someone's honor and chastity is a crime in Islam??" I couldn't suppress my fury, "I would never deign to give them any proof, but I'd be happy to do it for you, Dad. I know the mosque means a lot to you."

"Yes, and I'm still a part of it. I don't have to be on the board to be a part of the mosque or the community." Dad sighed and leaned back. "The problem is that no one has said anything to me directly. All these rumors started from the women's side and Elisha conveyed them to her husband. We do know though, that if I stay on the board, they'll try to separate and create another mosque. I've heard men talking about it."

"And you don't want the community to split?"

"Sometimes wisdom is in letting go. If my leaving the board keeps everyone else united, then why not?" He sounded a lot more relaxed than I anticipated, or maybe he just wanted to be strong around me. "Their nonsense is not saddening me, Sarah, because I know it is all a lie. If it were true, it might have bothered me—but my daughter has excelled in a way I could never have imagined, and I am very proud of her."

I sat down by Dad's feet and rested my head on his knees. "I'm so sorry, Dad."

Dad lifted my head gently and said, "Sarah. A trial has come your way, and *inshaAllah* your repentance will erase your mistakes and raise your rank in the sight of Allah. Be patient, my child. Like your mother, Aisha, may God be pleased with her."

For the first time, I saw Dad's eyes well up with tears. All this time he had been strong, and it was about time that I be strong for him. At that instant, I made a pact with myself—a pact of indifference.

After that day, I didn't cry—not because of what people said about me, not because of how they continued to single me out, not because of how some families stopped their daughters from seeing me, not because of how they cut off ties with my family. I refused to shed a single tear because of them. Their words didn't hurt me anymore; their mistreatment didn't upset me any longer.

I built a bubble around myself—a safe shelter—taking myself above their cruelty. The only people who mattered to me now were Dad, Adam, and Jasmine's family.

From that day onward, I never set foot in Wickley's mosque again. The mosque my dad had founded, the mosque where I'd learned much of my faith, the very mosque where I'd discovered my Muslim identity. It was time for the fall semester to start anyway, and I found other ways to learn and grow and worship.

I buried myself in my studies at CM, and eventually found a place for myself in the MSA there. I immersed myself in volunteering at the children's cancer hospital in Pittsburgh, trying to keep myself distracted by helping others who were in need. I felt a sense of relief putting a smile on my drawn face, offering loving hugs to the kids. And after that, whatever time I had left, I spent it helping Dad with his businesses.

Adam started visiting us more regularly, and we'd meet at home about one weekend a month. I eventually told him what had happened, and he wanted to move back to be with his family, but Dad refused to let him without finishing his master's degree first.

As for Jason, I thought about him sometimes, but I no longer cried. There was a connection, now, between my memories of him and how I perceived myself as a Muslim woman. I realized that if Jason was meant for me, God would make a way for us to be together, a way that was pleasing to Him. And if he wasn't the one for me, then God would provide me with something better, as He promised. And he would bless me with contentment in my life, no matter how it turned out.

Glossary of Terms

Alhamdullilah – Thank God

Astaghfirullah – Seek God's forgiveness

Authubillah – "I seek refuge in God" usually said when in the presence of something worrisome or evil

Desi – From Indian-Pakistani decent

Du'a – supplication

Halal – permissible

Hijab – Head covering of a Muslim woman that she is obliged to wear in front of other men who are not from her family

Imam – Muslim clergy

Iman – faith

InshaAllah: God-willing

Kuffar – disbeliever

MashaAllah: Muslims use this term after complimenting something/one

Qur'an – Holy Book of Muslims

Rak'as – units of prayer

Salaam 'alaikum – Muslim greeting meaning peace be upon you

Salah – 5 daily prayers of Muslims

Fajr – Dawn prayer
Dhuhr – Noon prayer
Asr – Afternoon prayer
Maghrib – Sunset prayer
Isha – Evening prayer
Sheikh – a knowledgeable man
Shaytan – Satan
Yousuf – Prophet Joseph
Tajweed – Art of reciting Qur'an in proper pronunciation
Wa 'alaikum salaam – Reply of the greeting meaning and upon you peace
Wudu – ablution

Acknowledgments

All praises and gratitude are to my Lord for His infinite mercy on me and for making me capable of writing this book.

I am deeply thankful to my children for believing in their mother and for their support and patience when I was busy writing this story.

A special thanks to my parents for their prayers. Unfortunately, my father passed away before this book was published and he never got to read it, but his love and prayers stayed with me throughout.

I am thankful to Na'ima B. Robert for taking the time to review my work. I want to acknowledge and appreciate Zainab bint Younus for helping me edit the book. I am also thankful to Najiyah Maxfield-Helwani for all her time and suggestions. And many thanks to all my friends who took the time to give me their feedback. I pray that our communities benefit from this work of fiction, and we can learn to respect and understand each other.

CPSIA information can be obtained
at www.ICGtesting.com
Printed in the USA
LVHW091812180919
631478LV00004B/689/P